Messing With Magic

by

James Wearne

A Lynx Somerton Story

Messing With Magic

Cover Art by *Debbie Taylor*

The Wild Rose Press, Inc.
PO Box 708
Adams Basin, NY 14410-0708
Visit us at www.thewildrosepress.com

Publishing History
First Fantasy Rose Edition, 2016
Print ISBN 978-1-5092-0853-1
Digital ISBN 978-1-5092-0854-8

A Lynx Somerton Story
Published in the United States of America

I dove on Andy, covering him with my body as heat sizzled along my spine. The fireball missed and exploded amongst a shelf of expensive bags. The smell of burnt leather filled my nostrils, and we both slapped our legs to douse the flames. I glanced up to see what we were facing. A fire demon stood blocking the main exit from the room. It had skin like flowing lava, with black crust floating on crimson fire beneath. It brandished a sword of flames with one of its four arms, and its head almost touched the roof.

Its eyes found mine and locked on. It had come for me and strode toward us, knocking over the counters and displays in its way. For some reason I was overcome by an urgent desire to stand up, plant a staff in front of me, and boldly shout, "You shall not pass."

I was happy I didn't, for the luxuries within the room started to ignite around the fire demon, and it sent another fireball whistling our way. Retreat seemed a sensible option.

People were screaming and running. I saw a man fall as the demon passed him, horrific burns upon his face. I dragged Andy by his shirt. "Move."

Dedication

To Max Flory
"Rain keeps falling"

Though much is taken, much abides; and though
We are not now that strength which in old days
Moved earth and heaven, that which we are, we are;
One equal temper of heroic hearts,
Made weak by time and fate, but strong in will
To strive, to seek, to find, and not to yield.

~Alfred Lord Tennyson

Chapter One

I joined Supernatural Intelligence to serve and protect the people of Britain, not to scurry about London checking alarms like a brainless golem. Jamming on the handbrake, I yanked hard on the wheel of my yellow Mini Cooper-S. The back end slid around in the wet, and with a satisfying spray and hiss of tires, I parked illegally at the side of Trafalgar Square. I wanted a real case, but my near perfect scores and aptitude for magic meant nothing to my colleagues. As a young, athletic woman, with opal-blue eyes and lager-colored hair, I had no chance. They asked me to serve the tea at meetings, told blonde-witch jokes behind my back, and had a running tote about how long I would last. I ignored them and trained daily to exhaustion, but it still hurt. Political correctness among wizards seemed to amount to an agreement that the environment was a nice place to take a walk. Turning off the engine, I placed my permit on the dash, stretched my neck to both sides, looked in the mirror, and sought the warrior inside. Yet my inner Bruce Lee was on vacation. So I stuck out my tongue and tied my mop back in a ponytail. Since when had I started to expect that life was meant to be fair?

Bounding up the steps of the National Gallery, I paused by the tall white columns of the entrance, and looked back. At two a.m., traffic was sparse, and the only other person in view was a homeless man, engaged in a deep conversation with one of the bronze lions at the base of Nelson's column. This lifted my mood. For the last time I checked, the poor lions were as bored as military hairdressers. Cast from bronze cannons seized at the battle of Waterloo, they were spelled to rise and defend England if Big Ben struck thirteen times.

In the days of muskets and bayonets, a charging bronze lion would have been a mighty weapon indeed. Now, with their usefulness surpassed by the invention of explosives and the tank, the unfortunate lions had nothing to do all day, except endure the tourists who clambered upon their backs. Beyond, I could see all the way down to Big Ben and the Houses of Parliament. I felt my spine straighten. No matter what my colleagues thought of me, I was still an agent of the Crown.

A security guard stood behind the entrance to the Gallery. He took no notice when I hammered on the door but stared into the distance, as if focusing on something unseen. I swore. The alarm had rung true. Someone was actually messing with magic in there. I could spot that ensorcelled look a mile away.

I pulled a communication crystal out of my jacket. Much more reliable than mobile phones, the crystals never ran low on batteries or had poor reception. They were totally untraceable, and I never got angry looks from people if I used one on the bus. I just wished mine came with a digital camera, messaging, and Wi-Fi. Our equipment was behind the times. Thinking of my partner, Raven, I sent out my thoughts and put a spark of will into the crystal.

Raven's voice sounded in my mind, *"Lynx?"*

"Raven, this is serious. Someone has ensorcelled a

guard near the entranceway. I need back-up. " I thought back.

"Merlin's jewels," Raven swore. *"I can't help you at the moment love. Got a bit of a situation myself. You're on your own."*

I couldn't believe that he couldn't come and help. *"What's more important than a break-in at the National Gallery?"*

"I'll tell you tomorrow," Raven paused, *"and Lynx?"*

"Yes."

"I'm sorry for only giving you the crap jobs. You train harder than anyone else. I should trust you more."

Raven apologizing—had the world ended? And was that actual emotion I could sense? I didn't quite know how to take it. A computer had more feelings than Raven. Sent to boarding school at the age of six, he'd joined that traditional club of British men who viewed feelings as a sensory anomaly.

"Thanks." I didn't know quite how to take it, *"Why the sentimentality? Are you worried I won't be able to handle this?"*

"It's not you I'm worried about."

With that, Raven cut the connection.

I turned my attention to the doors of the National Gallery and tried to focus, but my mind faltered. Raven might have confidence in me, but the enormity of the moment was descending, and I really wished he were here. I could not think. Anything could be waiting for me on the other side of those doors, and in the back of my mind, the fear of failing to live up to my parents' legacy haunted me. I mentally kicked myself. There was no one else to do the job, and I wasn't going to get anywhere standing about, letting my mind go through all the things that could go wrong. Going back to basics, I closed my eyes, slowed my breath, and took a moment to ground myself.

Wizards, stuck in the musty libraries of the past, mutter Latin and make elaborate gestures to cast their magic. Witches, relying on superstition rather than science, invoke complicated spells using herbs, crystals, and all sorts of exotic ingredients. Sorcerers, whose worldviews have not developed since Dante, call upon demons to aid them. I believe in a simpler way. This was the twenty-first century after all. It was time to do away with the robes and the rituals and focus only on what was necessary and effective.

I was a Neon-Mage, forging a new magic that took power from anything that glowed. London was a playground for me, and to do my bit for planet Earth, I put to use all the wasted energy. I took from lights left on in empty rooms, the screen savers of monitors cycling endlessly in deserted office blocks, CCTV footage never watched, mobiles switched on in people's pockets, and motion-sensor lights triggered by rats. I reached out to the surplus energy of the city, directed it toward the lock, and uttered the word, "Break."

I felt a sharp pain in my fingers. The lock trembled briefly but then stilled. I allowed no doubt to enter my mind. Magic was a matter of faith. A wizard might explain it in terms of the possibilities of quantum mechanics and uncertainty principles. I liked to say that the universe wanted to roll snake eyes from time to time and with enough encouragement it would. I allowed the energy to flow again, ignoring the pain as it coursed through my hand and yelled, "Break."

The lock before me shattered. I resisted the urge to pump my fist.

Silent alarms would now be sounding in nearby police stations, summoning the conventional cavalry. While the police might not be the greatest backup against whoever was using magic in the Gallery, they were better than nothing, and it gave some comfort to my fluttering stomach as I walked inside.

The guard did not register my entrance. I went over, grabbed him by the shoulders, and shook him, but his expression did not change. He was gone from this world. Whoever spelled this guard was powerful. Most illusions could be overcome once a physical link was established back to the real world, but my shaking had accomplished nothing. The poor guy was sweating profusely, and I could see him curling and uncurling his fists at his side. I did not know what he was seeing, but it looked like he wanted out. While I might not be able to break the illusion, I had to do something. Calling upon the dim night-lights of empty halls, I whispered in the guard's ear, "Sleep."

He closed his eyes and tilted sideways as a deep sleep washed over him. I caught him, guided his heavy weight onto the ground, and made sure his head was supported. He'd be himself again, once he woke up.

My footsteps echoed in the marble hall. I could smell the lavender scent of whatever cleanser the night cleaning crew had used on the floors. The minimal lighting made for many shadows. I thought about going back to grab the guard's large baton of a torch but did not want to announce my presence. Silent faces, from priceless paintings above, watched me. Their eyes, from ages past, followed me around the room and judged me in my denim jacket and black leather pants. I did not care. The pants, which I had found in a second-hand shop, were ripped but comfortable.

I was ready for anything but this emptiness. Not counting the Sainsbury wing, there were over forty-six rooms in the Gallery, and I had no idea where I should start. Pulling my butterfly knife out of my pocket, I opened it, set it on the ground, and spun. Let the fates decide the direction. The knife stopped spinning and pointed straight back out. Great. I wondered whether I should take that as a warning.

After picking up my knife, I headed for the stairs on the right. This was the direction of the Impressionists. Almost everyone has heard of Monet, Picasso, and Van Gogh, and if I were a thief, you bet I would head straight for what would sell well.

At the top of the steps, the security doors stood wide open. My hunch looked good. The room buzzed with magic. All the heat, infrared, and pressure pad alarms had been circumvented. A latticework of energy held it in stasis. A noise from within beckoned me. In the soft museum lighting, a man was prising Van Gogh's *Chair* from its frame. Beside him sat a Renoir, pulled down from a wall.

An invisible shiver ran through my body as I moved to confront the man. 'Pay attention to your intuition,' Raven had cautioned me countless times. This silent shiver was a sure sign of something unseen. I just didn't know what.

I stopped.

Closing my eyes, I allowed myself to look with my magical sight and detected a ward spinning, chest high in the doorway. Anyone who walked through to disturb the man would trigger it. That was easy enough to get around. In true Neon-Mage style, I got down on my hands and knees and crawled, so much easier than trying to dispel the bugger. The hairs on the back of my neck stood up as I passed beneath.

Entering the room, I barely had time to rise, before the man turned and with a wave of his hand, struck me with a bright flash of light.

A stirring mass of orange, yellow, and green filled my vision. I gasped. I was standing in a huge field of tall sunflowers. I jumped to see a way out, but the sunflowers extended to the horizon. Where had I been sent? To the South of France?

No. I stopped jumping and thought about it. Sunflower fields don't usually stretch, as far as the eye can see, and where was the tingling feeling in my extremities that was a side effect of trans-location? I closed my eyes and brought to mind the image of the man waving his hand at me. What had he done?

I held the image until it dawned on me. Behind him on the wall had been Van Gogh's *Sunflowers*. I hadn't been trans-located. I was in an illusion. Somehow, he had used the painting to make me think I was in a field of sunflowers, when in reality I stood in the National Gallery with a dorky, ensorcelled look upon my face— just like the guard at the entrance.

A wizard, at this point, would have cast a counter-spell. A witch would have called on the little people to help her see truly. For me, either option was a waste of time and power. There was a simpler solution. To break the illusion all I had to do was prove it false. Find its weak point, the non-concordance with reality, the bee that didn't buzz, the flower that didn't smell. That would alert my brain that something was wrong, giving it time to catch up and reassert what it actually sensed.

As I looked around, finding a fault was going to be harder than I imagined. This illusionist was a master. Not only was I drawn by the beauty of the sunflowers, I could feel the heat of the sun on my face, hear the breeze through the leaves, and smell the freshness of the earth.

I centered myself. There must be a way out. Even as a master to how many levels did his reality go? I reached for the carry case on my back. It was a black tube, one in which I usually carried my yoga mat. When I was on the job, though, it held something extremely different. From it, I pulled my katana, my Japanese long-sword. Holding it steady in both hands, I slashed at the flower directly in front of me. It dissolved in a splash of yellow paint.

I had guessed right. The illusionist still thought of the sunflowers as a painting. I continued to slice my way forward, and the field dissolved in splatters of sun-colored puddles. My brain structured itself back to reality, and I found myself standing back in the Gallery, exactly where I had been, but now with my sword in my hand.

The man looked up and grinned. "So you want to fence, do you?"

With a gesture of throwing dust in the air, the painting on the floor next to him came alive, and I found myself standing on a Parisian street. It was drizzling rain. Great, I recognized the scene. I was in Renoir's *Umbrellas*. I tried to remember my grade school French but could only remember how to count to ten. That was the trouble about being home schooled by an old witch, she had battled to stop Napoleon and thought French was a 'filthy' tongue. Hence, my education was remarkably deficient in some areas.

I began counting.

Un. Two young girls giggled and ran past me.

Deux. The Parisians closed their umbrellas and pointed them at me. Uh oh—my spider senses were tingling.

Trois. The points of the umbrellas danced toward me, and I brought up my katana in response.

Quatre. For each umbrella I blocked, another jabbed me, and even knowing that I was in an illusion, it did not stop those jabs from hurting.

Cinq. I was hit from behind and had to spin, but that exposed my back to other umbrellas. Soon I was being poked from every side.

Six. I had to think of something.

Sept. The lady in blue was wearing a grin, just like the illusionist.

Huit. I feinted with my katana, leapt forward, and grabbed a fistful of hair. "Ow." The lady said in the illusionist's voice.

Neuf. Paris women don't have men's voices.

Dix. My brain dispelled the illusion, and the street scene dissolved with the rain.

I stood once again in the National Gallery.

The illusionist recovered first and pushed me hard in the chest. I fell backward, still clutching a lock of his hair and my katana. He grabbed the Van Gogh and ran out of the room. I rose to follow. A small part of my brain sent me a warning, but it was too late. I smacked straight into the ward that I had previously crawled under. There was a loud noise like a clash of cymbals, a flash of light, and everything went black.

Chapter Two

Through the closed lids of my eyes, a bright light shone red. My head felt like it had been placed between the ground and a jackhammer. Raising a hand to shield my eyes, I tried to control the throbbing in my brain while I blinked my eyes open.

A voice above me said, "She's coming round."

Propping myself up on my elbows, my vision came into focus to reveal two police officers looming over me. Each stood at such an angle I feared their bobby hats would tip off and fall, despite their biting chinstraps. The older one, with an uneven, red-tinged moustache, gripped my arm, ready to pull me up. He growled, "You've got some explaining to do, missy."

The other one held my katana up, and even though my brain was working like sludge, I managed to pull a thought through the murkiness and find the appropriate thing to say, "Wait. Let me show you my badge."

The policeman's grip relaxed minutely on my arm, and he asked, "You're police?"

"Military Intelligence. My badge is in my back pocket."

Still holding my arm, he cautiously reached around. I tilted my body. I was glad he wasn't making more of a fuss about retrieving my proof. Some of these types liked to cuff first and talk later. He pulled out the badge and flipped it open.

Even though it was a part of the British Military, MI-23 feared an outcry, if the public learnt that government funds were going to an agency that protected Britain from the supernatural world. So to maintain secrecy, Quentin, MI-23's tech wonder-boy, created magical badges that, when flashed, garnered instant authority in the mind of the recipient. It not only stopped awkward questions but also stopped the haggling over who had what jurisdiction. I knew that these police officers might have to make some creative additions to their reports, but for the moment, they would follow anything I said.

The policeman helped me to my feet. "Sorry about that. You aren't exactly dressed like the military."

Granted I wasn't in uniform, but it wasn't the greatest police work to assume that I was a perpetrator, just because I had been found unconscious on the scene. The other policeman handed me my sword, which I slid into the holder on my back. The pounding in my head thankfully receded, now that I was standing. I asked, "Did anyone catch the thief fleeing with the Van Gogh?"

"No. You were the only one in the building besides the security guards. We think they must have been hit with some sort of hallucinogenic spray because none of them claim to have seen anything. One was even fast asleep in the foyer. We're taking them all in for questioning, but I doubt we will find out anything more."

I did not dispel them of the hallucinogenic theory. They would likely take me straight to a mental asylum if I tried to explain the truth. The fact that there was a scarier, weirder world than they could imagine wasn't something most people were ready to accept. I said, almost to myself, "So, he got away."

The policeman's face sparked up. "You saw the thief?"

"Yes."

"Could you give us a description so we can put out an APB?" The police officer got out his notebook to record the details. He was using a silver, Schaeffer pen, and I wondered whether it had been a birthday present from his wife. It certainly wasn't standard issue. He was getting on in age, and the pen matched. Maybe his parents had given it to him, when he had joined the force, all those years ago. I bet that pen could tell stories. No one had ever given me as nice a pen.

I caught myself and came back to his question. Whatever the ward had hit me with was making my mind wander. It was probably part of the spell to give the thief greater time to get away. Concentrate Lynx, concentrate. I described what I recalled, "You're looking for a Caucasian male, mid-twenties, approximately six-foot-two, dressed in jeans, black shirt, cowboy boots, and a blue blazer. Stubble, maybe three days old."

"Hair?" he asked.

His hair. Looking down, I uncurled my fist. There it was. Strands of brown locks coiled in my hand. I had him. I looked at the two officers. They were looking at me, looking at the hair. "Um. It was brown." I said hesitantly.

One of them got out an evidence bag, "Is that his?"

I nodded.

He opened the bag and presented it to me. "Put it in here."

The police officer looked pleased. To them DNA evidence was king. I dropped a few strands in the bag, kept the rest, and told them, "I need to go."

"Are you sure?" The younger policeman looked concerned. "You were out cold a minute ago. You need a medic."

"I'm okay. Nothing broken." I touched the back of my head to make sure. Good, no leakage to report. The dull throb had become more annoying than painful. I told them, "I really need to go. I may be able to find him and get the painting back."

Pen still poised above the notebook, the officer asked. "Anything else you can add to his description?"

I thought about it. "He was easy on the eye and had a grin on his face that I imagine has, too many times, gotten him into and out of trouble. He brandishes it like a weapon."

The policeman did not write that down.

Exiting through the doors of the Gallery, I looked into a sea of flashing blue lights. It looked like every available police car in London had responded to the call. Shielding my eyes, I dodged a couple of officers running into the Gallery. Others were busy keeping the media back, who sniffing a big story on their police scanners had descended by the vanload. On the other side of the police tape, they clamored and elbowed each other in their eagerness to take footage.

Flashing my badge, I snuck through the lines, sidestepped the media, and wandered over to Trafalgar Square to sit cross-legged near the base of Nelson's column. I felt in my pocket for some gum. The idea of bad breath mortifies me, so I always carry a pack.

After chewing it till it was soft, I spat the gum into

my hand, tried not to be grossed out, and pressed the illusionist's hair into the sticky mess. I removed the necklace from around my neck. It was a pure silver chain and a medallion of the Tree of Life. My mother had left it to me after she died. I attached the hair and gum to the medallion, then reached in to my other pocket and pulled out a glow stick. I cracked it, so the highlighter lemon-yellow glow could power the spell while I followed its directions. Holding it and the necklace in one hand, I closed my eyes.

This was the tricky part. Sympathetic magic wasn't my strongest field. I worked better with the smash and grab of elemental energies. Still, a finding spell with such a strong link as hair should be easy. I bound the glow stick to the medallion with intention, and said, "Find."

I cried as the pain of casting tore through me. The medallion spun crazily. Finally, it settled, off the gravitational line and clearly pointed down the Strand. For the medallion to be pulled as much as it was, he was close. I smiled. The illusionist was mine. Placing the tugging chain and stick between my top and bottom front teeth for a moment, I removed a small bottle of juniper-scented, hand sanitizer from my jacket pocket and thoroughly cleansed my hands. I popped two aspirin I found in my other pocket. Ready, I held the chain and stick in my right hand and set off.

Running down the Strand, the medallion turned when I reached the Savoy Hotel. Looking at the imposing front edifice, I paused before starting down the drive. This was the exclusive territory of the very rich and was exactly the type of place a buyer for a freshly stolen Van Gogh would stay. With the medallion pulling me, I continued to the entrance and ignored the doorman's quizzical look as he opened the door to let me inside.

Entering the lobby, I imagined the sort of money it took to stay here. When I went to France for a holiday last year, I only stayed in hostels. I swear I never knew women could snore until I shared a room with eight of them. One day I would love to stay here. Yet, for the moment, I put the luxuries of the lobby firmly from my mind. I was an agent not a tourist.

The medallion pointed upward, so I headed for the lifts, my boots clipping loudly on the black and white chessboard marble.

A voice called after me, "Excuse me?"

Somehow, the voice managed to sound both snooty and polite at the same time. I wondered if there were special classes for that. I didn't have time to spare, but knew I needed to placate the staff before I could continue. I turned and answered, "Yes."

It was the night manager, speaking from behind the desk, "I am sorry, but that section is for house guests only."

Looking down at myself, I smiled. I guessed torn, black-leather pants, a white silk blouse, and a denim jacket were not exactly what ladies of the upper crust wore. I reached in my back pocket, pulled out my badge, and held it up.

He moved like he did not appreciate having to come out from behind his desk. He was dressed from the Edwardian Age, right down to tails on his suit, a crisp double Windsor, and a collar starched with slopes steeper than the Matterhorn. This guy exuded the pompous air of one who served the very rich.

He inspected my badge, sniffed, and said, "Sorry. We do have to respect the privacy of our guests. And dressed like that, well you would have to be a rock star to afford the Savoy or…"

His voice dwindled, and even though I noted a slight increase of the polite and decrease in the snooty as he spoke, I felt my face flush. Were my pants that tight? Still I wasn't going to let some night manager get the best of me. I asked, "Or what?"

The man had the good grace to blush in turn, "Dear me. I must have lost my train of thought. I can't remember what I was going to say. Now is there any way I may be of assistance?"

"There is one thing you could help with." I really didn't want to go breaking down doors. It is a surprisingly hard thing to do, even with magic. "Do you have a pass-card I could borrow? I've reason to believe a suspect is in one of your rooms."

Alarm and excitement showed on the man's face. I imagined the graveyard shift could be terribly dull, and anything out of the ordinary was a welcome relief. He asked, "Is the suspect dangerous?"

"Nothing to worry the other guests about. Alert your security team, but tell them to stay well back. I guarantee I'll be as discreet as possible."

The night manager handed me a pass-card from his pocket. "Please do. We can't have the Savoy's name tarnished."

I noticed he ignored my medallion, which was defying gravity by sticking straight up between us. Most people don't register magic, even when it is being worked right in front of them. I think it's a coping mechanism of the brain.

The lifts were formidable in Edwardian black and gold. I pressed every button, not knowing which floor to choose. The medallion pointed up for the first four floors but flattened at the fifth.

I slipped my hand inside my jacket, feeling for my gun, and removed the safety. When it came down to it, modern technology was a great leveler. A gunshot would kill a wizard or a witch as easily as a mundane.

Following the medallion down the corridor, I saw a flash of light, coming from under the door of the room ahead. I quietly advanced and sure enough, the medallion pointed straight at the room. Releasing my magical will from the medallion, I let it drop into my jacket pocket. I would remove the hair and gum later.

Poised and ready to use the pass-card, I hesitated. This illusionist had tricked me twice. He had overwhelmed me with the power of his illusions, and now I was about to enter a hotel room on my own to face him. I should call for back up. I fingered the crystal in my pocket but pride stopped me. What would my parents have done? I did not want people saying I could not handle it on my own. This was my arrest. I would get that painting back.

I readied myself for attack, borrowing energy from the lights in all the empty corridors of the hotel and imagined a shield in front of me. "Protect." I opened the door. The art-deco suite had an entrance foyer and a sitting room to one side. The illusionist lay sprawled, eyes closed, in the middle of the floor of the sitting room. I dropped my shield and went over to check his pulse. He was unconscious but alive.

Keeping a watchful eye out, I checked the bedroom. It was empty. Moving into the bathroom, there was no one there, but on the mirror someone had written in red lipstick, *There is enough for everyone's need but not for their greed.* The illusionist didn't look like the type to carry red lipstick, and the writing seemed oddly feminine, with an old way of printing the A's, as if the person had learned with a fountain pen.

With dwindling hope, I went through the rooms thoroughly to see whether the painting was anywhere. I checked the shower, the cupboards, under the bed, and even looked to see whether the air vents had been tampered with, but there was no sign of the painting. I went back to the illusionist, who was still out cold, and patted him down. He did not have any weapons or the painting. I drew his wallet from his back pocket and looked at his license. Gazing down at the comatose thief, I said, "Well, Mr. Andrew Daniels, you're properly nicked."

Taking my handcuffs from the back of my belt, I rolled him over and cuffed him. Unlike police issued shackles, these cuffs were covered in complex runes to stop any practitioner from casting a spell. Checking the illusionist's head for visible damage, I could not see anything. I went to the bathroom and poured a glass of water. Going back, I threw the water in his face.

His eyes shot open. "NO!"

I put my face in his. "No what?"

He blinked, tried to move his arms, and looked helplessly to either side before he realized he was cuffed. His eyes focused on me. They were azure and gray. He said, "You were at the Gallery."

I poked him with my boot, "I'm the one asking the questions."

He grinned at me, but his face was pasty and the

effect was lost. "I wasn't asking a question. That was a statement."

Okay, I would concede that point. He still had his wits about him. But I needed to show him who was the boss here. "Don't get smart with me." I pulled him up by the lapels of his blazer, leant him against the white and black sofa, and asked, "What happened to the painting?"

He stretched his neck to either side and blinked twice, as if trying to clear a headache. His eyes darted to the table. "It's gone."

There was a bit of water left in the glass, so I offered it to him. I had to play both good cop and bad cop at the same time. I mentally sent out a growl directed at Raven, wherever he was. My partner should be here to celebrate my first arrest and help with the questioning. "What do you mean gone?"

The illusionist downed the glass as I poured it in his mouth. Finishing with a gulp, he said in a somewhat froggy voice, "I was double crossed."

"By whom?"

He looked around the suite. "I don't think I can tell you."

I had given him that glass of water too soon. It was time to play bad cop again. Resisting the urge to poke him once again with my boot, I told him, "All right, you're going to jail."

He replied, "No problem."

Mr. Andrew Daniels looked like a cat taking a cream bath.

"Don't think it will be a prison that you can waltz out of with a quick illusion." I narrowed my eyes, "It'll be the Isle of Skragrock for you."

This time, his smugness was a little less sure as he took up a defiant tone. "Never heard of it."

"Didn't think you would. It's off the northern coast of Scotland, unmarked on any map. It's bitterly cold. Once a month a boat drops off supplies and is the only contact with the outside world. The prison is specifically designed for persons such as yourself, for the Isle is dead to all magical energy. You'll never be able to use your magic to cast an illusion and escape. You'll be there until your sentence is finished." I put the empty glass of water on the coffee table. "So you better start talking. Assuming, of course, that you want to come back from the Isle some time before you're eligible for a pension."

He breathed out. "Well this is the first time I've been handcuffed in a suite, at the Savoy hotel, with a beautiful woman, so I guess there really is a first time for everything."

I raised him to his feet. "Great. Have it your way."

"No. Wait. You don't understand. I meant I'll talk for the first time. I'll help you get the painting back."

He sounded sincere.

"You will?" My naïve excitement betrayed me. I cringed. My voice had come out like a thrilled teenager. I wished I had said something tougher, like, 'so talk' in a raspy, blues-singer voice.

He seemed not to have noticed. With his head lowered, he answered, "Yes. The only problem is that I don't really know who hired me to get the painting, let alone who took it from me."

I looked at him incredulously.

From behind his fringe, he looked back and with a sigh said, "It's true. I needed money, and I was given this job. They said I'd get ten million pounds if I brought the painting to this suite. When I got here, there was no one around. I put the painting down on the table and waited in the chair. I heard something in the bathroom. When I got up and turned around, there was a flash of light. Next thing I knew I woke up wet, handcuffed, and with you."

I could not help but think he looked cute when he was pleading. He was turning it on. He really wanted to be believed. I was having none of it. I flashed him my best million-dollar smile. "Well then it looks like it's off to Skragrock for you. Do not pass Go. Do not collect ten million pounds."

"Wait. Let's not be hasty." He stiffened as I grabbed his arm. "I can tell you who got me the job."

I was pretty good at spotting if someone was lying to me. "Who?"

He was getting nervous now. The reality was starting to sink in, and for the first time he was looking at me not as a pretty, young thing, but as the person who would be the start of the end of his free life. "Let me know what the deal is first."

I thought of what I could actually promise and offered, "I'll tell the court you cooperated."

"Can't you just let me go?"

He made it sound so reasonable, but I was having nothing to do with his charm.

I put on my best judge's voice. "You broke into the National Gallery and stole a priceless work of art, violating section 3.6 of the British Use of Magic Code, and that doesn't even touch the civilian statutes."

He looked away. "It sounds bad, when you put it that way."

I punctuated with a finger in his chest. "It *is* bad. Further, Van Gogh's *Chair* is one of my favorite works of art. In it, he transformed a simple and humble part of his life into a brilliant composition of color and lines. I could feel the texture of the chair just by looking at the painting. It's a symbol of the simple tragedy that was Van Gogh's life and you...you just hacked it out of its frame."

He was looking at me intently, his head slightly cocked to the side. "I didn't think—"

I interrupted him with an angry retort, "No you didn't."

There was a knock at the door. What now? I did not want anybody to come in and spoil my first arrest.

The illusionist had a strangled look upon his face.

He whispered, "Don't answer it."

I rolled my eyes, pushed him onto the sofa, and went to the door.

Chapter Three

Through the peephole, two men, big enough to quell a riot with a glance, crowded the hallway. They were dressed in identical, gunmetal gray, three-piece suits. The sort of fashion that would have been worn by a Victorian pugilist. They sure as hell weren't hotel security. One delivered a deliberate and measured knock with an old fashioned cane. Had they not seen the bell? Aggressive men of size raise my hackles. It was time to take these guys down a notch.

"Please don't open the door," the illusionist pleaded, looking genuinely scared. "It's more trouble than you can handle."

The one thing that annoys me more than aggressive men, are men who assume they know what I can or cannot handle. I needed to see whether these guys knew anything about the missing painting, so I ignored Mr. Daniels and pulled my Beretta Nano from its shoulder holster. A small, easy to conceal 9mm, it packed a large enough punch to stop just about anything. I did not actually want to shoot these guys, but a little intimidation never hurts when dealing with Neanderthals. I steeled myself for the gorilla twins, opened the door, and pointed my Beretta at them.

The man knocking on the door paused mid tap. He brought his cane to the floor evenly in front of his body, clasped it with both hands, and said, "Hello crumpet.

That's a nice little toy you got there. May we come in?"

His disregard for my gun made me feel uneasy. I could tell they were not strangers to having guns pointed at them. That was a warning sign. My other hand went up to double the grip on my weapon. I asked, "Who are you, and what do you want?"

He sniffed the air and looked past me into the suite where the illusionist was seated on the sofa, before he answered, "My name's Weasel, and this is my associate Dave. We need to have a little talk with your friend in there."

"He isn't my friend. He's my prisoner," I replied. They hadn't made a move to enter the room, and I considered slamming the door in their faces. However, their size told me they would have no trouble knocking down the door, and I wanted to avoid hurting them, if possible.

"Look whatever floats your boat. It'll be just a little chat. He owes us money." He turned his attention away from me and using a louder voice, asked, "Have you got the money you promised us, Andy?"

The illusionist shook his head. "Sorry, Weasel, I don't. I thought I would. That's why I called you here. I was supposed to get paid, but I got ripped off."

"Well then, you know the rules Andy. Your week is up." Weasel looked at me. "I'm sorry, miss, but if you'll excuse us, this is going to get messy."

I pulled my ID badge. "No it's not. I need him."

Weasel laughed and turned to his partner. "How long have we been in business, Dave?"

"Long enough, Weasel. Long enough," Dave retorted.

Weasel turned back to me as he asked, "Long

enough for what?"

"Long enough not to be intimidated by a little piece of crumpet with a badge and a gun." Dave almost sighed as he took a step toward me.

Something glowed in both of their eyes. Involuntarily, I took a step back and kicked myself. How could I have missed the signs? These were the famous Werewolves of London, hired muscle from the bad end of town. No one messed with them. I was in serious trouble. Werewolves were practically impervious to magic, and my gun was worse than useless. I looked back at Mr. Andrew Daniels. His face had turned an odd shade of gray-green, and I imagined I could feel his shaking from where I stood. I steeled myself and turned back to face the werewolves. I was not about to let a man be murdered before me. Not on my watch.

Weasel took a step through the doorway. Despite myself, I took another step back. The werewolf growled, "Ask yourself, is this joker really worth the trouble?"

I thought frantically. My magic could probably freeze one of them, but I would not have anything left to stop the other one from coming through and killing us both. Even if I had my katana out, I doubted I was a physical match for a werewolf. I asked, "How much does he owe?"

Weasel stopped and scratched his head. "About five million pounds?"

"I think it actually was closer to six million, once we include the interest," Dave chipped in.

"Yes, that's right." Weasel smiled at me with teeth that had far too many points, "Six million pounds,

Dorothy, now click you heels three times and think of home."

Maybe I could appeal to their greed. "Wait. You take him now, and you won't see that money."

Dave seemed resigned to the fact. "True."

Weasel walked up so the gun was pointing directly at his chest. "The thing is, we still get paid...either way."

I knew I could squeeze the trigger, and he would keep on coming, so I lowered the gun. I only had one die to roll. "What if I go surety for him?"

"No, kill me now," the illusionist yelled.

Weasel considered. "How are you going to come up with six million pounds on a government salary?"

I held his eyes. "That's my problem."

He asked, "Why?"

I didn't know what he wanted. "Pardon?"

"Why? What's your motivation for saving this muppet?" Weasel's gaze flicked to the handcuffs. "Are you screwing him?"

"No." I said, my voice going up an octave, and my cheeks hot as fire. "I am not sleeping with him. I care about the painting he stole. He's the only lead I have, and this is my first case. If you kill him now, I lose my best chance to find the painting, and you never get your money. On the other hand, trust me and we both just might get what we want."

"No deal. Do you think we are stupid? The moment you arrest him, you'll send him off to Skragrock. Then when you don't come up with the money, we have to wait till he gets out to kill him. Long after you're dead and dealt with—of course. No, crumpet, doesn't work for me."

Weasel moved to shoulder past me. I said, "Wait."

"Come on Dorothy. Shut your eyes."

Mr. Daniels was holding his breath and had the wildest eyes I had ever seen on a man. I could not let them do this. I raised my voice, "I said wait." Weasel turned to me. "This better be good."

"What if I promise not to turn him in until after you are paid?" I tried not to think about all the regulations I would be breaking.

"No whisking him off to jail or protective custody?" Dave stepped up right beside his partner, crowding me.

"No. I haven't called this in yet." I felt a surge of anger toward Raven. If he were here backing me up, then I would not be in this position, "All I want is to get the painting."

"Why should we trust you?" Weasel tapped me on the chest with the handle of his cane.

I grabbed the handle and looked Weasel in the eye, "Because even if he gets protective custody, I don't."

"True." Weasel laughed and again looked me up and down. "All right. We do get more if we collect. You have one week."

I immediately countered, "Make it two."

"Ha ha. I like you crumpet. You've got spunk." Weasel pinched my cheek. "Ten days."

The moment he let go of my cheek, I agreed, "Ten days. Thank you."

"Don't be thanking us." Dave pushed his chin forward. "If you don't get the money both you and Andy are going to meet with extremely nasty accidents."

Weasel sniffed the air around me. "And don't even

think of running. We've got your scent now and can track you."

Dave added, "Anywhere in the world."

It was no idle threat. They had been in business for over a century and had once tracked someone from London to a hut in the Brazilian rainforest. After word got around about what they had done to that poor fellow, suffice it to say, no one ran from the werewolves. They let it be known that the more anyone ran, the more gruesome the end.

They left. I watched them all the way down the hallway, before I closed the door. Slumping against the wall, I put my head in my hands. The Magus was going to be furious when he found out what I had just done.

Chapter Four

Screeching to a halt, I just managed to avoid crashing straight through four lanes of traffic. Replaying the confrontation with the werewolves in my mind, I was not paying as much attention as I should to the road, and a red light had appeared out of nowhere. Mr. Daniels squirmed in his seat next to me, pressing his foot hard against the floor. I could tell he wished that he had control of the car. There might be hope for him yet, for he was wise enough not to say a word.

After marching him out of the Savoy and down the Strand, I retrieved my car from where it was still illegally parked in front of the National Gallery. With a jacket thrown over his cuffs to avoid attention, I drove off without the media or the police taking any notice.

Safe in the Coop, it was hitting me what a colossal cock up I had made of things. My first solo run, and I was already aiding and abetting a known felon. I took a deep breath. I had saved a life, but at what cost? Before, I didn't have so much as a parking ticket on my record, and now I was breaking the law. Still, glancing sideways, I knew I had done the right thing. Beside me sat another human being who was still breathing because I had saved him. Yet, it had put me up the proverbial creek with no paddle in sight. Taking out my crystal, I tried calling Raven, but there was no answer. I couldn't go back to Bosley House, MI-23's headquarters, as there would be too many questions. So, I headed to my apartment in Notting Hill.

We took off from the lights. "So, Andrew…"

Mr. Daniels interrupted, "Don't call me that, only my mother called me Andrew, and whenever I hear it, I feel like I am in trouble. It's Andy."

"You are in trouble, Andrew." I took my eyes off the road long enough to give him my best imitation of a headmistress's stare. "More trouble than you've ever been in before. So it's time to drop the act and start telling me everything about the person who gave you the commission."

Andy's nostrils flared as he took that in. He didn't like taking orders from a woman younger than himself. But he controlled himself and said, "It was Tablet who organized the job. He might know more."

I checked, "Tablet from Gordon's?"

"Yes. You've heard of him?"

I nodded. Tablet was a contractor for all sorts of unsavory types. I changed down gears to execute a sharp right turn. "I have. Will he be there tonight?"

"He should be." Andy's reply came out as slightly strangled. He gripped the seat in an attempt to keep his body from being thrown to the left. "I can call him in the afternoon to make sure."

It was half a plan at least. We drove on in silence for a while. Then I couldn't resist, "And what was with the writing in the bathroom in red lipstick? Are you a cross-dresser?"

"No." It was Andy's turn to sound angry. I filed that away, a little too defensive there. I'm guessing he might like a bit of lace. Would look pretty in it too. He asked, "What writing?"

"When I got to the hotel, scrawled in red lipstick across the mirror were the words, 'There is enough for everyone's need but not for their greed.'"

"Wait, I know that quote." He looked at the roof of the car, as if hoping that would help him remember. Maybe it did, for he finally triumphantly said, "Mahatma Gandhi."

Points for general knowledge aside, this man was a bit of a conundrum. A thief, with a rich boy air who spoke like he read Classics at Cambridge. "Aren't you the smartarse?" I said. "Still doesn't help, for we still don't know why they wrote it."

"I don't know. It's probably a dig at me. They expected me to wake up and see that." Andy shifted in his seat. His arms were still cuffed together on his lap under the seatbelt, and I could see the belt riding up toward his neck. I took the next corner especially hard.

Maybe it was more than a dig. It was a mistake. It gave me insight into whoever had taken the painting. They were arrogant. They were cultured. I asked, "So tell me, why can't you just cast an illusion on the werewolves, so they think they've been paid?"

"Won't work." Andy shook his head and looked down.

"Why not?"

"The werewolves can smell their way through any illusion. Their noses are so sensitive that any false impression is bound to fail. I can fool a human because I know how it should smell to them, but a werewolf, well I just can't recreate the complexity of what I can't even begin to understand."

So, it would be up to me to come up with something. I really needed a cup of tea and a soft chair.

Andy asked, "Where are we going now?"

"My place."

Andy shifted in his seat again and put on a smirk. "Really. I usually don't do that sort of thing on the first date."

I guessed he was trying to be charming, but I fixed him with a withering look, imagining I was Cyclops from X-Men burning him to a crisp. I said, "Just don't. I'm not in the mood."

Andy looked out at the buildings flashing by the car and was silent for a while. He then said, "Thank you."

I looked over at him. "For what? Arresting you?"

He spoke softly, "For saving my life."

"I didn't do it for you. I did it to get the painting back." I saw a flash of pain cross his face, which he tried to cover by staring out the window. Interesting. "But you're welcome."

Andy looked over at me. I pretended to be concentrating upon the roads. He smiled. I may have been committing a felony and had ten days to come up with more money than I had ever known, but a warm feeling spread through me. We said nothing until we came to Kensington Rd. Parking was tough. I had to go down the road a couple of blocks to find a space.

Getting out of the car awkwardly, Andy asked, "So how do you afford a place in Notting Hill, on your salary?"

I closed the door for him and pressed the lock button on my key. The mini made a satisfying beep. I liked being sure it was locked. "I don't. It was my parents'."

"Was?"

Even after all these years, I still had to push down the loss. "Yes. They were killed when I was young. This place was held in trust until I turned eighteen."

"I'm sorry. What happened to them?"

"I've no idea. All I was told was that they had been killed while on active duty. One of the reasons I joined MI-23 was to find out."

"Tough not knowing?"

I grunted in reply. Of course it was.

Andy pressed, "Have you found out anything?"

"Nothing." I had asked about old case files but could find nothing that referred to their last two years of service.

Andy changed subjects. "So why else did you become an agent?"

"Well there isn't much career opportunity outside the service."

"Rubbish," he sounded shocked, "I know a dozen people who would employ you in an instant."

"Criminals?"

"Well…"

"You see the legal opportunities are far and few between. It isn't as though I could hang a big sign on my door, '*Lynx Somerton, Witch*' and expect to get customers."

"You might be surprised. Still, it had to be more than the employment opportunities."

He was right. I really hadn't considered doing anything else—ever. "It was what my parents wanted me to do. They started my training young."

"My parents wanted me to be a doctor. You don't have to follow what your parents want for you."

"I know, but I watched them heading off, prepared

to risk their lives to protect people. It made them happy living a purposeful life. They ended up paying the ultimate price, but I want to believe that it meant something."

Andy seem to be digesting my words. "I get that. What happened to you after they died?"

I decided to answer, recognizing that in doing so, he would now know more about me now than most of my fellow workers. "I went and lived with my great-aunt. She has a place in Devon, on the Moors."

"All lonely and desolate?"

Why did everyone think of Brontë when I mentioned the Moors? Totally wrong moor, yet they still imagined me pining for Heathcliff. "Outside, yes, but inside was a different matter. It was warm—color everywhere, pets underfoot, there was always something delicious smelling on the stove. Poor old dear had no idea what to do with a girl who had lost her parents, so she taught me her trade, witchcraft."

"Didn't you go to school?"

I wonder what it would have been like if I had. There were times growing up when I dreamt of having friends, but how could I have brought them home to an aunt who may have invited a dryad into her kitchen for tea. "No we were in too remote an area. We did it by correspondence. Besides, the things she was teaching me were much more interesting."

"I could tell that you didn't grow up with other kids," he stated, like it was the most obvious thing in the world.

Obvious…

He was treading on dangerous ground. I asked, my voice dropping ten degrees, "What do you mean you can tell?"

We were still a block away from my apartment, and he seemed unmindful of the fact he was jabbing at someone who had the keys to his cuffs. Was he stupid as well as immoral?

"It's obvious you are a loner," he blithely continued.

"You think you're such an expert on character that after a mere hour with your arresting officer you can make such a blanket statement?" I stopped on the sidewalk.

He turned to me and asked, "Who's your best friend?"

"Raven." I answered immediately and started walking again, with assurance that I had won the argument with the promptness of my reply.

Andy didn't move, and I was annoyed that I had to stop. He was quiet for a moment before speaking again. "Another agent from work?"

Damn him, how could he have known that? I admitted, "Yes."

"Doesn't count then." There was a spring in his step as he started to walk again. "Name one of your female friends."

"Ummm..." I had tried sharing my apartment last year with an Australian girl called Eve. We had gotten on well enough, but I hadn't been able to stand her habit of inviting just about anyone back for drinks. There was Amy, but truthfully, she was a cousin I hadn't seen in at least a year. Then my aunt, but I don't think she would count, having raised me and there was the apparent generational gap. Wendy and I had struggled through Sandhurst together, yet I hadn't heard from her since she had been sent to Afghanistan. Charlotte I loved like a sister, but we fought like sisters.

I was taking too long.

He said in a slimy voice, "Don't have any. Do you?" He taunted in the same oily tone.

I protested, "I've been busy."

"Bet you push all the men away too."

My nostrils flared, but I didn't have a comeback as he was dangerously close to the mark. I stormed on in silence and was glad when we arrived at my building. There was a twenty-four-hour convenience store on the ground level, and I really needed that cup of Earl Grey. "Just a moment, I have to get some milk."

We entered, and the elderly clerk called from the behind the counter, "Hello Lynx."

I think he had been there since the days when every item sold had been wrapped in brown paper and string. I greeted him back, "Mr. Adams. How's the hip holding up?"

I had half an eye on Andy. He couldn't think I was such a loner, if I was chatting with Mr. Adams. Andy wasn't paying attention. The pig was looking at the pictures on the front of the men's magazines and not even hiding his action.

"Not bad, only twinges occasionally now," Mr. Adams answered. "Is this your new fellah?"

"No." I stood in front of Andy so Mr. Adams wouldn't see the cuffs as I purchased the milk. "Just a work associate."

"It's about time you got a man. You young girls are all too concerned with your careers, so you can't keep anybody. It isn't right, and you'll regret it later." He always found time to give me a lecture on the problems of youth, but I didn't mind. He meant well.

I peppered him with a smile. "I just haven't found the right one yet."

"You haven't been looking," he scolded. "I know the long hours you keep at work. Finding someone to love should be a priority, it's the juice of life."

How is it that people of his generation are capable of living with the same person for fifty years? I had yet to get past the two-year mark.

"I will put it on my to-do-list." I took my change and the milk. "Send my love to Mrs. Adams."

"I will."

Andy and I trudged up the stairs to my apartment. Entering my living room, I tried to remember the last time anyone had been over. I breathed a sigh of relief that the place looked clean. All the walls, the wood, the couch, the bookcase, the lamps, and the cushions were in various shades of white. Pearl, cream, eggshell, ivory, as well as linen were all in evidence, making the place look pristine and peaceful. My books stood in perfect alphabetical order on the bookshelf. Under my breath, I whispered, 'Light' and the vanilla scented candles sprang to life in the corner.

"It's a bit sterile," Andy remarked, as he plonked down on the couch and put his feet on the coffee table. His shoes were still on. Where was this boy raised?

"Get your feet off the table," I ordered.

"Otherwise what? You'll arrest me?"

I just glared until he put his feet on the floor. I then felt a blush coming on, as I realized his feet had been covering a book, titled, *Finding the Love You Want*. Generally, I detest self-help books. Buying one feels like an admission of defeat. I got the book in a moment of weakness. It's not like I believed happiness was only possible in a relationship. I felt complete without one. Truly. Andy followed my eyes to the book, and the heat on my face grew hotter. God I am pathetic. Thankfully, I was saved further embarrassment by a ball of white fur, which leapt up on the couch, right behind Andy.

"What the…" Andy exclaimed, startled. He looked behind at my cat, who head-butted him.

"Oh I hope you aren't allergic. That's just Mr. Particularis."

Rubbing the cat under the chin, Andy queried, "You named your cat, Mr. Particularis?"

I was a little annoyed that my cat had gone to check out the newcomer first. Sometimes I swear he punishes me for leaving him at home when I go to work. "I named him that for he is as fussy as they come. I once ran out of cat food and instead gave him a tin of salmon. Now he refuses to eat anything else."

Andy looked at the size of my cat. "It shows."

"Don't be rude. He understands English, you know."

I guessed I should be the hostess. "I'm going to make myself a cup of tea. Would you like one?"

He crinkled his forehead, and I could instantly tell he was a coffee drinker. I cannot understand those who do not appreciate the wonders of tea. "Do you have anything to eat?"

Men are always thinking of their stomachs. He was like every boyfriend I have ever had. Admittedly, there had been only two, but he was exactly the same as both of them, so despite the small sample size of three men I felt had a right to extrapolate to their whole gender. I mentally went through the contents of my fridge. "I could make you an omelet."

"Anything will do."

Was that a yes, please? That would be lovely, thank you? No. I opened my mouth to give him a piece of my mind, when I realized what I was doing. The man was a thief, who had burgled the National Gallery. How could I possibly hope to correct his manners, when he had no compunction about committing grand larceny? I beckoned him to follow me into the kitchen and hoped my disapproving silence would be enough to show him the error of his ways.

Andy watched, with what looked like amusement, as I looked up a recipe for an omelet on my iPad. "You don't do a lot of cooking, do you?"

It's true that some may think an omelet is a simple thing to make, but ask any chef, and they will tell you that a perfect one is hard to master. "That's not true. I cook all the time. I just like to follow recipes."

"It's an omelet."

I found an appropriate recipe that matched the ingredients I knew I had in the fridge. "Yes and I like to do it properly."

He lounged against the fridge. "Don't you get sick of being a perfectionist?"

"I'm not a perfectionist. I'm not good enough to be one."

Sometimes I wish I had more of an inner censor. I pushed Andy out of the way, opened the fridge, and angrily put items on the counter. I calmed as I measured the milk, the salt, diced half an onion, a whole tomato, grated a third of a cup of cheddar, cracked four eggs, sliced fifty grams of ham, chopped some fresh parsley, and sliced some mushrooms. There is something about cooking that takes away the stress of the world and thankfully, Andy had the good grace not to talk while I worked on the omelet. Once each ingredient was in a new bowl of appropriate size, then and only then, would I start the cooking process.

"I could help, if you took these cuffs off," Andy offered graciously, holding up his hands.

Barely looking up, my concentration fully on my preparations, I said, "Do you think I'm a sucker?"

He laughed. "Can't blame a man for trying. Don't be so serious. Don't you ever have fun?"

I almost threw an egg at him but could not help but smile. I responded, "As a matter of fact I do. Just the other week I took a whole night off to watch documentaries on the banking crash and sub-prime lending."

"Ooh fascinating. You really know how to let your hair down." His grin told me he knew I was joking.

I went back to cooking. It was almost time to flip half the omelet over. I adjusted the gas, it is important to not cook omelets on too high a heat or they go brown.

He offered, "If you uncuff me, I promise to not cast any illusions at you."

I flipped and with satisfaction looked down upon an exact semi-circle. I pressed the mixture down a little to let the juices run, ignoring him.

He hopped up on one of my breakfast stools. "You really have got to start trusting me at some point."

I didn't have to do anything of the sort. Just because a man is in my kitchen doesn't mean I have to start trusting them. Usually it means the opposite. I turned, brandishing my spatula. "Whatever gives you that idea?"

He swiveled on the stool trying to find a comfortable balance. "Because it is the only way we are ever going to pay off the debt."

I was about to give him a piece of my mind when a gong sounded. It was my communication crystal letting me know I had a message.

I slid the omelet onto a plate, finishing it with a sprinkle of parsley. Passing it to Andy, I said, "Excuse me."

Trust him? That man was a dreamer. I picked up my crystal and went to the other room to listen to the message.

I watched through the doorway, as Andy attacked the omelet two-handed with a fork. Then the message from MI-23 came through, sending ice through my heart. *"Raven's dead. Tower of London. Come."*

Chapter Five

Rolling up the garage door, I revealed my pride and joy, a 1972 Jaguar E-Type Roadster, perfect in British racing green. It used to be my father's and was faster than the Mini. I would have loved to claim all original parts, but to survive what I'd put it through, I'd outfitted it with modern Brembo suspension and Hawk ceramic brakes. I also added a Supersprint exhaust, to boost the horsepower and scare the dogs for a two-block radius every time I started the car. The final touch was a fantastic new Bose sound system, complete with a subwoofer in the trunk.

We were quickly on the road, flying past the early morning traffic as the pre-dawn light brightened the sky. Normally I loved driving the Jag, but this time, while Andy inanely tried to chat beside me, I was too distracted by Raven's death to appreciate the marvellous ride. I drove on automatic, so when banks of lawn appeared, rolling up to the imposing walls of the Tower of London, I truly wondered how I had gotten there so fast. I could hardly remember the journey at all. It was like finding yourself in bed after being at the pub, but not being exactly sure how you got there.

I left Andy in the car, although he complained. Seeing him handcuffed to the wheel, I only felt a little bit bad. I probably should have told him what was going on, but I wasn't ready to talk about what had happened.

The police held back the media. The press was having a field day. First, the break-in at the National Gallery and now an attack at the Tower of London. That should fill their little, sensationalist, blackened hearts for at least a week. I squeezed through and showed my badge to a young officer. He offered to escort me through to the crime scene. Away from the entrance he asked, "Homicide or Theft?"

"What do you mean theft?" I stopped, "I was called here because my partner was reported dead."

"I'm sorry for your loss, miss." He held my eyes for a moment before going on to explain, "There was a break in at the Crown Jewel exhibit. A diamond was taken."

I asked, "What diamond?"

"The Koh-I-Noor." He scratched his head. "It is missing from the Queen's Crown, and they can't work how someone snatched it without breaking the glass."

"The Koh-I-Noor?" It made no sense. It was the centerpiece of the Queen's crown. As one of the most unmistakable diamonds in the world, it would be impossible to sell or wear. I vaguely remembered its legend. "Isn't that the one that is cursed?"

"Only for men." The policeman moved through the grounds. "Every man who ever wore it lost his throne or had some other misfortune befall him. Women, however, seem to prosper when wearing it. Originally, it was taken from India as spoils of war for Queen Victoria, and she did all right with it in her crown."

"So we're looking for a woman?"

The policeman shrugged. "That's above my pay

grade. It'll be years before I make detective."

I looked at him. He was younger than I was. I forgot that people could be. He nodded self-consciously and continued walking on, but I stopped him with a hand on his arm. "Look…"

The Tower ravens lay dead on the grass. I went over and nudged one. Its feathers were as brittle as a burnt brandy snap. The raven had burned from the inside out. The body was charcoal all the way through. Only magical fire could do that type of damage. Wings clipped, the poor things wouldn't have had a chance. Brushing my hands ineffectively on my leather pants, I rose. This was more than random destruction. Legend held that England would not fall as long as there were ravens at the Tower. I wasn't superstitious, but a shiver ran up my spine. The unnecessary killing of the birds was a message. Who was threatening Britain?

"It's not only the ravens." The policeman ventured as we walked on, "The men guarding the place were found like that too. Not the Yeoman Warders, the guards that are on show during the day. The dead ones were the hard men you don't see that guard the place at night. The men prepared to die for Queen and Country, and who carry automatic weapons."

I did not respond. It was too close to the truth of Raven. There was a hard man whom no one saw.

He filled the gap. "Sorry miss…I just hope you get them."

I saw in him a reflection of my own insecurities and did not want to leave him flailing, so I agreed, "Thank you. So do I."

The grass behind the White Tower resembled a miniature Olympic opening ceremony, covered with hundreds of white flags. The forensic team was busy marking and photographing the fall of every shell casing. It seemed the men defending the Tower had emptied thousands of rounds. Not that it had done them much good. Among the white flags were the blackened remains of at least twenty men. The shock must have registered on my face for the policeman said, "Nasty business, I feel that way myself."

I nodded gratefully and then put back on my professional face. "Thank you Constable, I can take it from here."

He tipped his hat and left.

I moved forward and asked one of the forensic guys who was crouched down with a clipboard, "What happened here?"

"Too early to say." The man stood up, and I could see the worry on his face. I guess he had never seen anything like this before, it didn't fit with his idea of the world.

I asked, "What would be your best guess?"

"There were no actual explosions, so a couple of the guys are saying flamethrowers," he offered, with a raise of his left shoulder.

"But you don't believe it…"

He shook his head and gestured with his hand. "Flame throwers don't burn a guy uniformly to charcoal. And how anyone could have gotten close enough in that storm of bullets to actually use one…"

He trailed off surveying the area, scratched his head, and turned to me. "You got any idea?"

"I do, but you wouldn't believe me."

"You are…"

"Military Intelligence."

He looked me up and down. I didn't like wearing a uniform, but until I got a bit older, it might come in handy. I was getting sick of that incredulous look. Still he asked, "So what happened?"

I wanted to tell the forensic officer exactly what happened, but once the door of knowledge to the world of magic is opened, it is incredibly hard to close. I offered him a choice, red pill, blue pill. "Do you want to know for yourself or for something that you could put in your report?"

He scratched his head. "For my report."

His reply disappointed but did not surprise me. I told him, "Flamethrowers it is then."

He went back to placing the stakes in the ground— probably hoping that once everything was categorized and marked, the scene would make sense.

I stepped over a charred body of a dead man, not looking too close at the horrific grimace of pain etched upon his face. My mind shut off at some level, but I knew that I would pay the price later for what I was seeing. I was thankful for the hours of meditation training. It helped me maintain a professional demeanor despite the horror. I felt soiled, and somewhere deep inside, I was screaming. This went against everything that I believed in. Not only had someone murdered these men, they had used magic to do it. It was incomprehensible to me.

When I was filled with power, I became hyper-aware of all that was around me. That included other people's emotions. It was hard to comprehend the lack of soul one would need to be able to massacre so many in a killing spree, when filled with the life affirming force of magic. Whoever did it would have been vibrantly aware of the agony and fear each man suffered as he died. An absolute monster did this—an evil sorcerer of power.

I moved on. Looking for the one corpse, I had come to see.

Near the entrance to the Crown Jewels lay Raven. He was burnt but not beyond recognition. I knelt beside his charcoal corpse, scared to touch him lest he crumble away. He had been so strong in power. The number of people I knew who could have had a chance at killing him I could count on one hand, without including my thumb.

I placed my fingers ever so gently upon his brittle brow. I whispered, "Don't worry Raven, I will find your killer. May you travel peacefully to the other side."

"Be careful when you touch him. He's as dry as the Sahara in the noonday sun…" a voice behind me said. I turned to see Wharf Rat, an agent from MI-23, approaching. "…and likely to dissipate in a puff."

I rose to my feet. Wharf Rat was a five-foot tall Londoner, with a Cockney accent and a nose that involuntarily twitched. He sniffed, as he adjusted his gaze to look up to me. If there ever was someone with small man syndrome, it was him. Wish, his studious, stick-like partner, stood slightly behind him, watching through his coke bottle glasses. Wish might have turned out to be a decent human being, but with Wharf Rat, he was a Spock whose Captain James T. Kirk had turned out to be a soccer hooligan.

Great. This was the last thing I needed. Of all my colleagues, these two were perhaps the most backward. They were mundanes. That is, people with no magical ability. Yet, they had been assigned to our section from MI-5. They knew what we did. They had seen magic and resented the fact they had none. Seeing me shunned by the others, they came down hard on me as an object of their resentment.

Wharf Rat hawked and spat at Raven's body.

I rounded on him. "What the hell are you doing? That's Raven."

Wharf Rat had grown up tough. When I looked carefully, I could see the scars from fights on his face. I let him catch me looking. He didn't like to be examined. He was the type to smash a pint glass and shove it in someone's face, just for smiling. Like many in the service, I suspected he drank too much. I had seen him taking swigs from the flask in the top drawer of his desk. Not that I would say anything. He spat again, grinned evilly at me, and said, "He's a slimy traitor, and it is no less than he deserves."

He was a diminutive bully. Sheltered by my upbringing I wasn't used to such types. He pushed my buttons, and I found myself thinking of the perfect comeback long after he had gone. However, spitting at Raven was not something I could let slide. I put my finger in his face. "Do that again and there will be trouble."

The forensic team turned to watch. I glared at them, and they reluctantly went back to their work.

Wharf Rat had his own face in mine, well, more in my chest but as close as he could get, "What are you going to do? It's what the traitor deserves."

"Why the hell are you calling him a traitor?" I scrunched my hands into fists.

"It's only logical," Wish interceded, while Wharf

Rat and I continued to glare at each other. "Someone had to disarm the wards around the jewels to get to the diamond, and the wards on the Koh-I-Noor were set by Aleister Crowley himself. Only someone at MI-23 could have known how to get past them. Here we find Raven, someone capable of disarming the wards, suspiciously on the scene, even though we know no call was made to MI-23. Ergo, he's a traitor."

I shook my head. "But Raven—he would never."

Wish looked grim. "Why else would he be here? He had to know what was going on to have been here on time."

I argued, "Who killed him then?"

Wharf Rat said, "Raven got betrayed by another wizard after he retrieved the diamond. At this stage that is the best theory we have got. There were no witnesses. Everyone at the Tower was killed."

"All you have is flimsy circumstantial evidence."

Wish stepped up beside his partner. "Where were you last night?"

"Don't worry about her, Wish." Wharf Rat's eyes glared maliciously at me. "She wasn't clever enough to be involved. Raven got her out of the way by sending her off to the National Gallery. How did you go there, Lynx? Did you stop the robbery? Did you get the painting back?"

"I have a lead." I couldn't tell them about Andy sitting in the car.

"You lost a national treasure."

I hated being teased. Heat stung my face, and I growled, "I'll get it back."

"We all know you have no business being an agent." Wharf Rat poked me in the shoulder with his finger. "You couldn't even tell that your partner was a traitor to the Crown."

My pent up exasperation got the better of me, and I punched him, a straight left that put him down on his arse. He shouldn't have poked me. I pounced, aware I was making some sort of screeching sound. Blood poured from his nose, but he grabbed my arms, and I was surprised by the small man's strength. He growled and cursed at me, but I had trained in Brazilian jujitsu and was preparing to put him into a lock, when I felt huge arms come around my waist and pull me up and back. I struggled, but to no avail, my feet flailing in the air. Wharf Rat scrambled up. Jensen, another agent, had come over and pulled me off.

Jensen looked like a punk bouncer from the seventies, complete with a green Mohawk and safety pins in his ears. A giant of a man and one of MI-23's chief enforcers. I, however, knew him as the teddy bear he was. He had worked with my parents, and after they passed away, he sent me birthday and Christmas cards, looking in on me whenever he could. But seeing him now was the last thing I needed. I felt like a little girl as I struggled and demanded, "Put me down."

Jensen ignored me. Holding me with one arm, he pointed at Wharf Rat and Wish. "What are you two doing where I can still see you?"

Wharf Rat protested, "She punched me."

Jensen just gave him a stare. "One, Two…"

He didn't need to get to three. Wharf Rat and Wish were sensible enough to flee. It was not only the fact that as a wizard the hierarchy of MI-23 placed Jensen far above them, the primate instinct to obey the alpha male overtook them. Jensen would not hesitate to grind their bones to make bread.

Jensen spun me around and put me on the ground in front if him. A tear betrayed me, and I quickly wiped it away before it had time to roll down my cheek.

I was glad to see Jensen. Last I heard, he was overseas on a mission. I hadn't seen him since I had started working at the agency. With Raven's death, the Magus had apparently called all hands.

"How you holding up love?" Jensen smiled with a set of bad British teeth.

"You know, holding." I worked hard not to meet his eye.

"Nasty business this." Jensen shuffled his feet. "I owe Raven. He helped make me the man I am today."

"Me too." I looked up. "Well the woman I am today."

Jensen did not smile. I continued, "The best way we can repay him is to find his killer."

"*You* aren't looking for anyone. The Magus wants to see you back at Bosley House."

"What?" I protested.

"It's orders, Lynx. You're to report at once." Jensen indicated Raven's body. "We invited you down to say your goodbyes not to investigate. Sorry."

"But—"

He interrupted, "Don't worry, we heard about the National Gallery, and no one believes you were mixed up in all of this."

"Surely you don't believe their lies."

Jensen looked at me with eyes that had known treachery before and I marked his words as he said, "You never know who could betray you."

"I don't believe it of Raven."

"Neither do I, but I have seen too much to discount that theory." Jensen shielded his eyes as the sun came out from behind a cloud. "You know, if there is anything else I can do…"

"I'll let you know."

Jensen looked relieved. I bet he was happy I hadn't broken down. "Okay then—well I better see what is going on inside."

I stalked across the lawn, feeling troubled. Raven surely couldn't be a traitor. Yet, he had sent me off to the National Gallery by myself. A sliver of doubt entered my mind. I needed to know what happened. While there were no live witnesses to interrogate, maybe I could see whether there were any dead ones.

Chapter Six

The stonewalls of the aptly named Chapel of St Peter-in-Chains held centuries worth of the pleading, whispered prayers of prisoners facing execution at the tower. Here, both the guilty and the innocent came to terms with their Creator, before they faced the stone block and the axe. I found little inside that would inspire worship. The rows of sharply angled, hard pews and unforgiving, cold stone walls and floors were punishment in themselves.

I came to raise a ghost. Surprisingly, not a particularly hard thing to do. It requires no innate magical ability. Anyone can communicate with the spirit world, and most spirits seemed eager to talk with those of the flesh. I was hoping to contact one spirit in particular, the educated Queen Anne Boleyn. While most ghosts wouldn't think twice about lying and mostly moan about their own ends, I had a hunch that Anne Boleyn might be one Tower spirit who had something intelligible to say about what happened last night. Her ghost had been sighted walking to the chapel from the Queen's house. So, in deciding where I should do my séance, I used my aunt's advice and went straight for the bones. Anne Boleyn was buried under the floor of the chapel, so I sat down on the Victorian pavement, near the shield and heraldry that marked her grave, drew a circle around myself, lit a candle and said, "Spirits attend me. Anne are you there?"

My aunt taught me that not much more is needed. All the rest is smoke and mirrors.

I spoke again, "Anne Boleyn. I wish to talk."

Nothing seemed to be happening. Maybe mid-morning wasn't a prime time for ghosts. Maybe it was the chapel, consecrated ground and all that. I suddenly felt stupid sitting there, hoping for a ghost to show up. I stood up, smudged my circle, and made for the door at the back of the chapel. As I approached, a gust of wind howled out of nowhere and blew it shut. The old pipe organ at the other end of the chapel started to play a funeral dirge. The hairs on the back of my neck stood up. I felt glacial. Turning around, I saw a figure hovering near the altar.

I ventured, "Hello?"

An invisible force took hold of me and threw me against the door at the back of the chapel. I started to think I might have made a mistake.

The figure glided closer and said, "It was stupid of you, dear, to call me and then smudge your circle."

Two smaller figures seemed to be running circles around the figure addressing me. I tried to move but couldn't. Luckily I could still speak, "I didn't mean you any harm."

"Hah!" The figure came into view. It indeed looked like the long dead queen, Anne Boleyn. I recognized her from the painting in the National Gallery. Although why she was still wearing that white frill around her neck, I had no idea. She asked, "How do we know you mean what you say? I sense power in you."

I offered, "You have my word."

"Henry once gave me his word and see where I

ended up!" She lifted her head in her hands and removed it from above her shoulders. Her disembodied head continued to speak, "Besides which, you think I am stuck in the past? That I don't have eyes to see the world? Giving your word means nothing in your modern society. No one has any concept of honor anymore."

I felt the pressure against me increasing. "Look, I agree our society has lost its values, but it doesn't make what I said untrue. My word means something to me. All I want to know is whether you saw anything last night."

The pressure eased slightly. "What is it worth to you?"

The question threw me. I had not expected her to want to bargain. "What have I to give a ghost?"

The pressure pinning me against the door dropped completely, and Queen Anne put her head back upon her shoulders. She said, "Your time and company. It gets lonely here. If I appear before anyone, they generally scream and run away. Would you come and visit me? I am dying for some conversation."

It took me a moment to realize she had just made a joke. I answered, "That would be agreeable. It wouldn't kill me to visit."

The Queen's eyes sparkled. "And of course, if you don't, I can always find you and haunt you—giving me something to do to counter this grave boredom."

"Perish the thought. I will come when I can." I offered, "They even made a movie recently about your sister. Perhaps I could play it for you."

She sat down on a pew. It amazed me how ghosts forget that they aren't real people. She was insubstantial, so sitting meant nothing, but as I talked about her sister, her humanity shone through, and she adopted the mannerisms of the living. She said, "Oh how I loved Mary. We had our fights, but in the end, she even lied to the king for me. They were lovers as well you know."

"I'd be glad to bring it for you." It was time to seal the deal. "So what can you tell me about last night?"

Queen Anne Boleyn whispered conspiratorially, "Last night we saw many things. The moon, clouds, and magician's fighting. What did you want to know?"

"What happened?"

Queen Anne rose and as if she were on stage, pointed to the east. "Well around ten, I think the moon started to rise in—"

I interjected, "I meant about the magician's fighting."

She smiled again. It was refreshing to see that despite centuries as a ghost, she still had a sense of theatre. "One arrived in the middle of the night. He was a huge fellow. He started killing all the guards and the ravens. He went into the Jewel House and came out carrying the hugest diamond I have ever seen. I never had anything like that in my crown. A terrible cut, but it was enormous. Then another magician arrived to confront the one who had taken the diamond. All of a sudden, they started throwing fireballs at each other. It was prettier than Guy Fawkes Night. The little ones loved it."

I didn't want to be distracted but had to ask, "The little ones?"

"Yes Richard and Eddy." Beside Anne, two little boys manifested. They were dressed in ancient white nightgowns, encasing them from neck to toe. "I have been looking after them since I became a ghost. They had been running around the Tower with no one to guide them before I came along. The poor dears were murdered in their sleep! Suffocated with their own pillows. How could you do something like that to ones so young? Now remember your manners boys."

"Pleased to meet you, miss." The two boys spoke in unison and bowed at the waist.

"And very nice to meet you both too." I smiled at them and bowed back. They must be the murdered Princes of the Tower. I bit back questions that many a historian would have loved to know. I must stay on the task at hand. Turning back to Anne I asked, "So what happened next?"

Queen Anne said, "Well the big one, the one who arrived first, ended up killing the little one, who was trying to stop him. Isn't that the way history usually goes?"

I could not believe someone had beaten Raven in a straight fight. You didn't get to live two-hundred years without being able to survive some pretty nasty encounters. Still, I had confirmation that Raven arrived after the theft of the diamond and the guards were murdered. That should be enough to clear his name. I asked, "Can you describe the big one to me?"

"Not really, he was all wrapped up in a robe. I can tell you that when I say big, I mean big. He had a touch of giant about him."

"Thank you. You have been extremely helpful." I wasn't sure how to curtsy but dredged up remembrances of medieval movies and hoped I did not embarrass myself. It was only proper to do so to a

Queen, even an ex-Queen.

"Anytime, my dear, anytime." Queen Anne nodded her head slightly to me as I straightened up. "Now don't forget to come and visit."

"I won't."

With that, the ghost of Anne Boleyn faded away. I could not contain my excitement. I had an eyewitness who had cleared Raven's name. It was time to face the Magus.

Chapter Seven

The car park, at Bosley House, was as empty as a wizard's fridge. The Magus must have sent everyone possible out to find Raven's killer. Whether or not he believed the preposterous notion that Raven was a traitor, it would still be all hands on deck until the killer had been found. It was the MI-23 way. No one touches our agents. I parked the Jag in an unusually prime spot.

Andy pleaded, "Please don't handcuff me to the wheel again. I am not going anywhere. I promise."

"And whatever makes you think I should take your word?"

Andy did his best impression of a puppy dog. "Because we are in this together."

I dramatically unlocked one handcuff. Andy's eyes lit up, and I could not help but feel a little bad, when I did not release the other one, but instead fastened the cuff firmly to the steering wheel. "Sorry, but I make it a sound policy not to trust criminals."

I gave him my best fake smile, got out of the car, and hurried across the lot.

"Can you at least bring me back a sandwich?" Andy shouted after me. As I leapt up the steps I heard a faint, "I'm starving."

It felt good to not even deign to reply. I had more important matters on my mind than the state of his stomach. What did the Magus want? I went over the events of the night. The Magus would want no excuses. I would have to defend my actions. My partner was dead, and I had lost the painting. No matter how I put it, last night had been an epic failure.

Bosley House was protected by both magical and mundane means. To enter the building, I reflexively put my hand onto the scanning plate, and the door opened. At the security check, I handed in my gun and went through the metal detector. The place felt eerily quiet as I made my way up the grand stairway. Usually the place was bustling by this time of the morning.

The Magus's secretary was not at her desk, so I knocked on the door of his office. A gruff "Come in" emanated from inside.

I would have expected more trappings in the office of someone who had guided the powers of Britain since the Victorian age. A crackling fire blazed in the hearth. I wondered whether the flue needed cleaning, because it wasn't drawing properly and the place smelled of smoke. On the mantel of the fireplace sat an old photo of the Magus standing next to Queen Victoria. To one side stood a locked, glass bookshelf. This was the Magus's personal library. I would have loved a chance to sneak a look at his collection of spell books. Like most wizards, though, he guarded his secrets jealously. This made the rebel in me want to scan the books and post them on Wiki-leaks.

"Aah Lynx. Good to see you. I'm sorry about Raven. Are you taking it well?" For the most powerful magician in Britain, the Magus didn't seem like much. He was dressed in a drab, gray suit, wore round spectacles, and apart from a slight potbelly, looked like a fierce wind could knock him over. He was speaking like a concerned uncle, but I could in no way underestimate the man. Without breaking a sweat, he could handle more power than I could comprehend.

I spoke, before I thought, "No. I'm not taking it well. Especially when I hear Wharf Rat and Wish accuse Raven of being a traitor."

The Magus indicated for me to sit in one of the chairs facing his desk. So, it was to be a more formal meeting, not the two comfortable, chairs indicating a fireside chat. That was not a good sign. The Magus said, "Good investigators should look at all possibilities."

Resisting the urge to stamp my foot, I protested, "But it isn't true."

For the first time I felt the force of his eyes and could see the strength within. He was willing to accept that Raven whom he had known for the better part of a century might be a traitor. He considered it—despite the pain it caused him, because he believed it was the right thing to do. He said, "We don't know that."

I played my trump card. "I do. I raised the ghost of Anne Boleyn at the Tower, and she witnessed the whole thing. The first magician stole the diamond before Raven even got there. He was only there to try to stop the theft. That was why he was killed."

The Magus sadly shook his head, "Maybe I have just been around too long, but I can't take the word of a ghost."

"Why would she possibly lie?"

"Ghosts do things for many reasons. You know that their testimony is inadmissible in court. I will inform Wish and Wharf Rat, though. Raven was killed by another wizard and whether or not they were in cahoots or not, is actually unimportant to retrieving the diamond." He indicated the seat again and said, "Now please sit."

"Why are they on the case anyway? It should be wizards investigating Raven's death."

The Magus cocked his head to one side. "You mean yourself?"

"Yes."

The Magus squared some papers on the desk as he explained, "Wish and Wharf Rat are on the case because we need someone independent to investigate Raven's death."

"Independent? They're as biased as anybody?" A chill overcame me as I considered another reason for them to be on the case. The number of people who could have killed Raven in a magical duel was extremely limited. One of whom was now opposite me. I really shouldn't entertain the idea, but what if it was the Magus who killed Raven? I heard Jensen's voice in my mind urging me to trust no one. Maybe the Magus was putting Wish and Wharf Rat on the case so the killer would never be found. I had to step carefully.

The Magus's voice cut irritably, "Commander Somerton you know this is political. The Queen's crown has been violated for God's sake, and I will follow proper protocol. Now will you stop whining like a teenage girl, sit down, and suck it up?"

It doesn't do to ignore a request from the Magus a third time, especially one delivered with such authority. So, even while I was smarting from the fact that he wasn't agreeing with me, I complied. Once I sat, he continued, "There is another reason I cannot let you investigate your partner's death."

"What—"

"As the newest member of MI-23, I wouldn't want to expose you to whoever took out Raven. You'll confine your investigations to retrieving the Van Gogh. How is the investigation going?"

I sat there controlling my breathing. Who cared about a stupid oil painting when Raven was dead? I ordered my thoughts. I considered lying about Andy, but the Magus would see right through me. So, I gave him an accurate report of all that had happened in the last twenty-four hours.

"Let me get this right. You have the culprit, but he's not in custody."

I started, "Yes, but—"

He interrupted, "And you owe six-million pounds to the Werewolves of London, having gone surety for the culprit."

It sounded bad when he put it succinctly like that. He had missed the bit where I had saved someone's life and tracked down the perpetrator. Still, I hung my head, not wanting to meet his eye. He had stuck his neck out by allowing me to become the youngest agent ever to join the department. This would not reflect well on him at all. I said, "Yes."

"This is not the way we work at all. I may have made a grave error in making you an agent. You do understand that there is no way the Ministry can help you to financially pay out that amount of money."

Wanting to sink into the carpet, I said, "I do."

He poured a small tumbler of whiskey, from a bottle in one his drawers and tossed it back. I noticed he didn't offer me one. He continued, "As far as I am concerned, I am unaware you have apprehended anyone. Use him to get to the painting. Find the ones that hired him. Follow the money. But don't show your head around here until you get that painting back."

I smoothed the black leather trousers along my thighs, and then picked at the knee that was torn. "Okay and once I have the painting back?"

The Magus looked at me, "Mr. Andrew Daniels violated a national treasure. What we do to him should send a message to the magical community, so that no one will ever dare to think of doing anything like that again."

"But I told him I'd tell the court he cooperated."

The Magus took off his glasses and started to wipe them with a cloth. "I can't see him making it to a court."

A chill ran through me. What was the Magus saying?

The Magus put back on his glasses and asked, "Can you do your job and follow orders? Or should I give this to someone else?"

I needed time to think. The Magus was telling me to kill Andy. I didn't want to be a coward, but I was sure I would never do what the Magus was implying. It went against everything I believed in. I had found a family in the Army and had been programmed to follow orders, but to kill someone who wasn't a threat? That was unacceptable to me. Yet, I couldn't let him take the mission away from me. I would think of something. I went into autopilot, stood up, and saluted. "I won't fail you, sir."

"See that you don't."

I pushed down the side of me that recoiled at the proclamation of Andy's fate. I certainly didn't want the

Magus to sense how I felt. I left with a nod of my head. "Magus."

"One more thing, Lynx."

"Yes. Sir."

"You haven't been making friends touting your theories of magic among your colleagues. I have been hearing complaints."

"But it is what I believe."

"The rituals we practice, the ones you think are unnecessary and archaic, are there to protect the caster from the energy being manipulated."

"It's only a bit of pain."

"Pain that could cripple you, burn you out, and leave you mentally incapacitated."

"Only if you draw too much."

"And you have the experience to know how much you can draw?"

"I'm careful sir."

"Be that as it may. I highly recommend that you stick to the ways of doing things that have worked safely for hundreds of years."

"I'll consider your recommendation."

He could see I wasn't going to. "Your parents were as stubborn. Do what you want. I wash my hands of you, but at least have the decency not to tell wizards who have years of experience that you know a better way of doing things."

"Even when I do?"

"Even when you do. Why do you want to get into it with them anyway?"

"They were calling me a witch. I'm a Neon-Mage."

"I don't care if they were calling you the frikkin' tooth fairy. Put your head down and respect the fact that these agents have kept Britain safe for hundreds of years."

"But—"

"But nothing, Commander Somerton. That is a direct order. You're embarrassing yourself. I took a chance on you, and I don't want other people thinking that I made a mistake. Dismissed."

I had no choice but to salute, turn and leave, but on my way out, I heard the Magus call after me, "And Lynx."

I turned back. The Magus had wandered over to the window and was looking out. I looked on him in a new light knowing he could order the death of another human being. "Yes?"

Magus did not look at me as he said, "Go and visit Quentin, please. He has a few things to give to you."

"Yes, sir." I saluted.

"And one last thing." He pointed out the window. "May I ask why someone is trying to remove the steering wheel from your car?"

Chapter Eight

Andy pretended to be asleep. His head rested on the dash, and his left hand was held dramatically up to the steering wheel. I could hear overacted snoring as I approached. The steering wheel was still triumphantly secure. Old cars were built to last. The idiot hadn't realized there was no way he was going to get it loose without tools. I walked to his side of the car and punched him hard on the shoulder. "That's for asking me to trust you."

Andy's eyes shot open. "You should!"

So much for pretending to be asleep. "Oh how is that exactly? I am in a meeting with my boss. I look out the window and what do I see? You trying to remove the steering wheel from the car."

Andy rubbed his arm. "You can't blame a man for trying."

It felt good to take the last twenty-four hours out on someone. I raised my voice, "I just did."

I wasn't actually angry with him, but with the Magus. I know I signed on for the cloak and dagger stuff, but to me, that did not cover killing Andy. He was not a bad man. A criminal? Yes, but really just a human being trying to live in the best way he knew how. What the hell was I going to do?

Andy, oblivious to my inner dialogue, protested, "Well it isn't fair to hit a handcuffed prisoner. It is against the law or something."

I started the engine. Wishing my voice sounded like the deep purr of the 5.3litre V-12, I queried, "Or something?"

"Yeah, like ethics. You ever heard of them?"

"Don't push me."

We drove in silence. Andy, at one stage, rubbed his arm again in a vain attempt to make me feel guilty. I gave him a stare. He looked away sulkily. I was glad of the silence. It gave me time to think. The Magus's order bothered me on many levels. I never really considered that I might be asked to kill a civilian. I knew killing was part of the job but had always considered it would be a last resort against the most evil of men. My whole career was starting to look shaky before me.

I was lucky to find a parking spot on Gaunt St. "Come on, you better come in with me. I can't trust you alone and unsupervised."

"Thank goodness. I'm sick of waiting in the car." Andy opened the car door clumsily, his hands still cuffed. An older woman, pulling an old, cream, box vinyl shopping-cart, looked alarmed as she passed. I flashed her a reassuring smile. The woman took in my black leather pants, looked again at Andy with the cuffs, and returned my smile with a disapproving sniff.

"Where are we going?"

"The Ministry of Sound."

Andy's brow furrowed as we came to the closed gate. "I don't want to spoil any fun you had planned, but I think it is a bit early for a nightclub."

I knocked twice. "Believe me there is not just coincidence in the name."

A suited man opened the gate. I flashed him my

badge, and he beckoned me inside. Bouncers handled things at night, but it was MI-5 security during the day. We proceeded into the nightclub. At the back of the cloakroom, I pushed a panel to reveal a secret staircase. We followed it down to a passageway, which ended at a steel door. We were somewhere underneath the dance floor of the Box. I put my hand on a finger print panel, and the light turned green. I turned and waved at the camera.

The steel door opened and a man, dressed in a white lab coat, Atari t-shirt, and jeans, stood there with a smile on his face. Quentin was a tech-geek, who proudly claimed that nerds were the new cool. "Good to see you, Lynx."

"You too, Quentin." I leant in for a kiss. The fact that technology and science could be combined with magic seemed incomprehensible to most, but Quentin had turned it into an art form. He had even made a working magic app for the iPhone. Not that he had released it, yet. He beckoned us to follow him inside to his inner sanctum.

A techno-clad girl lay on the couch. She was watching some sort of display on a pair of blacked out glasses and was hooked into a sound system with a pair of headphones. I wondered what worlds she was exploring. Her clothes consisted of pink, shaggy leg warmers and a neon green mini-skirt. Her legs were open, and I could see a lace G-string. I jostled Andy by his arm to stop him from staring.

Quentin explained, "That's Lucy. She wandered down here the other night, and for some reason I let her in. Now she doesn't want to leave and well, it is handy to have someone to go to the door to get the Chinese delivery when I am hungry."

"Chinese. Yeah I bet that's all she does," Andy piped in.

I glared at them both. What was worse was that I knew Quentin supplemented his income by producing magical designer treats for the partygoers. I said, "Drugs aren't good for her, you know."

"Ah Lynx, you're so old fashioned. Modern designer drugs are our chance to change our brain chemistry for the better. Didn't you take mushrooms with that Celtic shaman?"

"Yes, but that was a ritual." I never should have told him that story. He was endlessly using it against me.

"Can't you see that dressing up and going out is but another sort of ritual?"

He had a point, but I still said, "You're trying to justify permanent damage to people's brains. The long term effect can be devastating."

"And you are being closed minded. Do you think my brain has suffered?"

It was the same argument we had every time. I knew it would end up with his claim that at least his drugs were pure and didn't contain a lot of the harmful additives that the criminal community put in theirs. I'd prepared a brilliant retort and was preparing to launch into it, when Andy cleared his throat and Quentin's attention switched.

"This is Andy," I said to Quentin, "He heisted the painting yesterday."

"Oh yes." Quentin rubbed his hands. "The one who got deliciously double-crossed and then caught."

I wasn't surprised that Quentin had heard the story

already. There was little that Quentin did not know or hear, and the Magus must have updated him before we arrived.

"It was anything but delicious, I assure you," Andy retorted.

"Nonsense, from where I stand it was the greatest lesson for you." Quentin punctuated the next words with his finger in Andy's chest. "Crime. Does. Not. Pay."

"Consider me instructed." Andy brought his handcuffed hands up and gently moved Quentin's hand away. "Hey, is that a Rolex?"

Quentin smiled. "Yes. Well crime might not pay, but the drug business is rather lucrative."

"That is crime, Quentin." I pointed out. Not that he ever had to worry about being caught. He stood far too high on the food chain to be bothered by normal police. His genius made him a national asset.

Quentin shrugged. "Not in my book."

I let it slide—there would be no changing his view. We followed him into his laboratory. There were worktables full of half-finished projects. Quentin liked to wander from one to another, while he worked. I could not even begin to guess what half the mixtures of electronics, mechanics, chemistry, and ritualized spells were meant to do. A huge floor to ceiling crystal stood in the center of the room. On one wall, hung a map of the world with a spell cast over it to show the current location of British submarines in red and whale pods in blue. He had a direct link to the Navy and often ordered them to change course to protect the pods from the active sonar. He was quite the environmental activist and beached whales upset him immensely. Andy pointed at the crystal in the middle of the room, "What's that?"

"It's an energy conductor." Quentin looked up lovingly. "When all the kids are dancing upstairs, an amazing amount of energy is built up. We're able to use the crystal to channel the energy down here and charge all sorts of magical items."

Andy was taken aback. "You take from the kids' energy?"

"No it's not like that. They just open the channels to the universal energy that is all around." Quentin looked at Andy and myself. "Some may call it love. I just happen to be able to harvest the emotion."

I felt bothered. What was that look for? I changed the subject. "The Magus said you have something for me."

"Not something." Quentin's eyes were light like a child's laugh. "Many things."

He darted away and came back with a pair of high-heeled, black leather boots. "Try these on. I had been thinking about your leather pants...No not that way, Andy...and wanted to make something to match."

I tried them on. They were a perfect fit. "Thank you. They are lovely—"

"No, no, no. You haven't seen the best part, yet." Quentin grabbed my arm. "Try walking up the wall."

"Up the wall?"

"Yes, just do it."

I went with some trepidation toward the wall. How exactly do you try to walk up a wall? I put the toe of one boot on the wall and my axis seemed to shift, suddenly the wall was down, and I was walking on it.

"Aren't they brilliant?" Quentin seemed delighted.

"I still haven't decided what to call them, spider-boots, floor shifters, wall grabbers, or something. Now try the roof."

Once again, I put a foot out to the ceiling, and my axis changed again. I was walking upside down. "These are so awesome."

"Yes, they will work on any reasonably flat man-made surface. No cave roofs or cliffs I am afraid. The spell gets too confused by the irregularities."

I ran to the wall and then pushed off and landed upright on the floor. Quentin rummaged through another box. He pulled out some rose-tinted, round, 'John Lennon' sunglasses. "I heard about the National Gallery and thought you could add these to your kit."

"What are they?"

"When wearing them, you will be able to see through any illusions or enchantments. They also, funnily enough, can help see when someone is lying to you."

I put them on and turned to Andy. "Are you planning to run away the first chance you get?"

"No."

Through the glasses, I saw him nodding. I took them off and his head was still.

"Liar." I turned back to Quentin.

Quentin held something behind his back. "This, Lynx, is not from me. It belonged to your mother. I know she would have wanted you to have it, though."

I could not believe it. Something from my mum? Quentin brought into view an old black bowler hat. I recognized it from some old photos I had seen of my mum. It was her favorite. I thought it had been lost. I took it and placed it on my head. It fit perfectly. There was a tear in my eye as I said, "Thank you, Quentin. This means a lot."

"You're welcome my darling, but you don't know the half of it. Spin the hat one-hundred and eighty degrees upon your head," Quentin instructed.

I spun the hat and found myself sitting in a burgundy Chesterfield chair in a domed library stacked floor to ceiling with books. Where on Earth had Quentin's lab gone?

A lady in a white cardigan, with brown hair, pulled back into a tight bun, walked up to me. "Welcome to the Repository."

"The Repository," I repeated lamely.

"Yes," the lady answered. "We are in a spirit world parallel to the real world. Here in this library the wisdom and knowledge of over a thousand years of British magicians and witches are stored. I am the Keeper. You need but to ask a question, and I will supply the requisite knowledge."

"Any question?"

"Those pertaining to the uses and application of magic are most likely to get a response. I am also well versed in lore and history. I am afraid I cannot help with anything too current, for until something has been written and filed I have no knowledge of it."

"Do you have all the old MI-23 files?"

"Yes."

"Do you have the case file for when my parents were killed?"

The Keeper seemed to look in the distance. "The Somertons?"

"Yes."

"I do have the case file, unfortunately it has been

marked 'F.M.E.O."

"F.M.E.O."

"Yes. For Magus's Eyes Only. You will have to get his permission to access those records."

I felt a kick in my guts. My whole teenage life I had dreamed of finding out what had actually happened to my parents, now it was denied me by a simple classification. Still it was not the Keeper's fault so I said, "Thank you, for checking."

"Is there anything else I can help you with today?"

"No. Except." I sounded sheepish. "How do I get back?"

The Keeper smiled. "All the agents have different ways of getting here. Yours, if I see correctly, is your mother's. To leave, she simply spun her bowler hat."

I spun the hat, and the world returned. I was back in the room with Andy and Quentin.

Quentin explained, "You'll find that no matter the amount of time that you're gone in the Repository, it'll only be an instant in the real world. The hat is tuned to you and you alone. No one else will be able to use it. Now, that is the end of my presents. Is there anything else you need?"

I thought for a moment. "Do you have anything that is particularly effective against werewolves?"

"Let me see." Quentin fished around in some boxes and came out with a container of bullets. "Here we are. These are made with silver nitrate and should help stop a werewolf. They've also been dipped in Holy water from the Grail Well at Glastonbury, so should give any vampire problems as well."

With my mother's hat, the boots, and those bullets, I felt like we had a chance.

Chapter Nine

To go through the door of Gordon's Wine Bar was to step back through time to another age. Gone was modern London, replaced by her darker, gruffer, more dangerous cousin. The roof of Gordon's was black from the smoke of ever-present candles. The only electric lights were centered around the bar. Stacked barrels of wine and sherry were tapped, forgoing the need for bottles. A chalkboard detailed the prices of the offerings. The walls made the place feel more like a cave than a room. I could imagine Guy Fawkes, plotting to blow up the Houses of Parliament, cosseted in the corner, at one of the squashed wooden tables, with his goatee and hat, speaking passionately in the overloud whisper of someone sharing a secret who has had too much to drink.

The only thing that spoiled the atmosphere were the people tapping away at their mobile phones. The textaholics made me glad I used crystals. I wanted to scream at them to sit up and talk to their friends, but I knew it would be a losing battle. The illusion of connection in the cyber world was easier than relating to people in the real.

Ordering two glasses of the house Chablis, we took our drinks to the table where Tablet was sitting. Andy had to duck to avoid hitting his head on the low roof. Tablet saw us, and his lip curled up on one side.

"Andy. Why you bringing the cozzers?" Tablet raised his portly frame, half out of his seat, and then plopped back down, when he realized any attempt to leave would have to involve squirming around us both.

I wondered why criminals recognized me as the law, but no one else had a clue. It wasn't fair. I constantly had to flash my ID to get a modicum of respect, but the moment someone from the shady side spotted me, they instantly guessed my profession.

Andy grabbed a chair, spun it around, and straddled it to face Tablet, and placed his wine upon the table. "Relax Tablet. This is Lynx. She isn't here to arrest you."

"I'm not scared of her, you idiot!" Tablet gave me a desultory glance up and down. "I'm scared to be seen talking to the Law. Half my business would walk out on me if they thought I played both sides."

Andy pointed one finger at Tablet. "Listen you fat muppet, forget about her. I got gypped on the Gallery job, and I want some answers."

Tablet shook his head. "No you don't."

Andy's eyes narrowed. "What do you mean, no I don't? Yes, I do."

Tablet pointedly took a big swig of wine and swished it around his mouth. He narrowed his eyes at Andy. "No. You. Don't. That's one big can of worms that you'd be better off leaving well alone."

"I need that money. Who set up the job?"

Tablet leant back against the wall, tipping back on the legs of his chair. "I like you too much to tell you, so sod off."

I hung back, but with Andy getting nowhere, I put one foot on the edge of the table and kicked out with my new leather boot, pinning Tablet between the wall and the table. The wine spilled and red rivers washed down the table, staining Tablet's lavender shirt, before the goblets smashed on the floor. Tablet tried to push back with his arms but couldn't find any purchase. He comically tried windmilling his arms before giving up to glare angrily at me and protested, "Hey. No need to get physical, young lady."

I could see the barman looking in our direction, so I produced my badge. He nodded and went back to cleaning the bar with a rag. Turning my attention back to Tablet, I said, "You know Tablet, you're exactly right. There is no need to get physical."

He looked at me suspiciously.

I reached into the top left outside pocket of my denim jacket and pulled out a small crystal blue bottle. I sniffed it, replaced the cap, and nodded sagely to myself.

"What's that?" Tablet's eyebrows pulled together, and if his head weren't already against the wall, he would have leant further back.

"Something my aunt taught me how to make. Well, I say aunt, but really she is my great, great aunt. She's an old school witch, you see. After my parents died, I lived with her out on the moors of Devon. I learned a lot. Anyway, she told me to use this little potion on men who weren't courteous." I shook the bottle in my hand. "Now you do want to be courteous and answer my questions, don't you, Tablet?"

I saw his mind working overtime. People always expect the worst from witches—it's a cultural bias.

He looked at Andy. "Are you going to let her threaten me?"

Andy showed Tablet his cuffed wrists, which he had been hiding under his blazer. I shoved hard with my boot and waved the little bottle in Tablet's face.

"Andy isn't in any position to tell me what I am allowed or not allowed to do."

Tablet looked around the bar. Many were watching, but no one was moving to interfere. I think they were more interested in my bottom rounding out the black leather, than what actually happened to Tablet. I un-corked the bottle and started to count, "One, two

"Ok. You win. Put that away. We can be civilized here." Tablet almost yelled the words.

I removed my boot from the table and put the bottle of harmless perfume back in my pocket. "The word is courteous."

Andy asked again, "So who gave you the job?"

Tablet righted his chair, sopped at the wine that had spilled with a napkin, put his elbows on the table, and leant closer. He said in a hushed tone, "I was contacted by a Director of Indra Corp and—"

He didn't get to finish his sentence. A bolt of red energy streamed across the bar to strike him in the chest and slam him against the wall. I felt it sizzle past my arm and was worried I would blister from the heat. A sound like a jet engine roared through the bar. A wind blew out all the candles and smashed all the lights, plunging us into instant darkness.

I grabbed Andy and threw up a shield, just as two more bolts of energy were flung in our direction. I carried Andy to the floor. My shield held, but each bolt felt like I was being hit in the face with a frying pan. Patrons fled. The lights of their mobile phones waving everywhere in their haste.

I crawled to Tablet and felt for a pulse on his wrist. There was nothing. Damn. I felt for his eyes and closed them. Another bolt came out of the darkness and smashed into my shield. I couldn't hold it for much longer. Whoever was attacking us was much stronger than I was. They also stood between us and the door.

Andy whispered in my ear, "Let me out of these cuffs."

Another bolt smashed into my shield. Through gritted teeth, I replied, "No way."

"It's the only way we'll get out." Andy grabbed my shoulder. "I can cast an illusion that will make whoever is throwing those bolts, think we are still here."

I breathed in. I knew from the force of those bolts I didn't have the power to win a duel with this wizard. Truthfully, it was all I could do to keep us alive. I reached into my pocket and produced the cuff key. I knew I was going to regret it, but I really didn't have a choice. Another bolt exploded on my shield, and I realized it would only hold for another couple of hits before I passed out. I released Andy.

He placed his hands over mine for a moment and then pulled me out from behind the shield. I saw another bolt whiz over our heads to explode where we had just been. I pulled back. Andy whispered, "Come on. It still appears as if we're there. I'm cloaking us. Just trust and follow me."

I crawled with him. Ahead there was a huge figure in black robes. A cowl obscured his face, but I got a glimpse of a gold mask inside. From a black staff, bolts of energy were being thrown at the place where we had been cowering underneath the shield. Crawling right past him, we didn't stop until we made it outside.

In the distance, I saw some police officers running toward the crowd of milling patrons. I couldn't let them in there. The warlock would not hesitate to kill them. It was up to me to make sure no one else died. I reached into my jacket to pull out my ID. It wasn't there. I must have dropped it after flashing it at the barman.

The police reached us. I shouted, "Stop."

One of the policeman said, "Not now, miss. We have reports of a disturbance inside."

I put up my hand in an effort to stop them. "But…"

The one that had been speaking to me just brushed my hand aside and growled, "I said not now. We'll take your statement after we're finished."

I fumed. I couldn't let them die. I turned to Andy. "You stay here. If you run, I still have your hair and will hunt you down wherever you go."

"You still don't trust me? After I saved us in there?"

I almost thought he sounded hurt, but I still reached in my pocket and moved to put my rose-colored glasses on.

Andy put his hand on mine. "Look at me. You don't need those stupid glasses to read people. Trust yourself. I'm not going to run away."

I held his gaze and said, "Please don't."

He nodded once. I turned and followed the policemen. I drew energy from the underground tracks of the nearby Circle Line that I could feel pulsing in the Earth. Normally I would not do this, as it would shut down service on all the trains currently on that line. But I needed power to cover the policeman from the warlock. Their only hope was if I could buy them the time to retreat and get outside. The energy filled me and I was surprised I did not glow with the power.

I entered the bar, ready for war. The policemen shone flashlights the size of batons around the room. Yet, apart from Tablet's dead body, the room was empty. There was no one there.

Chapter Ten

Sheltered from the cool night breeze, I rested my hand on the gray stone base of Cleopatra's Needle. The Needle, once dedicated to the Egyptian sun god Ra, pulsed with energy gathered during the day. Cleverly positioned along one of Britain's major ley lines, the Needle was one of the many monuments that reinforced the field protecting London. I opened myself to the excess energy. It felt better than a dozen espressos.

Andy stood making faces at one of the two Sphinxes at the base of the Needle. The Sphinxes face inward. They were lampooned when the monument was first built. Critics alleged that the Sphinxes facing inward were positioned backward—they should be facing outward as guardians of the Needle. However, they were not placed incorrectly. The Sphinxes' real function was to act as gatekeepers for the magical community of London. Pass between them, and they offered anyone, with power, a riddle. If answered correctly, they revealed a glimpse of the future.

However, as to the merit of their answers I have my doubts. When I passed through, the Sphinxes riddled me, "No nose, no mouth, no gills, no lungs, I yet breathe and age. What am I?" Having just consumed a robust Chablis, I knew the answer at once. Yet, as to my future, all the Sphinxes revealed was that I would die twice. Considering CPR, modern medicine, and the line of work I am in, I thought this was neither insightful nor helpful. I was hoping for some information I could actually use.

Andy looked frustrated. I wondered what riddle the Sphinxes had posed for him. He didn't seem to be the type to do the Sunday crossword, and by his gesticulations, he was having a lot of trouble finding the answer. I couldn't help. The Sphinxes' riddle was for him alone. Besides, I didn't fancy helping. He was the reason I was in this mess in the first place.

A siren wailed a long way off. By the river, the noise of the city was both muted and clearer at the same time. I watched the silver, gold, and blue lights play in the slow moving current of the Thames and allowed my thoughts to drift over the events of the evening. I felt guilty for Tablet's death. It was my job to protect the people of London, even the low life scum. If I had played it differently, he might still be alive. He didn't deserve to die. Especially like that. If we hadn't come along, he would still be in Gordon's drinking his wine, making his shady deals.

I looked at Andy. He felt my gaze and came over, giving up on the Sphinxes.

"Bad business that."

Surprisingly, Andy hadn't tried to run away. Idiot. I had been too tired to argue with him, when I tried to get him back in the cuffs. It was easier to trust him. I didn't have the energy to do otherwise. I answered, "The worst. I can't believe we got Tablet killed."

He looked at me strangely, like I was the idiot. "We didn't get him killed. The warlock was tying up loose ends. That we were there was just a coincidence. If they'd known we were coming, they would have killed Tablet sooner, rather than risk the information getting out. The warlock was probably planning to kill Tablet quietly, but the moment he saw an MI-23 agent on the scene, he came in all guns blazing."

Andy was right. Why had I assumed the warlock had only come because we had shown up? Even a petty illusionist thief was thinking more clearly than me. I still felt guilty. There must have been some way to protect Tablet's life. Annoyed that Andy had one-upped me, I spotted a flaw in what he said and triumphantly asked, "Why are you assuming the warlock was a he?"

Andy laughed. "Did you see the size of our attacker? Not counting the female Scottish caber-toss team, I don't think God has ever made any woman that big."

I slumped against the base of the Needle and watched a barge slowly make its way against the current. Even it seemed faster than me. I conceded, "You're right."

"What's wrong?"

"I'm not thinking clearly, and I feel like the deeper I get into this mess, the worse things are becoming. I don't know whether I am cut out to be an agent. I haven't made a right move since this started."

Andy squatted annoyingly close on the step below me. "Hey don't be too hard on yourself. You did manage to catch me."

I put my hands to either side of my head. "You were bloody unconscious at the time and now look at you. You aren't even wearing cuffs."

"I'll put them back on if that will make you feel better," he said consolingly.

I gave him my Cyclops impression again, but he

must have some sort of invisible force field, for he just squatted there smiling at me like a loyal Labrador and didn't explode in a ray of energy. I said, "I don't need coddling."

Andy put a hand on my knee. "Well can we put an end to the pity party then? You seem to have forgotten that we have a lead."

I looked across the river to the London Eye, the huge Ferris wheel in the heart of London. It brought things into focus. I actually had two leads. Not only did I have Indra Corp from the lips of a dying man, I also had the Gandhi quote left in the bathroom. It may have just been all the excess energy, but I felt a tingling in my toes. I stood and pulled Andy up with me. "You're right. Let's head down to MI-6. I have a friend who can tell us everything we need to know about Indra Corp. I'll just call to see whether he is there. He usually works the desk at night."

I took out my crystal

Andy seemed glad to see the shift in me. "You can call normal phones on those crystals?"

"Yeah, they hear my thoughts as speech. It's all free too."

He brightened. "That's a plan I'd like to be on."

"It's a perk of being an agent."

It can potentially be awkward calling on a crystal, as it isn't obvious when you are actually using it. There is no holding it up to the ear, and if someone you are with starts talking at the same time, it can make for some strange non-sequiturs flying through the psychic channels, if you don't have a firm handle upon your mind. I was thankful Andy didn't talk while I complete my call. Coming back, I said, "He'll meet us at a bar in half an hour."

"And he'll just give you the information?"

We started walking. "Sure. He knows where I work. We do this all the time. MI-6 has better records on the mundane world than my agency and to go through official channels takes too long. They in turn pass anything our way that has a whiff of the esoteric."

We walked a while in silence. Then I asked, "So how did you end up owing so much money?"

"I didn't." Andy looked pained. "It was my brother. When my father died, he took over the family business. I didn't pay much attention. I was enthralled with my studies of magic. Anyway, he started living the high life, cocaine, women, drinking, parties, and then came the gambling. He started to lose and borrowed against the business. He lost that and then went to the seedier side of town to borrow to support his habit—in an attempt to win it all back. Of course, that didn't work.

"When they found out he couldn't pay it back, I had a little visit from the werewolves. They already had my brother and just wanted to know whether I would like a chance to have him back. I said I'd take over the debt. They gave me a week. I had no idea how to raise so much money, but I thought Tablet might know. I had been introduced to him as a source for arcane books on illusion. He has a talent for locating items on the black market. We built up quite a relationship, and he hinted that he had done work for a good illusionist."

I looked down at the pavement for a while and was reminded how children play games trying to avoid stepping on any crack or line. In the end, they always end up making a mistake or simply forget and give up.

"So you went to Tablet to help your brother?"

"That I did."

My aunt was the only close family I had left, and I knew I would do anything for her. I grabbed Andy's hand. "I have to tell you something."

"What?"

How do you tell a man you have been ordered to kill him? I fumbled for something to say. "Um…We need to arrive at MI-6 anonymously. I don't want anyone to trace my car. Let's take a taxi."

We went to a taxi stand. Andy held the door open for me. Maybe it wasn't too late to teach him manners.

Seated in the back seat, I kicked myself for being a coward and not telling him the truth. After saving me in Gordon's, he'd earned it.

Chapter Eleven

A train rumbled above as we entered the bar. Built under the tracks, the place was decorated in the blue of a famous Portuguese football club. A few older men with oversize moustaches perched on bar stools, as they nursed drinks and stared at a flat screen TV. I saw why Percy had picked this bar—no one so much as glanced our way.

Percy, himself, sat in true espionage style, at a table near the back. He faced the entrance and lifted his chin in acknowledgement of our arrival. Dressed in a full three-piece suit, his dark overcoat lay folded on the chair beside him. I would put money on the fact that there was a gun, in easy reach, within the folds of that coat. Percy was textbook. Well at least when it came to spy stuff. His personal life was flamboyant. As was his lime colored, silk tie.

A couple of years ago, Percy had almost been killed by a Persian Djinn, during an investigation of a suspected Al Qaeda terrorist cell. The Islamic extremists planned to use the Djinn to strike a major blow against Britain and had brought it over in a bottle of Grappa. While it isn't true that a Djinn grants three wishes, a localized twister at Heathrow could have been a major disaster. Yet, when all seemed lost, Raven stepped in, saved Percy, the airport, the planes, and banished the Djinn. Ever since, Percy felt obligated to

Raven. I knew that courtesy extended to me.

As we approached, he rose and came at me with a big hug and a chaste kiss on the cheek. "Lynx darling, it's been too long."

I held him in the hug for a moment and then stepped back to look him up and down. "Percy it's great to see you. How's the analyst's desk treating you?"

"Well it isn't as exciting as the field but has done wonders for my constitution." Percy smiled. "And yourself, has Raven finally set you off on your own?"

"Raven's dead." I sat down in one of the chairs. Each time I said those words, it became more real.

"How?" Percy asked in a hushed tone. I could see the shock on his face and I realized, in that instant, what Raven had meant to him. Here, in front of me, was someone whose life had literally been saved by Raven, and the knowledge of Raven's passing made, for Percy, a less secure world.

"He was at the Tower." I needed no further explanation. Percy could extrapolate from there. It's what analysts do.

"Nasty business that." Percy brushed his hair back with both hands and continued, "I did not hear MI-23 had an agent down."

"It wouldn't be in any of the reports."

"Of course it wouldn't be in the official ones, but I still expect to hear things. We are MI-6 after all. Intelligence is our business." Percy tapped the table. "I take it the flamethrower theory is inaccurate."

"Grossly." I fought back images of Raven's charred body. "It was a rogue warlock."

"Makes sense. I thought the official report was a bunch of codswallop. Totally implausible."

It was a strange world we lived in. One where a rogue warlock was a more plausible explanation than the spin they put on the news. It was important for Percy to know something else. "The warlock also took the time to burn the tower Ravens."

"To shake the old legend." Percy caught on immediately.

"Yes. It was a message. They're attacking England."

"Who?"

"I don't know, yet."

"I will alert my contacts in MI-5. We'll put everyone on alert." Percy shook his head. "Damn the press will make a field day when they learn of this."

"Don't worry. They'll probably be focusing on the one bird that survived."

"Survived?" Percy cocked his head to one side.

"Yes, a raven called Rocky. He was smart enough to hide, despite his clipped wings. The warlock missed him."

Percy looked down at his tapping fingers. "How bad is this?"

I trusted Percy, but did not know how much to say or even how much was allowed. I guessed it wasn't wrong to let him know how I felt. "I don't really know, but my feeling is we've only seen the start. Something much bigger is going on."

"Raven was a good man. We need to drink to him." Percy changed the subject and signaled a waiter. "Three Ginjinha's, please."

The waiter bustled away. What on earth was a Ginjinha? Percy had the weirdest taste.

"There's something else you should know. They're

trying to pin the break in on Raven. Someone took down the wards protecting the Crown Jewels. It had to be someone from MI-23. Another mage could've perhaps blown them, but these were dismantled properly. His body being found at the tower was enough for them to think it was Raven." I pushed the cutlery in front of me to one side. "I don't believe it though."

"In this business you never know." Percy produced a folder from underneath his coat.

"I know for sure. A ghost witnessed it. She swears that Raven came to the Tower after the diamond was already stolen and was only trying to stop the warlock."

"A ghost?" Percy's eyes went wide. "Ghosts are real?"

"Yes. I thought you would have seen enough with the Djinn to know that most of the supernatural tales are true. Just about everything that we fear is out there and lots more that we don't even know about." I paused, how much should I tell him? He couldn't look anymore shocked, so I continued, "I went into the chapel at the Tower and raised the ghost of Anne Boleyn to get some answers."

"You talked to Anne Boleyn?" Percy's jaw dropped.

"Yes."

Percy rubbed his hands together like an excited child about to open a Christmas present. "I wish I could tell my sister. She did her doctorate on Anne's influence in the Tudor court."

I offered, "I promised to go back and talk to Anne. She's lonely, the poor dear. Maybe your sister could come?"

"To talk to a ghost?" He laughed. "I don't think she could handle that. She still thinks I work for the Department of the Environment, Food, and Rural Affairs. She would be shocked to discover that I am a spy, let alone that ghosts are real."

"It's a pity." Having to hide the truth about the supernatural from just about everyone, I never thought about MI-6 agents having to hide what they do from their families.

"I know. Sometimes I really want to share with her what is really going on in my life, but instead I tell her about the salmon count in the Thames. Believe me, dinner at her house can be almost as dreary for me as it is for them." Percy brushed his hands together. "Okay, down to business."

He pushed the folder across the table.

"I've the information you want on Indra Corp. It's 'Eyes Only'." He looked pointedly at Andy and then back to me. "I hope it helps."

"Thank you." I took the folder.

"I can tell you that if Indra Corp is involved, I couldn't see Raven having anything to do with last night's mess. Their CEO is Amanda Singh, a Telco billionaire from India. She has financial links to the Kashmiri separatists, the Hizbul Mujahideen."

I had to come clean. "I'm not actually on the Tower case. They won't let me investigate Raven's death. Did you hear about the National Gallery break in?"

"Please." Percy looked offended. "I am in the intelligence game, and that story has been splashed across every newspaper in London. Is there a magic angle?"

"Yes. This one here—" I indicated Andy with my thumb "—used illusions to pull it off. He spelled all the night-guards and somehow fooled the alarm systems. Indra Corp hired him to do the job."

"So where is the painting now?" Percy glared daggers at Andy.

"We don't know." I jumped to Andy's defense. "Andy was double-crossed. He was unconscious at the handover when I found him."

"Indra Corp has offices in the Docklands." Percy suggested, "Maybe they took it there."

"Or at least there may be some clue as to its whereabouts. We can check it out."

"It's worth a try." Percy looked excited. "Are you sure Indra Corp has it?"

"No, but it's our best bet. We do know they hired Andy to steal the painting and finding that out cost our informant his life."

"How?"

"At Gordon's wine bar. A warlock came and killed him. A very powerful one. We barely escaped alive." Saying it, I felt a tremor in my body, and my nostrils flared. Damn it, I did not have time to deal with post-traumatic shock. I built a cell in my mind and imagined throwing all my fear in there. Locking the door, I'd deal with it later.

"Well, it makes sense to at least try Indra's offices." Percy mused, "That is the only real estate they own in London, and even if the painting is not there, it is your best bet to get an idea where else it might be hidden."

I sat on my hands to hide the trembling. "We'll go in tonight."

"That's my girl. Not wasting any time. Will you need MI-6 support?" Percy offered.

I didn't want anyone else to protect if that warlock turned up again. Andy was enough to worry about. So, I said, "No. I think I can handle a simple break in on my own."

"Well keep me informed. We would love the chance to take anyone down who finances Islamic extremists." Percy rubbed his hands together enthusiastically.

At the back of my mind a small voice kept whispering but was not quite loud enough to be heard clearly.

"Something about Amanda Singh is ringing a bell."

"What do you mean?"

"I don't know. I can't quite connect the dots." I stood up. "Thanks again Percy. There is one other thing…"

The waiter interrupted us at that moment with the drinks. I'd forgotten about them. I sat back down. With a quick salute to Raven, we downed them. It turned out that a ginjinha was a berry liqueur drink, which was bitter, sweet, and as sticky as cough medicine. Percy popped the cherry that remained in his glass into his mouth. I put my glass back on the table. No cherry for me, I wanted all my wits about me when I did the break in and had no idea how long those cherries had been soaking in liqueur.

"You were saying…" Percy brought me back.

"Do you have any parachutes?"

Chapter Twelve

Lying on the paved ground, I rested my feet on a metal bench and with my hands behind my head, tried to count the floors of Canada Square. I wanted to mark where we needed to go, but the clouds racing past the heights gave me the sensation the building was falling toward me, and I kept losing count. I hadn't stared up at a building like this since I was a child.

This was a powerful spot—a fortress almost fifty stories high, with a pyramid on top to funnel magical energy. A billionaire, like Amanda Singh, had to be arrogant. Any normal person would be trying to get the painting overseas as fast as possible. She though would want it close, somewhere where she could look at it underneath, as it were, our noses. The painting could well be inside.

Andy sat on the bench. He put his arms out wide and stretched his legs out straight before him. He tilted his neck back at an acute angle to look at the building behind him. "It looks bloody high. Are you sure you don't want to go with my plan?"

I rolled my eyes and was disappointed he wasn't looking to see. "No Andy. I won't let you ensorcel the guards. It's wrong and against the law."

He protested, "But you are the law."

"Doesn't mean I want to arrest myself."

"I guarantee the guards will have a good time."

I looked up. It was the second tallest building in Britain and Indra Corp was on the 47th floor. Was Andy scared of heights? I remembered how green he looked when I mentioned the parachutes. I said cruelly, "No. We're going up, all that way. Right to almost the top."

"It's all right for you, you're wearing the boots."

He was being jovial, but I could see the whites of his knuckles where he gripped the bench. I softened and offered, "You can stay here, if it's too much."

Andy considered that. He stood up, and I admired that he was prepared to face that which terrified him, "No. We've been through this already. These people ripped me off, and I want to see it through to the end. Besides, you need me to keep us invisible as we go up. You don't want to end up with a million hits on You Tube. 'Spider Woman walks up skyscraper.' "

I rolled backward, sprung up to standing, and pointed with my thumb to my back. "Okay, hop on."

"You sure this is going to work?" Andy looked at me with eyes squeezed half-shut.

"Stop being a big baby. We don't know till we have given it a try."

"That's what I am worried about."

I crouched down, and Andy got on my back. He was heavy, but I could do this. I knew all those hours doing squats at the gym would one day count for something. Heaving myself up, I walked over and put my boot on the building's wall. To my relief Andy's weight transferred as I started up. First problem solved. Now it was a simple task of walking approximately two hundred meters with his weight on my back.

Andy said in my ear, "Remember to count the floors."

I shifted his weight. "Can you? I'm kind of exerting a bit of effort here."

"Sorry. I've my eyes shut, and I'm afraid if I open them, I might throw up." Andy buried his face in my neck, and I could feel the prickly stubble from his chin.

I briefly wondered what would happen if I dropped him, then shook my head, and started counting. I tried not to look down myself. Well, behind me as it were. I held onto Andy tightly. The winds buffeted me harder, the higher I climbed. We reached the 47th floor just as my quads started to scream and were ready to give out. Now this was the tricky part. "Andy?"

"Yes." Came the strangled reply.

"We're at the right floor, and I need you to do something."

"I seriously can't open my eyes, Lynx. I will faint. I get vertigo on stairs."

"Okay. Keep your eyes closed, but use one hand to reach into my jacket. I need you to get my gun out of the shoulder holster."

Andy reached into my jacket.

"Andy?"

"Yes."

"That isn't my gun."

"Sorry, I got distracted."

Andy reached a bit further and after some fumbling with the clasp, removed the gun.

"Now I need you to aim the gun at the window below us."

Andy pointed the gun downward.

"Not that much you'll break the window at my feet."

He raised his aim. "I hope you know what you are

doing, Lynx. These windows look mighty tough. The bullets might bounce back."

"Don't worry. The bullet in the chamber is a special one, just fire."

Andy squeezed the trigger and upon impact, a circle of blue energy, approximately one meter in diameter, leapt across the glass dissolving it. I stepped through, and we landed upright on the carpet.

Andy turned to look at the hole. "What was that?"

"Upon impact the bullet shattered and spread Hydrofluoric acid in a bounded circle."

A simple spell. I had etched HF on the bullet and drawn a circle around it. Alchemy, for me, was about intentions and simplicity, not runes and esoteric knowledge.

"What the hell is hydrofluoric acid?"

"Hydrofluoric acid dissolves glass."

"You thought of that yourself."

"I graduated with a first in chemistry from Cambridge." All people saw was the blonde hair. "Are you surprised?"

"No. I just—"

"Does it surprise you to know I am more than just a pretty face?" After learning potions with my aunt, chemistry had been a breeze for me.

While Andy floundered, I touched my bowler hat. Damn my unconscious. The truth was the Keeper had given me the idea of spelling a bullet. Andy was never going to find that out though. I said, "Now this is a conference room. We need to find Amanda Singh's office."

"Do we need to worry about alarms?"

"Not on this floor. There are two guards stationed

at the elevator. It should be fine unless they make a sweep. Then we'll have to move."

"On account of the big hole in the window and all?"

"That might give them a clue. Now be quiet and follow me."

I made my way through the offices. The CEO's door was locked. I bent down and pulled out my lock picks.

"What?" Andy asked, "No magic?"

I felt the first tumbler click. "I could explode the lock, but I want to shut the door behind us. If the guard comes by, he'll think nothing is wrong. Now shush. I'm concentrating."

In under a minute, I conquered the lock.

"After you." I opened the door for Andy.

Walking into the office, I was struck by its austerity. A modern executive desk in dark wood, a white leather chair, and a matching three-piece lounge, was all the furniture in the room. A genuine Jackson Pollock dominated one wall. At least, I assumed it was genuine. If I was right, it meant Amanda liked her art.

"Through here I think." Andy slid the Pollock painting across to reveal a metal door. There was a biometric scanner beside the door. I stared at it for a moment. My lock picks were useless against that. I wondered whether there a spell to defeat the scanner. I swiveled my bowler hat.

Chapter Thirteen

The world spun, and I found myself within the sanctuary of the Repository, relaxed in the burgundy Chesterfield chair. The Keeper must use something magical to make the leather so soft. The Chesterfields at Bosley House seemed to have centuries of hardened polish on them, and it paid to be careful, for if you sat too far back then it was a scramble to get out again. This one was more comfortable than my bed.

The Keeper appeared. This time her cardigan was a lavender color. I wondered whether being a being of spirit, she actually had a wardrobe or just appeared how she wanted to be seen.

"I have a small bedroom behind the stacks if you must know." The Keeper smiled at me.

"You can read my mind?"

"To a certain extent yes. It helps with inquiries. Many an old wizard will come and ask for, 'That book. You know the one with words in it.' Rather than frustrate myself with their blatherings, I pluck the title out of their mind. Still I do like proprieties. So," she inquired in orderly fashion, "how may I assist you?"

I briefly gave her a run down of the situation and then asked, "Is there a spell to fool the scanner?"

The Keeper pushed her glasses back on her nose and seemed lost in thought. "I have scanned my knowledge of case files, and there isn't one example.

You could just blow the door."

"I'm afraid that there might be some nasty magical defenses if I try that."

"Yes. It does pay to be cautious."

"Oh well. I'm going to have to improvise." I spun my hat and said, "Thank you."

It seemed not everything was going to be solved by a spin of the hat. I wish I had Quentin's magic app. Then I could just take a picture of the problem and the appropriate spell would appear. I told Andy, "I've no idea how to get past this."

Andy offered, "Maybe I could try."

"How?"

"Well I think this is an Iris scanner, not a retinal scanner and might be fooled by a simple illusion. Do we have a color photo of Amanda Singh?"

I shook my head. "I think all the photos in the MI-6 files are black and white."

"I need something in color to make an illusion of her eye."

"Will that work?" If it didn't, I would force the door with magic and just hope I had enough power to shield us from any ward.

Andy replied, "If I can see her eyes with enough detail it will."

I spied an Indra Corp annual financial report on the small coffee table to the side of the sofa. I went over and on the third page, there was a large photo of Amanda Singh. She was sitting back on a chair, with the type-written CEO address on the opposing page. In her forties, she was dressed in a traditional silk sari. There was a tightness to her smile, as if it was an unfamiliar expression, and the bindi between her eyes looked slightly askew. I called softly to Andy, "How about this?"

He came over, perused the photo, and declared, "Perfect."

After studying the picture for a while he closed his eyes. There was a shimmering in the air and then before me stood Amanda Singh. A scent of sandalwood filled the air and once more, I was in awe of the depth of Andy's illusions. Even as a spell-caster, I would have no idea that the person in front of me wasn't Amanda Singh, nor that there was magic being worked. Andy-Amanda walked over to the retinal scan, pressed the button, and let the scan go over her eye. The door slid open.

"It worked," I said, "I could kiss you."

Andy changed back. The scent of sandalwood still lingered in the air. "Anytime you want."

I pouted. "Not till you've at least had a shave."

Andy waved his hand over his face. He appeared clean-shaven.

"That's cheating, and it doesn't count. I'll still get stubble rash."

What was I doing? Flirting with him? I hadn't been this close to any man since training and fraternization had been against regulations. Andy's lips beckoned, but I ignored the yearning in my own. I patted him on the cheek and turned to the room. We'd a job to do.

Inside was an ornate orange room. Two china tigers guarded the entrance, and a golden Ganesh statue sat against the opposite wall. On an ottoman inside was Van Gogh's *Chair*. Andy moved past me. As he did, a gong sounded in the air.

He froze immediately. "That didn't sound good."

"You're an idiot." I wasn't talking to him but myself. I knew he had just run through a magical ward. I was trained to think of such things. Andy was not. It was my task to stop him before he set it off.

Andy didn't know I was talking to myself and thought I was having a go at him. "Hey that's a bit harsh."

I started to explain, but stopped. From behind the ottoman rose six giant, hissing, king-cobra snakes. I drew my katana.

"Ummm Lynx..." Andy remained frozen in place halfway to the ottoman. He had also seen them.

"Stay still. Snakes respond to movement." I moved beside him as one of the snakes slithered over the ottoman and came toward us.

"Are you any good with that thing?"

"I've trained in Kendo since I was six. My parents were agents and saw the spark in me early, so they decided to train me in every art that would keep me alive until I could come into my magical maturity. Somehow, my magic complemented the training. So while I may not be able to beat a wizard in a magical duel, my magic has supported my martial arts to a degree that most would find surprising."

Andy mused, "Like Mortal Kombat?"

"Just get behind me, and you can have all the Sonya Blade fantasies you want."

The cobra struck at me. Its jaws seemed obscenely wide. I sidestepped and brought my sword down hard, slicing off its head, letting the weight and sharpness of the sword do all the work. That was easy. The other snakes hissed angrily and started to slither toward us, coming around the ottoman at all angles. I took a step toward them.

"Aah Lynx," Andy said from behind me.

"Not now Andy." There were still five to kill. They went down pretty easy. I was faster with my sword than they were with their bites, so I was confident but still had to concentrate.

Andy ignored me and said in an even tone, "But Lynx I think the snake you just struck is growing another head."

I looked down in alarm, just in time to see the snake I killed rise up again. It struck out at my leg, but I managed to dodge. It rose to its full height, hissing and glaring. It struck at me again. I dropped my sword and this time I grabbed it behind its head. It started to loop itself around my arms. I said, as I kept an eye on the other snakes coming at us. "Spin my hat Andy."

"What?" he asked in confusion.

"Spin my hat!" I longed to be back in the army where people just followed orders and didn't ask questions. Why did he have to know the reason for everything? "I've got my hands full at the moment."

The snakes slithered further toward us. Andy spun my bowler hat. The room disappeared and once again, I found myself in the Repository. To my surprise, the snake had hitched a ride, too. It tightened its grip on my arm and hissed again, as if angry it had been brought here.

"Lynx." The Keeper queried, "Back again so quickly?

The snake squirmed in my hand. I tried to freeze it using my power. There was nothing there.

The Keeper said, "Unfortunately your magic will not work here. We're in the spirit world, and the elemental energies are not available. So please hold on tightly to that snake. I would hate to have to hunt for it through the stacks."

"Believe me, I won't be letting this one go." I held the snake out at arms length, but it somehow turned in my hand. I could see in its eyes hatred and a desire to bite me.

The Keeper, sounding as if it were a tea party conversation, asked, "I take it you got past the scanner?"

"Yes, but now we're in some strife. We've found the painting, but it's guarded by King Cobras that don't seem to want to die. I cut the head off this one, and it grew it back. There are five others back in the world slithering toward me."

"Exceptionally interesting. In Hindu traditions, the Nagas are the immortal King Cobras that guard treasures. For someone to have them as guards, you are dealing with a very powerful adversary." The Keeper smiled encouragingly.

I thought the smile inappropriate considering her choice of words. "You say immortal?"

The Keeper took a seat on a stool opposite me. "Yes. There is no way to kill them. You can chop their heads off, and it won't have any effect. Legend states they tricked Garuda, the Hindu eagle god, into giving them some elixir of immortality. Indra, the leader of the gods, took it away from these evil creatures, but some spilled on the grass. The Naga licked it up and became immortal, but in doing so, they cut their tongues, and that is why snakes now have forked tongues."

I let her words sink in, and then asked in defeat, "So there's no way to overpower them?"

"I did not say that." The Keeper actually wagged her finger at me. "I only said that there was no way to kill them. Really, Lynx, you should pay more attention. I should lend you a book on listening skills."

I didn't have time for a lecture. "I don't care about my listening skills. What should I do?"

"A young lady should never stop looking for ways to improve herself," the Keeper chastised.

I, at that moment, could not wait to be of an age where people actually stopped thinking it was all right to give me unsolicited advice and actually paid attention to what I really wanted help with. I made a strangled noise of frustration as the snake hissed and struggled.

The Keeper must have been able to translate my cry into English. She continued, "Well whoever goes in there must have some way to disarm the Naga. I have heard of the High Priestesses kissing King Cobras on their heads to bless the harvest. My guess would be to try that."

"Kiss this snake on its head?" I asked incredulously.

"Yes. If I am right, it will be like a deactivation switch. The priestesses are trained to do this from birth and who would think to replicate the feat?" She reached over and patted my knee. "Is there anything else?"

"No, thank you." I took a moment, got one arm free, and then twisted my hat to go back to the real world.

I brought the snake wrapped around my arms up to my lips and kissed it on the head, holding it with the fangs pointing away from me. Almost instantly, it unwound itself from my arm. I tentatively, put it in on the ground, and it wriggled away.

"What did you just do?" Andy asked.

"I kissed it on the head." I swayed in front of another Cobra. "Now be quiet while I kiss the rest."

A snake struck out at me, and I sidestepped it nimbly. As it righted itself, I kissed it on the top of the head and it immediately relaxed. I replicated the feat with the other snakes. They crawled over to one side of the room and seemed to fall asleep in a pile.

"I've never seen anything quite like that. Jolly good show." Andy beamed at me. "Now let's grab the painting and run."

"Wait one second." I spied a laptop on a desk in the corner of the room. I went over and took out a thumb drive, placing it in the USB port I threw my will toward the drive and muttered, "Copy."

The drive flashed green for a second.

"You know you can actually do that without a spell."

"My way's faster." I grinned at Andy. We were about to leave when I saw against the wall an old painting of an ancient Maharaja, and for some reason it drew me. At the bottom of the frame it read, 'Kharak Singh". Something clicked in my head.

"I knew it. How could I've missed it before?"

"Knew what?" Andy asked.

"That the two break-in's were connected." I pointed to the enormous diamond in the painting that was in the center of Kharak Singh's turban.

"Is that what I think it is?" Andy peered carefully at the painting.

"It sure is." The details were all flooding back to me. "Kharak Singh was the original owner of the Koh-

I-Noor diamond. The Dutch East India Company confiscated it, back in the nineteenth century. They gave it to Queen Victoria as a gift."

"So…" Andy asked, but I could see he had caught on.

"So…" I smiled excitedly. "Amanda Singh is his descendent. She probably set you up to be a distraction and to draw MI-23 to the gallery, while the important theft went on at the Tower. Somehow Raven knew and sent me off alone to the gallery, while he went to the Tower by himself."

"They didn't really want the painting?"

"No." I went over and grabbed the Van Gogh from the ottoman. I carefully rolled it up and put it in my jacket. "You were just a distraction. That you succeeded was a bonus. They probably expected you to fail."

"Son of a…" Andy punched a wall, then looked sheepishly at me, "Sorry, I don't like being used."

"I understand," I said. "Now, if you are over your temper tantrum, we need to get out of here."

One added bonus was that I could now legitimately pursue Raven's killer, without defying the Magus's direct order—for the two jobs were by the same people. I stopped in my tracks. This meant that the warlock at Gordon's wine bar was Raven's killer. I'd felt the heat of his power and knew it was him. Unless of course Amanda Singh had two warlocks with immense strength on her payroll. I tried not to think of that scenario.

Making our way toward the boardroom, I heard a noise and glanced behind me to see one of the two guards coming around the corner.

"Stop there," he shouted. He fumbled at his belt for his gun with one hand and with the other tried to press the two-way on his shoulder. I sighed. It would be so easy to take him out. I only had contempt for his crossed hands. Who trained these people? He probably got his security license from a cornflake pack. Yet I'd told Andy that he couldn't enscorcel the guards, so I couldn't now take one of them out physically. If I did, I knew he would never shut up about it. I grabbed Andy and ran to the boardroom. We just made it through the door when I heard a bullet whistle behind us.

I manhandled Andy to the hole in the window. "Jump."

He didn't move. So, I grabbed him by the belt of his pants and his collar and threw him through the hole, praying he remembered to pull the ripcord.

The guard made it to the door behind me. I waved as he raised his gun, and then jumped through the window. I looked down in relief. Andy's parachute was open. I started to free-fall through the night.

Chapter Fourteen

At a conservative estimate, Van Gogh's *Chair* would be worth one hundred and fifty million pounds. At auction it might easily bring a better price. Walking down a London Street, with something of that much value stuck in my jacket, made me twitchy. Beside me, keeping up, was a jubilant Andy.

"I've never done anything that crazy before." He looked like he was about to break out into a song and dance routine and start swinging off the lamp-poles. "I thought I was going to die and then the blessed parachute opened above me. It was the best feeling in the world. I could've kissed the ground when we landed."

"Keep it down. We don't want to attract attention."

We had landed near the river, quickly cut our lines and dumped the chutes in the Thames, yet I was still worried about pursuit.

"Sorry Lynx I can't. I just base-jumped for the first time. What a rush." He screamed the last sentence in the air and did that ridiculous fist pump thing that men do—usually when they're drunk and watching their favorite sporting team score. This was why at the academy they drummed into us that four-out-of-five agents who are compromised, were working with amateurs. It's the nature of the beast. All the tradecraft in the world won't help when working with someone clueless like Andy, who was drawing everyone's eyes. Still I had to admit I was feeling pretty jubilant myself. We'd done it. We'd got the painting back. I gave Andy a quick hug then said, "Now come on and keep it down."

I pulled him into an all night eatery just as a series of blue lights flashed past. Finding a booth near the back, I placed the priceless painting on the orange vinyl next to me. Andy sat opposite, sliding in and placing his arm along the top of the booth in proprietary ownership. I ordered a fruit salad, praying that it was not out of a tin. I took the offer of tea. Andy ordered an omelet with the lot and a beer. Suddenly I was annoyed. "Weren't you satisfied with the one I made?"

"No...I mean yes," Andy answered, once he realized I was referring to the omelet. "The one you made was great."

"Great?" I scowled. He thought I couldn't take the truth. "So great that you had to order another the next day. Seriously, what was wrong with my omelet?"

Andy shuffled his cutlery. "Jesus, Lynx. I just like omelets and am hungry. It has nothing to do with the one you made me."

I leant across the table to reposition the knife in its proper place. Did the man have no sense of aesthetics? "I'm a grown woman, and I can take it if you don't like my omelet. I just want you to be honest with me so next time I can improve."

He stubbornly moved his knife back on an angle. "I am being honest."

I grabbed a paper napkin from the stainless steel, box holder and placed it upon my lap. "Fine then."

Andy at least knew enough about women to know

that fine meant anything but fine. I knew he didn't want to, but he couldn't help but rise to the bait and the question seemed to escape his lips, despite every attempt to smother it. It came out almost inaudibly, "Fine?"

I leapt at the question. "If I can't trust you I can't trust you."

He came back with anger, as if that would work better than rational argument. He had so much to learn. His voice rose, "Why can't you just believe that there was nothing wrong with your omelet?"

With men, it is important to point out the obvious. He set me up at the net and I smashed it into the backcourt. "Because you're lying."

"Okay, okay. Let's see. Your omelet." Andy covered his eyes with his hands and rubbed his face before he looked up and offered, "It could have done with a bit more cheese."

I pushed back in the booth and crossed my arms. "You didn't like my omelet because it didn't have enough cheese?"

Andy blew out his breath. I could see his frustration. "No. That isn't what I said. I liked your omelet, but it could have had more cheese in it."

I fixed him a glare.

He added lamely, "I like cheese."

"How much bloody cheese do you need in one omelet? Next time, make your own." Game, set, and match.

He opened his mouth but thought the better of it and shut it again. I berated myself. I realized what I was doing. I was angry at myself, not him. It wasn't that I didn't trust him, it was that he shouldn't trust me. We sat in silence.

I felt guilty and had been taught by my aunt that it wasn't right to eat with bad feelings between people. It was bad for digestion. Still I wasn't going to apologize. I asked instead, "How did you end up as an illusionist."

Andy refused the olive branch. "You don't want to know."

I hated people telling me what I wanted. "Of course I want to know, otherwise I wouldn't have asked."

"You think you want to but you don't." He refused to look at me and instead was trying to get a white napkin out of the stainless steel, box holder. It tore, then he grabbed again and this time came out with a handful. He took one and left the rest in a messy pile.

I straightened the pile. "So it's all right for me to answer all your questions about my past, but I can't ask any of you."

Andy threw up his hands in exasperation, "Fine then."

He took a moment to compose himself, looking away in the way people do when they want to actually see what they were remembering, He started in a quiet voice, "One day my father came home from the pub when my brother and I were playing Playstation. I froze when I saw him standing in the doorway. He was stony silent. That was when it was the worst. When he yelled he was usually too drunk to hurt us and could be distracted easily. He took two strides, grabbed my brother by the hair, and flung him into the wall. He turned to me, and I poured all my will into him not seeing me. To my surprise it worked. I was still there in the chair, but he thought I had run away. He could not see me.

"I sat there and watched him beat my brother. Max ended up in the hospital that night. I would have done anything to have been able to protect him as well, but at that stage I didn't know how to cast an illusion over someone else. I sat there like a coward, while my father thrashed him. I know I couldn't have done anything to stop it, but to this day I regret not stepping in. Bones heal, but I still feel the shame."

A tear rolled down my cheek. "I'm so sorry that happened to you. You know, it's not your fault."

"Some days I believe that. Most of the time it still feels like I'm to blame."

I didn't know what else to say. I was touched he had shared but was feeling slightly uncomfortable myself. I hadn't expected him to go that far and now didn't know what to say. I reached for a safe topic. "So how did your other talents develop?"

"Other talents?"

"You know, like the wards you set at the gallery."

"Wasn't me. All I can do is illusion. I was given the ward on a scroll. I read it out loud once I was in the room."

It made sense. A scroll would work for anybody. It also meant Andy was a Talent, someone with instinctive magical ability, but who doesn't use spells. It would explain why his illusions were so powerful. A Talent usually can only do one thing, but they can do that one thing better than any spell caster could dream of doing. I wondered whether there was more to Andy being given the Ward. Perhaps it had been a trap set for me and Raven, knowing we would answer the call. I still wanted to know why Raven had stayed at Bosley

House. He must have had some clue regarding the traitor. Maybe I could find it? I asked Andy, "How did you break into the gallery, seeing as you've no other magic? Are you a professional thief?"

"I didn't have to break in. I just hid behind an illusion until they closed."

Of course. I should have figured that out myself.

"How about you?" Andy asked. "What sort of magic do you do?"

"The elemental kind. I want to be the Bruce Lee of the magical world."

"I like it." His words seemed genuine. "You want to break through and forge ahead with the mixed martial arts of wizardry."

He got it. He understood me. I felt excited and exclaimed in a surprised voice, "Yes!"

Just then the food arrived. I was pleasantly surprised that the fruit salad was fresh and not out of a can. We ate in a comfortable silence. Upon finishing, I produced my laptop out of my backpack, placed the thumb drive into the USB, and opened up the files I'd copied from the computer at Indra Corp.

Looking through them I stumbled upon a folder marked Kali. Opening it up I scanned the directory: Jewel House, Wards, Gallery, and Incarnation Ceremony. I opened up Wards and was shocked to see a copy of a *MI-23* file detailing the wards around the Crown Jewels. This was the first solid evidence that there was indeed a traitor in MI-23. Part of me hadn't truly believed there could be a turncoat, thinking there must be some other explanation, but here was a file that had been taken from the unhackable MI-23 Repository. The only way it could have gotten out was by a traitor leaking the contents. Who could I trust with the news? Surely the Magus was safe. Yet what if he were the traitor?

Opening up the gallery folder, a photo of Andy came up. The mission objective was indeed to draw the attention of MI-23 before the break in at the Tower. Andy had been a distraction. That he had pulled it off was merely a bonus. What I read next under Incarnation Ceremony tied knots in my stomach. Amanda Singh planned to become an incarnation of Kali the destroyer. She was going to use the Koh-I-Noor diamond as a focus to become a living deity on earth. From there she was going to unify India and Pakistan and use her power to wage war upon England, seeking revenge for Britain taking the diamond all those years ago.

Great, on top of everything else, I now had to stop a dark empress from trying to conquer England and crushing the brightest hopes for the future.

I filled Andy in and ended with an honest statement. "I've no idea what to do next."

Andy replied matter-of-factly, "Well first things first, we find a buyer for the painting so we can have the werewolves off our backs."

I should've guessed this was going to come up. "We're not selling the painting. We're giving it back."

"What?" He sounded outraged. "I jumped out of an office building just so you could give the painting back?"

"Yes. It's the right thing to do."

"But we owe six million pounds..." Andy was looking at me like I was the stupidest person on Earth.

I knew he didn't like my decision. I didn't like owing the money either, but for me there was no choice. I said in a consolatory voice, "I know we do, but we still have nine days to sort that out."

"Nine days. Oh that's all right then. I thought it was only eight."

"No need for the sarcasm."

"It's not like the werewolves don't like to eat people alive or anything."

He was starting to make me angry. "I said I'd think of something."

"What?"

"Listen, I don't have a plan right now, but if we don't stop Amanda Singh, it won't matter that we don't have six million pounds, because there will be a vengeful goddess stomping around Britain destroying everything in sight."

Andy was silent for a bit. I could almost see an angel and a demon on each of his shoulders talking to him. Could he see that it was the right thing to do? I hoped he could. He put his hands up in defeat. "Okay. Okay. We give the painting back."

I reached over and squeezed his hand. He made a face but did not take his hand away.

Chapter Fifteen

A traitor in MI-23 meant I had to be doubly careful. They would've heard by now that we had taken back the painting, and the guard at Canada House would've given my description, so I couldn't go back to my flat in case it was being watched. Neither could I trust anyone at Bosley House. I steered us instead toward a cheap hotel. I ignored Andy's raised eyebrow. He was kidding himself. I hadn't slept for almost forty-eight hours, and it was all I could do to keep on going.

The foyer smelled of air freshener, and the plastic potted plants were dusty, but it would do. I did not care for the look the night clerk gave me as he passed over the key to our room, while letting us know where the ice machine was located. Andy looked smug, and I felt soiled, but was too tired to say anything. Let the night clerk think what he may. Andy was wise enough to keep quiet, but I should've hit him for the strut he put on.

Opening the room door, I wasn't surprised by the queen-size bed, even though I had expressly asked for a twin. I grabbed the comforter and a pillow and lay down on the short couch, despite Andy's protests. My last thought was chiding myself for not packing a toothbrush. After being sleep deprived for so long, I didn't even remember falling asleep.

Morning came and I stretched myself over the

confines of the couch. My mouth felt dry and my teeth chalky. I couldn't remember the last time I had gone to bed without cleaning and flossing. My boots were splayed on the floor. I was horrified I hadn't neatly put them to the side. What would Andy think? I sat up, quickly stood the boots up next to each other, and looked over to the bed. Andy wasn't there.

I sat up confused and then with a sinking feeling, I looked over to the desk where I had left the Van Gogh. It was missing. How stupid could I be?

I got up and jammed on my boots. He better run fast. I was going to hunt him down hard. I patted my shoulder holster. For the first time I actually felt capable of doing what the Magus had asked.

The door opened. I whirled around ready for action. In came Andy carrying two cups of coffee on a cardboard tray with some pastries in a bag. The nerve he had, to think that it would be okay to waltz straight back in after he had taken the Van Gogh. He must have given the painting to the werewolves and wanted me to know that I was in the clear. I walked up to him and as he passed me a coffee, I snapped one cuff on his wrist, twisted his arm, and threw him to the floor. Coffee spilled everywhere, and I grabbed his other arm to cuff the other wrist.

I dug my knee into his back and squashed his face into the carpet with my hand in his hair. "I can't believe you came back. You are under arrest for the theft of the Van Gogh from the National Gallery. You do not have to say anything, but it may harm your defense if you do not mention when questioned something, which you later rely on in court. Anything you do say may be given in evidence."

"trrrntvvvvnnnn," Came Andy's muffled reply.

I lifted his head. "What was that? Do you want to confess?"

"Turn the TV on," Andy said.

I asked, "Why?"

"Just do it."

"Okay stay there." I grabbed the remote from the stand and pressed the power button. A children's cartoon was showing. "There. Happy now?"

Andy sighed. "Put it on the news channel."

I reluctantly complied.

A picture of Van Gogh's *Chair* was behind the newscaster, who announced, "The thieves returned the painting last night. It was delivered to the front door of the Sun Newspapers, by an anonymous homeless man."

CCTV footage showed a bearded homeless guy walking up and leaving it at the front desk before walking away. "Anyone who can recognize this individual or with any information pertaining to the burglary, please call Crimestoppers."

I asked, as a number flashed upon the screen. "That homeless guy was you?"

"Yes. You could even smell the stale urine on me."

I took my knee off his back. "What if you'd been caught?"

"I was ready. It would have to be an agent to catch me. The police I can fool."

I unlocked the cuffs and looked at the spilled coffee. "What a waste."

"You're telling me. I've been up half the night."

"Andy…" I started.

"Look it was my fault. No need to apologize," he hesitated and scratched his head. "I should've told you what I was doing but you crashed right out on the couch. I thought it was best if we return it as soon as we could. Honestly I didn't want the temptation around."

I put out my hand and pulled him up. "It's hard for me to trust people, and I *did* catch you stealing the painting the other night."

"I get that." He said but made a show of rolling his shoulder around as if I had hurt him.

"Friends?" I offered.

Andy smiled as he shook my hand. "Friends."

Friends. Partners. I knew without a doubt that there would be no way I would ever carry out the Magus's orders. I should tell Andy right now. We could plan something. Maybe he could cast an illusion to fake his death. There would be some way round it. I would find some way.

"So what do we do now?"

I was struck by a dream that I had during the night. I had forgotten it with the painting missing, but it came back to me clearly now. Andy and I had been standing in Singapore airport together and a loud voice had said, 'Come.' A vision of a Koi pond had swum in my mind. I knew what that meant. Raven had told me as part of my training.

"We have to go and see the Oracle."

"The Oracle?" Andy looked puzzled.

"Yes. The Oracle sent me a dream last night to summon me."

"Where's this Oracle?"

"Not this Oracle, it's the Oracle. There's only one. He meets people in Singapore Airport, so that anyone, from any nationality with any past, may see him without having to cross any specific border."

Andy salvaged the pastries from the bag he was carrying, sat down on the bed, and started to munch on a Danish. "Why Singapore Airport?"

"It's huge. It's like a little city unto itself. It has movie theatres, restaurants, prayer rooms, fitness centers, hotels... Besides which, the Oracle's addicted to the curry puffs they make there."

"Okay and why are we seeing him?"

"Unlike most fortune tellers or psychics, he's the real deal. He sees into the future. It's often hard to understand what he sees, but it might just give us the edge we need. And since he's summoned me, I have to go. I just need to stop off at the apartment to get my passport and pack a bag." I'd have to take the risk and hope that we could avoid any surveillance.

"Okay, we can finish breakfast on the run." Andy pulled the other cherry Danish out of the paper bag and handed it to me. It wasn't too badly squashed.

Chapter Sixteen

There was something wrong. We were crawling ahead in a massive traffic jam, but it wasn't the frustration of being stuck. This was London after all—traffic jams were par for the course. No, it was something else, a disturbance in the Force. Spying a parking spot at the side of the road, I pulled over and placed my permit on the dash. Andy was pushed to keep up with me, as I power walked the block or two to the corner of Kensington Road. Emergency vehicles blocked off the street. A large crowd had developed and the media were there, rolling out cables and setting up.

Smoke was rising into the sky and I knew, I just knew, in the pit of my stomach what had happened. Andy started, "What—"

I shushed him. I needed to see and didn't want to talk. I told him, "Wait here."

I pushed my way through the crowd to the taped off area. From there I had a clear view of the space, which was now smoky air, where my apartment had been. My mind couldn't quite comprehend what it saw. I understood at some level, but in another it seemed surreal, like I had stepped outside of myself and into a cartoon, or a 1940's newsreel of the London bombings.

Firefighters were pumping water at the remains of the smoldering building. I flashed my badge at a policeman, who was standing on the other side of the

125

tape. He was holding the curious public back while stealing glances at the blackened ruins of what used to be my life. I asked him, "What happened?"

The policeman held up the tape to let me pass under. He explained as I rose on the official side of the tape, "The first floor apartment exploded in flames about an hour ago. The Hosers have been dealing with the fire ever since. No casualties so far. The guy in the convenience store downstairs made it out, and we think he was the only one in the building at the time." He leant forward and whispered, "One thing though, I overheard the arson investigator talking on the phone. This was no gas leak. It was a bomb. Burned too hot for a normal fire."

I thanked him and wandered toward the tattered remains of my life, lying exposed on the road. What had happened to all my clothes, my photos, and my passport? I spotted a burnt bit of a paper that looked like a pirate's treasure map. It was a list of things to do that I had made for the week. I could still read item number one: Clean Bathroom. An unchecked box beside it. That was going to be hard to complete now since my bathroom had no walls, ceiling, or floor.

Looking down at the tattered smoldering remnants of my couch, I began to laugh. Something was changing inside of me. I thought of how I had spent so much time trying to make my apartment perfect, but never had anyone over. Why had I chosen to live that way? None of what I thought mattered, actually mattered. I was waking up to the bigger drama. Almost dying put things in perspective. I didn't need the comforts and security of a home.

I needed justice.

I needed to stop the people responsible for this, for Raven, the men murdered at the tower, Tablet, Andy, the people of Britain, and now myself. I felt anger rise, but it was not a rage, it was a righteous anger. I looked down at one of my ivory, silk pillows now covered in ash. Then a dagger of fear hit me as one of the pillow's tassels reminded me. What had happened to my cat?

A voice called to me, "Lynx."

I tried to locate the voice. I spied movement from a stretcher ready to be loaded into the back of an ambulance. It was Mr. Adams waving. I ran over. In his arms was my cat. Party's pristine white fur was now a sooty gray, and he looked like he had just swallowed a bad mouse.

I patted his head. "Oh Party. I'm so glad to see you still alive."

Mr. Adams, took off his oxygen mask to talk. "I'm alive too, sweetie."

"Sorry Mr. Adams. Of course I'm glad that you're alive as well." Tears started to stream down my face. "I'm so sorry for what happened."

Mr. Adams put his hand on my hand as it stroked Mr. Particularis. "It wasn't your fault, Lynx."

I had to let him know the truth, even if he hated me. "Actually, I think it may've been."

Mr. Adams gripped my hand harder. "Nonsense child."

I was such a mess. Here I was, getting comforted by Mr. Adams, when he was the one about to be put in the back of an ambulance. I took a breath in. I had to tell him the truth. Well, at least as much as I could, without breaking the Official Secrets Act. "You have to know something. I don't really work at the British

Library…"

"Shh child." Mr. Adams pulled the blanket tighter around himself, and whispered, "Listen, I knew your parents. I know what they did for this country. I know they were cloak and dagger agents. I once patched up your dad when I found him collapsed upon the steps. He'd received quite a beating but refused to go to the doctors when I woke him. Said it was nothing."

"Really?" I asked, yet I could imagine the scene. My father had been the strong, let-me-suffer-in-silence type.

Mr. Adams coughed. He must have inhaled some nasty smoke. After a few deep breaths with the oxygen mask back on he finally got his voice back. "It's true. It's not the type of thing an old man would make up. I'm a little too old to be bothered with untruths and a little too young to have forgotten what the truth really is."

I smiled at his joke.

He continued, "I know what you do too. I wasn't born yesterday. The way your boots are always polished and tied in military fashion, the odd hours you keep, the look in your eyes… No librarian has that look."

It was a good reminder. Despite my best efforts, I'd been made by a convenience store clerk. "What look?"

"The look of capability. I wouldn't want to cross you Lynx, and I happened to be quite the pugilist in my youth." Mr. Adam's took some more breaths of oxygen before he continued, "Look, I don't know why they blew up your apartment, but it wasn't you that set that bomb off and even if it was aimed at you, it's not your fault. It was the evil men who set it in the first place."

"But you are sitting here with an oxygen mask," I protested.

"Please don't waste a single moment worrying about me. My mother survived the bombing of London and my father the landing at Normandy in WWII, so I will survive this. You just get the bastards who did this and keep your chin up."

"Thank you." I squeezed his old white hand gently.

A paramedic came up, almost absentmindedly pressed his fingers on Mr. Adams wrist to check his pulse. He then checked Mr. Adams blood pressure with a deliberate efficiency. Satisfied, he said to me apologetically, "We have to go now."

As they collapsed the stretcher in preparation to put him in the back of the ambulance, I asked, "Can you do me a favor, Mr. Adams?"

He put a hand out to pause the paramedics. "What is that?"

"Could you look after Mr. Particularis until I tie this up."

The Adams had a flat a few blocks over. I hated to ask, but I couldn't think of anyone else.

"It would be my pleasure. Laura can take him when she comes to see me at the hospital. If that is all right with these fine gentlemen?"

The paramedic nodded. "We aren't really meant to be bringing animals into the hospital, but I'll make a bed for him in the staff room. Your wife can pick him up from there."

"I'll visit as soon as this is all over."

Mr. Adams put the oxygen mask on and waved me away. They loaded him into the ambulance. Despite him telling me not to, I couldn't help but feel guilty.

That poor old man had almost been killed because of me. I didn't let it overwhelm me though. I would set this right.

I turned to see Andy ducking under the tape. The policeman pointed for him to get back on the other side. Great, just what I needed, for Andy to get arrested when we had to move. Whoever had done this was sending a clear message and could still be around—ready to fight. As much as I would love to smash whoever did this, a fight would be a disaster with all these bystanders about. They had already shown at Gordon's that they had no compunction about killing innocents. I went back to Andy, who was arguing with the policeman, and grabbed him. "Not now Andy. We need to move."

Andy indicated the rubble-strewn road. "But all your stuff…"

"It's gone." I breathed in. That was harder to say than I thought. "Whoever did this may still be around."

Andy nodded in understanding, took hold of my arm, and ducked us under the tape.

Seeing us come from the other side of the tape, a reporter jammed a microphone in my face. "Do you have anything to say on the terrorist bombing?"

I needed an outlet for my anger, so I channeled it into the microphone, blowing the circuits all the way back to the camera. The reporter dropped the microphone, shaking her hand. I put my face in hers. "It wasn't terrorists, you ghoul. It was a warning to me from a pissed off priestess of Kali the Destroyer."

Andy dragged me away before I could say more. The look on the reporter's face, though, was something money couldn't buy.

We made it to the back of the crowd and a gruff

voice asked, "Just where do you think you two are going?"

What now? I looked up to see the two Werewolves of London blocking the path in front of me. I took out my gun, glad I had just blown the camera.

"Did you do this?" I asked pointing back to the destruction of my apartment.

Weasel grinned a row of sharp teeth. "Of course not. It was your main asset. Why would we blow up what we want to take away? Now put that useless toy down and explain to me why you returned the painting that could have paid us off quite nicely. Our employers are far from pleased."

I took a deep breath and said almost to myself, "I'm not in the mood for this."

Weasel curled a fist. "I don't care what mood you are in. That's the great thing about not being one of the men in your life. Now give me an explanation."

I glanced down at my gun and then back up with a smile. "I'll give you two good reasons why you should get out of my face."

Weasel growled, low and throaty. "Don't even think of playing rough with me, princess."

"First reason." I brought the gun to bear. "Silver nitrate."

Weasel's ears pricked up. "What?"

I waved my gun at him. "My useless toy is loaded with bullets containing silver nitrate. I do believe that you may have a problem with that."

Weasel started to growl. He and Dave spread out widening the field of fire if they needed to rush me. Weasel put up a hand. "And the second."

I looked him in the eye. "We still have eight days.

Do you have a problem keeping your bargain? Or should I let everyone know that the word of the werewolves is no good."

Weasel started to laugh. Yet it was not a laugh that encouraged anyone else to join in. Quite the opposite. He stopped abruptly, nodded, and said, "Well played, miss. I am going to enjoy eating you if you can't make the payment. It has been far too long since I have enjoyed witch flesh."

With that they spun around and were gone.

Policemen were now running toward me. I lazily held up my badge.

Chapter Seventeen

Needing a space to think, I drove to Hyde Park. Fresh air and a walk would go a long way to helping me process my life going up in smoke.

Andy and I strolled past a homeless man, standing upon a soapbox at Speaker's Corner, haranguing the uncaring passers-by. Listening, I realized he was unfolding a story of how England had been secretly run by a group of sorcerers, since the sixteenth century. A few tourists were taking pictures. I pulled a fifty from my pocket and went up to the man. His eyes widened when he saw the note. As I passed it to him, I let fire flick over my palm, leant closer and whispered, "It was actually the seventeenth century."

He fell back off his soapbox and started to scramble away from me. Ignoring, the odious stench of stale alcohol, I followed, grabbed him by the lapels of his army disposal jacket. "What's your name?"

With eyes showing fright, he answered, "Russell."

I sat him up and squatted to look him square in his face. "Well Russell, not everything you have heard about us is true. We actually are here to help as much as we can."

He started to cry. "Please just go away."

I shook my head. "I can't do that."

"Why not?" he asked, as he wiped his nose with his finger and rubbed it on his sleeve.

I wished I had a tissue to give him. Trying to not let how grossed out I felt show on my face, I answered, "Because I see a spark of greatness in you."

"With your magic?"

It was like speaking to a small child. I answered, "Yes, with my magic."

I tucked the fifty into the pocket of his shirt. "I want you to take this fifty, get your stuff, and then go down to the London homeless shelter. Here's their card." I passed him one I kept in my pocket. "Ask for Father Donald and tell him Lynx sent you. He'll look after you and help you get back on your feet. But Russell..."

"Yes."

"You must give up your drinking. I'll be watching you."

He looked overwhelmed. I smiled and produced a rock that I kept in my pocket. I held it out to him. "Don't worry. You won't be on your own. This here is a luck stone. It's going to change your luck completely. Keep it on you at all times, and you'll find yourself on the path to contributing something great to the world."

The man took the rock. He stood up and for the first time straightened his shoulders. He nodded once to me and left.

Andy smiled. "Do you do that often?"

"Not often enough."

"Do you think he will actually change?"

"I have no idea, but at least I tried." I had seen the look on Russell's face, someone had said they believed in him and sometimes that was all it took.

"It was a good thing to do." Andy tipped the soap box Russell had been standing on back to an upright position. "Did you know that Speaker's Corner was built on the Tyburn Gallows? I do believe that they are trying to make amends for all those martyrs of free speech hanged here during its time."

Glad that he hadn't noticed my cheeks burning because he had paid me a compliment, I replied, "I heard that the reason why they allow free speech here is because the condemned were always allowed their last words before they were hanged."

"I never knew that." Andy seemed delighted I knew something he didn't.

I added, "I've been quite a fan of this place ever since my aunt told me one of my ancestors was hanged here as a witch. Have you ever heard of Elizabeth Barton?"

"Yeah, she was the one who told Henry XIII that he was going to die if he married Anne Boleyn. She should've kept those prophecies to herself. You're her descendent?"

"Her sister's actually." I thought back to Anne Boleyn. What had she thought when Elizabeth Barton was hanged? I'll have to ask when I pop back for a visit.

There was one part of the Park that I had been avoiding, but I knew I had come here to see. I got Andy moving. I wanted to show him. It was the memorial fountain for Princess Diana. More of a flowing oval than a fountain. My parents had died in Paris two days before Diana. Even when I was young, I suspected a connection and pretended that this fountain was built to honor them too. I wondered what they would think of their apartment being bombed. I stared at the flowing water and wondered why I could not cry. I was hollow inside and shut off from my feelings. Still watching the water flow felt soothing.

Andy led me to a bench, and we sat down. I pulled a family block of Cadbury's chocolate from my pocket and breaking off two lines, passed it to Andy, who declined. "Don't judge me. I drink a green smoothie for breakfast everyday."

"Wouldn't dream of judging you or your choice of diet."

I looked at the block and broke off another two lines. Chocolate has always been my weakness. Sure it wouldn't bring my apartment back. Sure it wouldn't pay back the werewolves or stop Amanda Singh, but it was luscious, rich and producing all sorts of calming, pleasure inducing chemicals in my brain.

Andy wisely didn't speak again until I finished the whole block. "So what's the plan?"

I looked at the empty wrapper in my hand and loathed myself. I felt sick in my stomach. "We have to get to Singapore. I just don't know how without a passport. I can't trust anyone at MI-23 to get a replacement."

Andy rested back on the bench as a woman went jogging by. He suggested, "We could go and see the Toad."

"The Toad?"

"Surely you have heard of him. Lives underneath Harrods. Guarantees that whatever you can't find in Harrods, he can find for you, as long as it still exists."

"He can get passports?"

"He can get anything."

"How will we get past customs? My face will be known to the computer. Yours too probably."

"Fear not, you are with the best illusionist in the world." Andy looked at me. "I'm going to have to teach you how to change your own face though. If we get separated, we can't have you reverting back to your normal visage."

"Great. How do I cast an illusion?" This I wanted to learn.

"Well first you need to firmly fix in your mind the image of what you wish to cast. Now it always helps to use what is already there. So, for instance, in the National Gallery I sent you to a field of sunflowers, as Van Gogh's painting was staring down at me."

"But that was an Impressionist piece. Not real sunflowers."

"Actually Van Gogh captured the soul of sunflowers in that piece, making it a far easier illusion for me to cast than any other. That is the true secret of illusions, if you capture the essence of what you wish to cast you will have more success than trying to imagine every detail."

"What do you mean?" We were watching dogs run around in a leash free area.

"Do you see that Great Dane there?"

"Yes."

"Imagine him as a cat. Not only what color, markings, eyes but also what sort of cat. Is he friendly to humans, or aloof? Does he disappear for days or mainly laze about the house?"

I closed my eyes and took a moment. I imagined a ginger striped, tomcat, half wild, who ate at a few different houses and would come and sit on the lap of the one person who didn't want him to. "Okay I've got it."

"So now cast your will at the Great Dane and force the change."

I complied but added speaking out loud the word, "Change." I could not cast any spell without speaking out loud. It is what releases my will. I notice that Andy always uses gestures.

Where previously there had been a Great Dane now stood a ginger cat. The other dogs froze then ran barking toward the illusion. The Great Dane still thought of itself as a Great Dane, so it was a very surprised Labrador that heard the ginger cat growling a warning that sounded like it came from a much bigger dog.

Andy said, "You better let it go before there is a terrific fight. Just think of the Great Dane again and will it back."

The Labrador suddenly was looking up at a much larger dog. It gave a frightened yelp and ran back across the field. The Great Dane, unimpressed, returned to sniffing the ground. Andy was laughing hard. I looked at him and said, "I wish I could just let go like you. We have a week to find six million pounds, stop a power hungry, megalomaniac becoming a god, and find the traitor in MI-23, yet you're still able to laugh."

"Plucking the strawberry, Lynx. Just plucking the strawberry."

"What strawberry?"

"One of my favorite Zen parables. A tiger chases a monk, and he slips over a cliff. He grabs a root and is hanging on for dear life. Below him is a river infested with crocodiles. Just then he sees a wild strawberry growing next to him. He plucks it, eats it, and says, 'What a delicious strawberry.'"

I smiled. "We certainly are facing some crocodiles."

"Yes and the tiger in our case is a pair of wolves."

I didn't want to worry about the money at the moment, so I asked, "Can we do another illusion?"

"I think we better not start a dog fight. I want you to now do yourself. Imagine another person. Once you have done that, change."

I fixed another person in mind and then cast the spell. Andy laughed. "Well done. However, you may have trouble getting through customs as the Archbishop of Canterbury."

I changed back.

"When we go through it would be better if you went as a woman. Remember that the illusion is only as good as your acting. If you went to the lady's room as the Archbishop of Canterbury, anyone might dispel the illusion."

I practiced a number of times and settled on one image. It was strange to be wearing a different face. We left, and emerging from the park, I felt connected again, nurtured by nature, ready to face the next task. We ditched the car, as it was too easy to track and went to find the nearest underground station.

Chapter Eighteen

The escalators weren't working at the Knightsbridge Tube station, so we trudged up several flights of stairs to reach the street. I was glad I was fit. Andy tried to hide the fact that he was breathing hard as he caught up with me at the top.

Harrods was a religious experience for many a fervent shopper, equivalent to a visit to the Vatican for a Catholic. Customers went home sporting the store's famous green and gold bags as proof that they had indeed traveled to the most elite department store in the world.

I could see them now in some backwater of Minnesota saying, "It's where the Queen herself shops. Well, at least, she did until the whole unfortunate Diana incident. Aren't the bags of such high quality?"

The motto of the store is Omnia Omnibus Ubique, or All Things for All People, Everywhere. Until I met Andy, I wouldn't have expected that to include a trade in false passports.

Fighting our way through the crowds, we descended to the basement level and the glittering gold Egyptian room. Ignoring the luxury displays, we walked up to a replica of the Sphinx. Andy placed a hand on its surface. "Toad? Are you in?"

The room spun, and I found myself in a candle-lit dungeon brimming with the most unusual and varied merchandise. There were boxes sprouting weird appendages that looked like they could, at any moment, animate and scuttle away. There were jars of glowing beads resting on shelves, beside products that would put a Chinese apothecary to shame. A full size mummy stood in its sarcophagus in the corner, and there was a RPG gun hanging on the wall. In the middle of it all sat an enormous man spilling over the sides of an office chair like a melting wax figure.

He wore tiny reading glasses and was staring down his nose at an invoice held at arm's length in one hand, while the fingers on his other hand tapped away at an old adding machine.

"Good day to you, Andy." He looked up and pushed his chair back from the roughly hewn oak desk. His voice would not have been out of place having tea at a garden party at Windsor castle. "And I have not had the pleasure…"

I offered, "Lynx."

The man placed his reading glasses carefully on the desk, rose, and strode over. He towered over us. I couldn't imagine fighting him. All he would have to do is fall forward and I'd be done. He took my hand and placed a delicate kiss on the back of it. "Enchanted. My name, much to my chagrin, is Toad. Whatever my humble establishment has to offer is yours. Though of course for an appropriate price."

Andy snickered. "Usually quite a steep price too, if I recall correctly."

"Please don't bore us with the figures, Andy." Toad placed his other hand over mine such that they were barely touching, and continued, "What I provide, Lynx, is anything that is unavailable everywhere else.

How can you put a price on that?"

Andy picked up a leather bound book and flipped through the pages casually. "You always seem to manage."

"Put that down. It's a rare copy of Gellar's treatise on vampire hunting." Toad let go of my hand, bustled over to Andy, snatched the volume away, and placed it on a shelf. "Now while it is true I manage to price the rarest of goods at quite a steep price, you can't criticize me. After all a man has to eat."

Andy leapt at the opening. "As much as you do?"

"Don't be mean. I can't help having ogre in my blood." Toad regarded me. "Have you ever heard of a skinny ogre?"

I tactfully avoided the question. "I've never had the pleasure of meeting any ogre before yourself."

Toad laughed. "You are a charming one, aren't you?"

He sat back down. From the creaking protest the chair made, I was worried it would buckle under his weight. Yet somehow he remained upright and pointed at a wooden chair in front of the desk, by way of an invitation to sit down. "Now what have you come here for? Eye of Newt, essence of Djinn, Theresa de Halin's Fabricomonica…"

I took his offer of the chair. Andy contented himself with examining a dusty apothecary jar. His face rested up close to the dusty glass, trying to determine what treasure was held inside. So, it looked like it was up to me to negotiate. "Nothing so esoteric. We were wondering whether you could do up some passports?"

Toad seemed to deflate to seven foot eleven. "Oh how mundane. Are you fleeing the country?"

I pulled my chair closer to his desk. "No, let's just say that we need to keep our departure under wraps. We are planning to return."

He winked at me. "Aren't you naughty? Is this to fool another man?"

"Not at all." I glanced at Andy, who was sporting his infuriating grin. "Andy and I aren't together that way."

"I am sorry to presume," Toad said, not daring to smile. He reached into a box and pulled out a digital camera, which looked like a matchbox in his hand. "Now for your passport pictures. Please step over there. I'll put up a white sheet."

"First I have to change my appearance."

Toad pointed to a wine barrel of a door. "The bathroom is back there."

"Thank you, but I don't need a mirror."

I shut my eyes. I always wanted red hair but did not like fake dyes. I held the image I had decided upon in the park and changed.

"Sexy," Andy commented.

I looked down and realized my hair was not the only thing I had changed. I had the body of a manga character. I was a couple of sizes larger in the chest, and the buttons of my blouse strained against the additional inches. The blush heating my cheeks matched my hair.

Andy also changed. He made himself older and heavier, with a touch of gray to his hair. I knew he had done that to make the point that he had no body image problems. Men!

Toad took a photo of each of us, instructing us not to smile. Since 9-11, smiling was disallowed on all passport photos. Someone told me it distorts the facial recognition software, but if that were true, all you would have to do is go around smiling and they wouldn't be able to track you through CCTV. I think they forbid it simply because they frown upon fun.

He fiddled on the computer to make sure the photos were the right size. Then passed us over a standard passport application. "Can you fill these out, please?"

We wrote down fictitious details about ourselves. I called myself Emily Elmsbury, because I loved the alliteration of Stan Lee.

Andy raised an eyebrow. "Emily Elmsbury?"

I replied, "Yes. Emily Elmsbury. Do you have a problem with my name?"

"No. God forbid."

"Emily is an architect who dreams of designing soccer stadiums, but when she talked about that with her therapist, she realized it was a vain attempt to get her father's attention. He always wanted a boy who could play soccer, but instead fathered three girls. Emily was born in Sheffield but hides her accent in the competitive world of London. She is more of a dog person, than a cat person, but hasn't actually had a pet since her goldfish, Hubert, died when she was thirteen."

Toad said, "That's all great, but all I really need is a date and place of birth."

Andy spoke up, "Don't worry about Toad. The more weird details you can keep in your mind about the character you are playing, the easier it is to keep the illusion in the mind."

"Weird details?"

"Don't take that as a negative." Andy continued,

"The weirder the better. It helps. Although who names a fish Hubert?"

I couldn't help the new rise of heat in my cheeks. If I had been thinking clearly, I suppose I could've illusioned it away. Andy caught on. "You had a fish called Hubert?"

"Yes. He died when I was thirteen."

"Ahem." Toad cleared his throat. "As much as it is thrilling for me to find out about your aquatopian past, could you discuss the passing of your Carrasius Auratus another time?"

"His name was Hubert."

"Yes, I am aware of that my dear, and now I need your date of birth."

I scribbled down a date. Andy shook his head. "That won't do Lynx. If you are going to be an architect, you have to be a bit older. At twenty-three you would barely be out of college."

"Do I look older to you?"

"Um." Andy scratched his head. "Even though I know you are wearing an illusion, why do I get the feeling that there is no way of answering that question without me getting into trouble."

I crossed out the year and put in another date. Toad yanked the form back. "That will do nicely. Now let me create."

He pulled out a laptop and plugged it in. It seemed that he did have electricity down here. The candles must be a simple marketing device or perhaps he just preferred the softer glow. He explained, "Now I am accessing the Home Office database."

"You can do that?" I asked.

"Yes, but I would consider it a professional

courtesy if you didn't arrest me. I have enslaved an Internet demon to tear apart the firewalls."

That got me interested. "An Internet demon? I've never heard of that."

"Wherever there is desire, demons lurk and the Internet has more than enough of that for their activity." Toad tapped away at his keyboard. "I had a run in with one a while back. He took all my money out of my accounts just out of spite. So I paid a hacker to put one of the lesser keys of Solomon into code. Ended up being as effective for trapping demons in the cyber world as it is in the physical world."

"So you get the demon to hack into…"

"Into wherever I want. It does my bidding."

"So you could get into the MI-23 mainframe if you wanted?"

"No way. Your boy Quentin has got that thing locked so tight, my demon can't go anywhere near it."

"Interesting. He never told me about Internet demons."

"He probably doesn't know what he is guarding against, but he has some very nasty and sophisticated guardians working to protect your doors."

"So you've tried?" I asked angrily, feeling all proprietorial about my branch.

"Don't get all riled up. Quentin himself hired me to test his firewalls. He wanted to be sure it was safe."

With a tap of the keyboard, Toad finished with a flourish. "Now you are both in the system. All we have to produce now is the passports themselves."

"How are you going to do that? Do you have another demon enslaved?"

"Let me show you." Toad went over to a door,

opening it up theatrically he said, 'Ta Da. It's called a printer."

"Very droll," Andy retorted.

Toad loaded the blanks into the printer and pressed a button. The printer started to whirr as it warmed up. "The tricky part is getting the blanks, especially now they have the biodata chips, but I have my ways."

"Let me guess, you bribed someone in the Home Office?" I couldn't help but ask.

Toad looked shocked. "No of course not. Someone stole them for me."

"So tell me again why I shouldn't arrest you when you keep on admitting to so much crime?"

"Because my dear, apart from the fact that it may be very useful for you to have someone on this side of the business, there is the fact that no one enters or leaves this place without my say so."

The room seemed to shrink as Toad took a step toward me. His affable nature dropped, and I glimpsed the monster inside. Instinctively I reached out for my power, but it wasn't there. The room must be warded. A growl seemed to emanate from Toad's throat, and his eyes begin to turn red. I remembered my ogre lore from training. Primarily peaceful, they were loners, for the males responded powerfully to any challenge of their alpha status. Fully-grown males would literally rip each other apart upon meeting, unable to stop the influx of hormonal rage. I had just come into an ogre's den and issued a challenge.

"Um Toad, Lynx didn't mean anything by what she said. She was just interested and wanting to know," Andy said in a worried tone. "Weren't you Lynx?"

I put on my brightest smile and tossed my hair

back. "I was just having a joke. Sorry if it was in poor taste."

The feminine charm seemed to work as the red cloud around Toad seemed to dissipate. "You have spirit, but little common sense, poking an Ogre in his den."

"Sorry."

"Not at all my dear. Just be warned that once the rage takes me, I cannot stop myself. That is why I live down here all alone. I don't want to hurt anyone."

I saw in Toad's eyes the pain he felt.

Toad continued, "I should also let you know, I have an unofficial carte blanche from the Magus himself. So even if you did manage to put me in cuffs, they would quickly be off once you took me in."

"The Magus knows about you?"

"He surely does. He is one of my prime customers."

I wondered at that. The Magus allowed this sort of thing to go on? I had this image of everything being black and white, but the further I experienced the more murkier it seemed.

Toad handed Andy and I our new passports. "So will that be cash or charge? Unfortunately Andy, your credit is no good here."

"Do you take credit cards?"

"Certainly." Toad pulled out a mobile machine from his drawer.

I put it on my MI-23 card. "May I have a receipt?"

Toad handed one to me and said, "It has been a pleasure to meet you, Lynx. Please come back anytime. Simply put your hand on the Sphinx, and I will teleport you down."

"How far down are we?" I couldn't resist asking.

"Believe me when I say you don't want to know."

With a wave of his hand, the ogre sent us back and we appeared once again in the Egyptian room at Harrods.

A ball of fire sizzled through the air, zooming straight at us.

Chapter Nineteen

I dove on Andy, covering him with my body as heat sizzled along my spine. The fireball missed and exploded amongst a shelf of expensive bags. The smell of burnt leather filled my nostrils, and we both slapped our legs to douse the flames. I glanced up to see what we were facing. A fire demon stood blocking the main exit from the room. It had skin like flowing lava, with black crust floating on crimson fire beneath. It brandished a sword of flames with one of its four arms, and its head almost touched the roof.

Its eyes found mine and locked on. It had come for me and strode toward us, knocking over the counters and displays in its way. For some reason I was overcome by an urgent desire to stand up, plant a staff in front of me, and boldly shout. "You shall not pass."

I was happy I didn't, for the luxuries within the room started to ignite around the fire demon, and it sent another fireball whistling our way. Retreat seemed a sensible option.

People were screaming and running. I saw a man fall as the demon passed him, horrific burns upon his face. I dragged Andy by his shirt. "Move."

We ran for the adjoining room. It was the Harrods's coffee shop. The fire alarm started ringing, and the sprinkler system turned on. I looked back to see another fireball streaking toward us. I pulled Andy down and flipped a table to shelter behind. The fireball smashed into it in a shower of exploding flame. I looked for a way out, but everywhere there were people running—except for one idiot who was filming the demon on his phone. I had to stop this demon here or more people would be hurt. I rose. Andy shouted, "Get down. Are you mad?"

I turned and said, "Run you fool."

Andy didn't run, much to my annoyance, but he did stay in cover behind the table. I put him out of my mind but stepped away to keep him out of the firing line.

The demon paused as it spied me, then, with what would pass for a smile upon its hideous face, it moved forward in anticipation. Two fireballs came hissing my way. I threw up a shield of blue energy, trying to keep a clear conduit flowing. I felt the heat, and as my shield buckled, a searing pain in the bones of my body. I was in trouble. I hadn't expected a demon to be this strong. I hoped I wasn't going to regret standing up.

The demon closed the gap in two huge strides and swung at me with his sword. I tucked and rolled, feeling the sparks as the sword smashed the ground beside me. I kept on rolling. The demon took two steps to the left to follow me and raised its sword to swing again.

"It was you who destroyed my flat." I accused trying to stall for time, while I frantically looked for a way out.

The demon checked its swing to answer. "I was following my Mistress' orders. But destroying your flat was fun."

A red-hot anger welled up in me, and I cast a burst of magical energy that hit the demon full in the chest. It smiled once more, as the energy vanished into his body. How did he manage that? I was in serious trouble. He swung again. I dodged back and then hit him with all the energy I could muster but to no avail. If anything he looked stronger. I picked up a shelf with my magic and flung it at him, but it bounced off his skin. I was in serious trouble. The flames around me rose. My stomach turned to ice. I was going to die.

With that thought I realized I was doing exactly the wrong thing. Raven's voice rose in my mind, 'Never feed a demon.' My anger and fear were fueling him. It's how demons work. I reached up and held the tree of life medallion my mother had left me. A feeling of calm infused my soul. I was not going to give up. The demon snarled, and I realized what I was doing was right. In controlling myself, I lessened his power. Now, how to banish him?

Looking up to the heavens I found my answer. I did two back flips and posed in a martial arts stance. As the fires raged around me, I beckoned the demon to attack. A look of fury at my defiance came upon his face, and he charged forward, to exactly where I wanted. I felt the water flowing in the pipes of the sprinkler, directly above the Demon. While ritual magic and potion mixing were not my strongest magic, working with the elements was something I always enjoyed.

I called to the water. "Come," I invited. Somewhere there was a huge reservoir of water to service the fire system, and I magically assisted it through the pipes to come jetting out of this one sprinkler in a huge stream. With the strength of a thousand fire hoses hitting the demon, the demon was flattened. Clouds of steam rose, but the water was too strong. The demon snarled in fury and then vanished, banished from whence it came.

I saw dots before my eyes. I had never moved that much water, the strain and pain had been immense. I reached out to stop the flow, but I had no energy left. I felt an arm around my waist as the water rose. It was Andy pulling me through the now waist-high water to where the escalators were. The fool hadn't run. I was going to have words with him, once I could see straight. The pressure of the water created a strong current, and I feared that we were not going to make it. Yet Andy struggled on, showing a strength that I hadn't guessed. From high above we heard sirens. I yelled as we gained the foot of the escalators, while I struggled to keep my head above water. "Andy we can't be detained now."

Andy looked back at me as he heaved us out the water and sort of blinked in reply. Hoping he understood, I let myself slip into unconsciousness.

Chapter Twenty

I woke to the sound of voices, blinking I felt a hand close over my mouth. Andy was there with a finger raised to his lips. I nodded my understanding—we were covered by one of his illusions.

We were on the ground floor of Harrods sitting in ankle deep water in the perfumery. Walking toward us were the Magus and Jensen. I heard the Magus growl, "Bloody disaster this. A whole floor of Harrods flooded, people claiming they saw a demon throwing fireballs backed up by footage from their mobile phones, and we have no idea where that girl has gone. Is this what she thinks an agent does? Letting everyone know magic is real. If it weren't for her parents, I wouldn't have accepted her as an agent. She was too young. Now that I have, it is my biggest mistake this century. This is a disaster."

Hearing the Magus say that was a kick in my guts. I stifled a primal sound. I knew I was trying my best, but from the Magus's mouth that obviously wasn't good enough.

"Sir, I think you are being a little harsh," Jensen said. I loved him for that. He was always on my side.

"Really Jensen?" The Magus turned to his Mohawked agent. "When was the last time a case you were working on was in the papers?"

"Well that would have been the Diana incident."

Jensen was working that with my parents? That was something I didn't know. I would have to ask him about it.

I caught my breath, as it almost seemed the Magus looked directly at me. "Lynx will have made the papers five times in the last two days. The stolen painting, the incident at Gordon's, the break in at the Canada Tower, her apartment blowing up, and now this. When will the girl learn discretion."

Jensen and Magus moved away surveying the damage.

"He's right, you know," I whispered.

"What about?" Andy asked.

"I am a disaster." Tears blurred my vision. "I'll never be as good as my parents. They were legends in the agency. I should just go and face the music."

"Nonsense, you just saved my life." Andy had his arm around my shoulders.

"Yes, but I ruined Harrods."

"Nonsense. It was missing a water level. Now they can sell all sorts of aquatic items."

I stifled a laugh and reached up and squeezed his hand on my shoulder. "Thank you."

****

Sneaking out of Harrods was harder than I'd imagined. There was a constant stream of police, fire, ambulance, and emergency workers going in and out. We didn't dare let our cover go. I couldn't afford to bump into anyone else from MI-23, especially after seeing the Magus so angry. Finally, I saw an emergency stretcher leaving, I nudged Andy, and we shuffled behind posing as extra paramedics.

Looking down at the old woman on the stretcher,

breathing through an oxygen mask, I wondered how Amanda Singh could possibly justify sending a demon into Harrods. I knew it was her. That fire demon had stepped right out of a Vedic tale. I'd taken the painting from her, but that was between us. Sure I was fair game, but to hurt an old woman was unthinkable to me. It was a shock to realize that the rules I played by, were not universal. I should've known. I felt hot steel forging inside of me. I wouldn't stop until I'd destroyed Amanda Singh's plans.

We squeezed through the door, nimbly dodging a stream of firefighters. The scene outside Harrods was mayhem. It took us a couple of blocks before we could escape the crowds.

"I wonder whether Toad is okay. Maybe he got flooded out."

"I wouldn't worry about that old ogre. It would take more than some water to worry him. He is bound to have a couple of exits out of there." Andy said, then added, "Of course his stock may not have faired as well."

"All those old books." I hoped that there was no one-of-a-kind.

"I'd be more worried about what happens when his magical supplies and potions leak into the water supply."

"Don't worry, the Magus knows about Toad. He'll send in a clean up team." I had faith in MI-23. They would handle it.

"That's like saying, don't worry about that oil spill we can clean the rocks on the shore."

"Oh come now, that's an exaggeration."

"Is it?" Andy asked. "What happens when you mix

eye of newt with dragon's blood or dare I say it, toe of frog?"

I thought about it. Andy was right, the results could be catastrophic. At best there were going to be strange happenings in Knightsbridge for months to come. I always trusted MI-23 to be able to handle any situation, but I wondered where my blind faith actually came from. Had I been indoctrinated?

We needed to put this behind us. "Let's head straight to Heathrow."

My crystal gonged in my pocket. I held it at arm's length, unsure as to whether I should take the call. What if it was the Magus ringing to chew me out? Why didn't these things have caller ID? I inhaled and exhaled. I would be the agent of which my parents would have been proud and face the consequences of my actions.

I answered, *"This is Lynx."*

"It's Quentin, darling." There seemed to be a lot of mind noise in the background, and I imagined him at his desk with all the displays on his desk beaming back news of the incident at Harrods.

I was happy it wasn't the Magus. I brightened. *"Hi Q. To what do I owe this pleasure?"*

"I have bad news. Under pressure for an explanation from the palace, Magus has declared you a rogue agent, working outside MI-23 authority. Sorry love, every agent is under strict orders to bring you in."

I took a moment to let the news sink in. *"So why are you telling me this? Couldn't you get in trouble?"*

"I could," he answered, *"but apart from the fact that I'm too valuable to the Magus to get much more than a slap on my wrist, there is something that I've never told you about your father and I."*

"What?" I knew that Quentin had joined the Ministry before my parents were killed, but he had always claimed that he hadn't known them well.

"In the early nineties, I fell in with a rather bad crowd of warlocks. I'd taken on the whole grunge ethos and loved to sneer at the establishment. I was a lazy stoner. The whole idea of doing sorcery and getting power for nothing appealed to me, and when it was suggested that we start to do some summoning rituals, I jumped at the chance. We tapped into some really bad stuff and pulled through more than we could handle. The Ministry was sent to shut us down.

"At the end of it, three people were dead, two in asylums, and then there was me. Somehow my mind was stronger than the others and I survived. Your father then offered me a choice. He said I could either choose to do something useful with my life, to do something good with my magic, or I could go to prison. He didn't need to give me that choice, but he was the first one to ever see a potential in me."

"I'm glad he did."

"It changed my life. I came into MI-23 and found that I had an aptitude for science and could apply that to making magical objects. Your father mentored me the whole time. When he was killed, I swore I would always keep an eye out for you. This is my chance to return the favor. Solve this case, bring me proof and I will make sure the Magus clears your name."

"I will. Quentin. I will."

"One last thing darling. Do you know how they found you at Harrods?"

"No. Did they follow me from my apartment? We were careful and ditched my car. I thought I had a *pretty good sixth sense and would know if I was being followed."*

"No it wasn't that. Sorry to hear about your apartment by the way."

"Thank you." It was still hard to know what I felt about that loss. *"It does suck."*

"Your credit card put you on their radar."

Of course, I was making rookie errors. The moment I swiped the card, they sent the demon.

Quentin continued, *"Don't use it anymore. I'll send you one to pick up at Heathrow, at the British Airways desk. Totally untraceable."*

Wait a minute. *"How do you know we're heading to Heathrow?"*

"I have my means." I could feel his smugness through the crystal.

I thought about it and smiled. *"You just overheard Andy and I talking, somehow through the crystal."*

"They're not called communications crystals for nothing. I'll teach you the trick when you get back. Don't tell anyone else."

He was sneakier than the detached scientist he portrayed. It would be a serious bonus, if I could find out what people were saying all over the Ministry. It certainly might not be fully legal, but if only Quentin and I knew then that might be the advantage I needed to take down the traitor. *"I won't. If I get suspicious about someone I'll let you know, and you can keep tabs on their crystal until you can teach me the trick."*

"No problem." Quentin laughed. *"Just don't tell anyone my secret. Many underestimate me, and I'd like to keep it that way."*

"I certainly will never underestimate you again."

His thoughts seemed to turn serious. *"Be careful."*
"I will."

I cut the connection. Turning to Andy I held up the new passport that had caused so much damage. "Onto Heathrow then. I do hope that whatever the Oracle has to say is worth all this trouble."

Chapter Twenty-One

During the obligatory farewell from the stewards, the humidity of Singapore snuck through the gaps of the extension that plugged onto the plane door. Even though it rained constantly in England, the air was never this wet. The whine of the jet engines thrummed outside as they cooled down, and with relief, we passed through to the blessedly cool air conditioning of the gate lounge. Wearing the same leather pants and shirt I had for days, I was longing for a shower and some clean clothes.

Vast tracks of travelators ferried people toward the terminal buildings from the gate. Keeping to the left, transit travelers hustled past us in their haste to catch their connecting flights. After fourteen hours on the plane, my body needed a good hour of hot yoga and a boxing class.

Andy eyed a massage chair eagerly. "Do we have time?"

"Not until we see the Oracle." Somehow I knew that the Oracle had already arrived and was waiting for us.

"Surely he can wait ten minutes. He would've foreseen that I need a massage after that ghastly flight." Andy tried to tug me toward the next set of massage chairs at the end of the travelator.

I grabbed his shirt and pulled the other way.

"Andy. Come."

He shook off my hand but started walking the way I wanted him to. "I'm not a dog or a small child you know."

"You're about as difficult."

Andy muttered something under his breath, which I graciously chose to ignore. We walked a bit further in moody silence, before he asked, "So, where are we going to find the Oracle anyways?"

"At the Koi pond. It's where he appears."

"Appears?"

"Yes. His actual residence is somewhere in Southern China. When he wishes to talk to somebody, he just appears on the bridge above the Koi pond."

Surrounded by lush orchids and greenery, an old man with a bald head and dressed in an oversized, red Hawaiian shirt, leant upon the little wooden bridge staring into the depths of the ponds—looking at the gleaming golden, silver, red, and multi-colored Koi. Despite the illusion and the fact I had never met him before, he waved to me. "Lynx, I'm glad you came."

"How could I not?" I gave him a short bow. I wasn't sure of the proper protocol when meeting the Oracle

The Oracle's eyes resembled a whirlpool. "Many that I summon do not come. They don't want to believe. They tell themselves it was just a dream. Yet dreams reflect reality, and they're just not wise enough to see."

I feared the worst. "What have you seen that made you want to summon me?"

"You face great danger and tread a perilous path," the Oracle started.

"Yeah we kind of already know that," Andy spoke

for the first time.

"Aah the Fool. Hiding behind the Warrior with your humor." The Oracle grabbed Andy's right hand and looked at his palm. "Be not afraid to care and love, some causes are bigger than yourself. When all is dark, ask what sort of man you wish to be. Do you want to run all your life? Or will you take a risk, to turn and face the pain of what you lost?"

"I..." Andy paused, and I saw him stop himself from making a remark.

"And you Lynx. I summoned you here for you need to know the stakes. Not only will the world suffer if you fail, but your soul will never know the peace it needs. For not only are you on the trail of a traitor who is helping to bring a Goddess of Damnation into the world, not only the killer of your friend and teacher, but you're also on the trail to find out the truth about who betrayed your parents."

I looked at the Koi swimming in the small artificial pond. I wasn't surprised. Somehow, I had known or at least suspected it. My parents had died in Paris, two days before Princess Diana was killed. I always believed that someone inside the Ministry had led them to their death. Something steeled inside me. I straightened my back.

"To stop the Dark One rising you must go to the seat of her Power, where the prayers of the holy float upon the winds of the world. To stop the traitor, remember the connection between all things, and most of all, the connection between things that are the same. Trust not the words of the one who is false. You shall know the lies by the pain they promise to take away. There are no short cuts. There is only the path."

The Oracle smiled at me. "Though your path is dark, there are those who are watching this world of pain who will be there to aid you in your time of need."

"Who?"

"That will be revealed. I cannot say too much."

The tricky line of seeing into the future is that it is not fixed but possibilities. I knew the Oracle was worried that by telling me too much, he might change the outcome and spoil any chance we had of winning.

"Look into the pond," the Oracle directed me.

I looked down and watched the elegant koi move almost imperceptibly and felt a moment's peace. Then at the edge of the pond moving inward I saw a black boiling cloud. "What's that?"

The Oracle answered, "It's what I see. What you are facing is nothing compared to what is coming. What you are doing now is important, but there is a greater evil upon the horizon. A greater force moving. I can see its influence building but am blocked from seeing more. There is darkness, conspiring to block my sight, and it is winning. I fear the end is coming."

"Like the end of all things end?" Andy asked.

"The end of everything as we know it. I can't see much through this darkness, but I can see that if we are to have any chance we must hold the North. Britain must remain strong and free, and for that cause I see you, Lynx—fighting and leading the charge. Magicians have held the darkness at bay, but the institutions that were, are failing. They have devolved into political tools. You are our best hope. A twenty-first century witch to carry the flame of light into the new millennia."

The Oracle handed me a white lotus flower.

"What's this?"

"You'll understand soon. Be brave, choose wisely. and be true to your heart. Now it is time for me to go." He turned back to the pond. "One more thing before I leave. When all is done and the danger past, look to the Caribbean to pay your debts."

The Oracle waved his hand in front of us and suddenly the koi ponds were part of a larger garden stretching in all directions. "I must go now."

I bowed briefly, but by the time I looked up the Oracle was gone, and we were back in the noise of the Singapore airport.

Andy and I joined the mix of people looking at the huge departure board. I spotted the flight we would need. We thankfully had four hours, enough time for a shower. I pointed at the board. "There we are."

"Which one?" Andy asked. "I didn't quite get what he said."

Andy would miss his head if he didn't have it attached to his neck. I said, "We need to go to the seat of Amanda's power, where the prayers of the holy float on the winds of the world."

He still looked befuddled. "And where exactly is that?"

I wouldn't want him on a quiz team. "The Himalayas. Indra Corp owns most of a mountain in Kashmir. It's there that we will find her and stop the ritual."

Andy was strangely quiet as we made our way to the Air India counter to purchase a ticket to Kashmir. I guess for someone who didn't like heights, he wasn't looking forward to exploring the tallest mountain range in the world.

Chapter Twenty-Two

Demons were far less frightening than driving in Kashmir. We were in a vehicle that should have been sent to the junkyard about the time I was born. I am not over-exaggerating when I say that it was held together in parts by rope and tape. On a normal road, it would have been bad enough, but we were driving on a single lane road, at night, up a mountain, with a sheer drop just meters to the side. The driver was playing Bollywood music, and could not seem to talk without taking his hands from the wheel and turning to face us in the back seat.

At least Andy was not complaining about my nails indenting his palm. I was squeezing his hand with all my strength. He petted the top of my hand in what I think he thought was a soothing manner but really just made me want to punch him—if I was not hanging on for dear life. We careened around a curve, and I shut my eyes but could still feel the centripetal force. I knew it was just one of the many massive switchbacks that went all the way up the mountain. That there could be a car coming the other way did not seem to enter the mind of the driver.

Andy was not perturbed in the slightest. Apparently his attitude was if we were fated to die here, then there was nothing we could do about it anyway, so why worry? The fact he was not worried at all made me more stressed. I do not like having no control of my fate.

With my eyes squeezed shut, I could tell the taxi was slowing down. I opened one eye, somehow we had reached the end of the road without dying. Once we stopped completely, I got out and took in our surroundings. A man squatted in front of a small teahouse, smoking a cigarette. He assessed us, probably trying to decide whether it was worth standing to get some custom this early. I shook my head. He ground his cigarette in the dirt and disappeared inside.

The taxi driver waved goodbye. I had paid him well and made him promise that he would be here again the day after next. The promise of more money would ensure he made the trip from Srinigar. Once the jewel of India, Kashmir had fallen on rough times. The tourist dollar had departed with the separatist troubles. It was sad, for the beauty of the place was astounding.

Standing on the side of the cliff, I watched the dawn spread, like an overturned can of pink paint, across the sky, while Andy tied his boots ready for the ascent.

Andy indicated the almost vertical path before us. "Are you sure you don't know a levitation spell or something?"

"No such luck," I replied. "And it's a pity these boots won't help either. It's old fashioned exercise for us."

The climb was harder than I had expected. I regarded myself as extremely fit, working out at least two hours a day, but I had never been at such altitude. My lungs heaved to pull in enough oxygen. We really should have started a lot lower to allow ourselves time to acclimate. Altitude sickness was a danger. Yet reviewing the plans we stole from the computer, the ritual was to be performed on the night of the dark moon, which was tonight. So we had a day to reach the temple perched another five thousand feet above us. The only thing that made me feel better about our journey was that Andy's face was redder than a beet. He was doing far worse than me.

The ascent made my muscles scream. I felt a little gloat of satisfaction when Andy broke first and asked for a rest break for lunch. We collapsed on a small rocky outcrop, too tired to even look in our small packs for provisions. The view was amazing. Snow-capped peaks of beauty and unimaginable height surrounded us and downward lay a sweep of green into a valley with a ribbon of blue marking a river.

"Quite spectacular isn't it?" A voice sounded behind me.

I scrambled up and turned to see a Buddhist monk standing there. He was bald and dressed in Saffron robes. There were prayer beads around his neck, and he was carrying a staff. Behind him rose a sheer cliff. He hadn't been on the path, and I couldn't help but ask, "How did you get here?"

The monk bowed. "Through the grace of the Buddha."

I let that one slide, remembered my manners, and bowed back. "We just stopped for a bite to eat, would you care to join us?"

After sitting down, the monk produced a small bowl and placed it in front of himself. He bowed. "I would be grateful."

Rummaging through my pack, I produced some

crackers, fruit, a few power bars, and some mini Edam cheeses, still wrapped in their waxy rinds. My hand touched beef jerky, but I pulled away, pretty sure a Buddhist monk would be vegetarian.

I divided the lunch, and Andy asked the monk, "So what brings you to this cliff top?"

The monk answered, "Yourselves."

It was a strange answer. I asked, "Have we met before?"

"No. But I can feel the darkness this night is threatening to bring." The monk's eyes shone briefly with a flame. "And while I will not battle, having chosen the path of non-violence many, many years ago, to those that will face this evil, I will aid anyway I can."

"That is most gracious," Andy said. There was something about this monk that radiated peace, and despite the tensions and the darkness we faced, I felt the sun shone brighter as we ate our lunch.

Once we finished, I packed everything away and lay back to enjoy the sun. The monk cleared his throat, and I sat up.

"Thank you for your gracious sharing. I, in return, have four gifts for you. The first is some elixir for you both." He presented us with a small gourd. "Please take a sip."

I put the bottle to my mouth but hesitated. I wondered whether it could be poison, but I had seen the monk's eyes shine and could sense benevolence radiating from his heart. I took a sip. It tasted like the sweetest nectar, perfumed by a thousand herbs. It spread warmth through my body, re-energizing every muscle and wiping tiredness from my mind. I passed the gourd to Andy.

"That was amazing. What is it?"

"My own rescue remedy," the monk said. I watched Andy's eyes widen as he sipped. "It's herbs I picked in the mountains and have blessed through Buddha's bounty."

"I feel so much better."

"Please keep the rest for your hike. You will need to be fresh when you finish." The monk continued, "The second gift I have to offer you is advice. To break the ritual, you must stop the priestess after she has summoned the power to the diamond, and before she has time to pick it up. It is then that she will be at her weakest, having expended her energy bringing Kali to this plane."

"That might be tight."

"You do not have the power to stop her before. She has almost two hundred years of ancestral anger and bitterness to fight with. She hates your country with a passion, believing you stole her birthright."

"Hatred runs deep in this country," Andy remarked.

The monk bowed his head for a moment. "Never stop believing that compassion can conquer hate. I am originally from Tibet, and when the Chinese overran our country, many turned to hatred. I was one such monk. I witnessed people protesting peacefully being dragged away and thrown from cliffs. I wanted to fight back but was taken by my master and told a story. There is an ancient prophecy foreseen by of one of the Panchen Lamas, which told of the day that Tibet would be swallowed by the great dragon. While many would suffer, it was time to accept that suffering, for that day would be our chance to take Tibetan Buddhism into the world. I allowed myself to believe that and now all these years later, the Dalai Lama has become one of the pre-eminent spiritual teachers, commanding respect from all quarters of the earth. Many Westerners have been introduced to Buddhism because of our plight. My hatred was converted into fuel for teaching the way of compassion."

"You don't hate the Chinese? Even after all they have done," Andy asked.

"They are beings trying to do the best according to their own understanding. I disagree with what they do but feel compassion in my heart for who they are. I see the divine Buddha within them all and hope that one day they see it themselves."

"You're a better man than I," Andy said.

"You may surprise yourself. Compassion and forgiveness starts with the self."

He looked at Andy and something passed between them, for Andy's eyes started to mist up. I let them have their moment and then asked, "So what's the third gift you offer?"

"When I was little we played a game to decide who would go first. You make your hand into a fist and bounce it three times. On the last bounce you make your hand either flat, a fist, or split your fingers." He showed us. "We call the game Roshambo or rock, paper, shears. Rock beats shears, shears cuts paper, and paper covers rock."

"We have the same game, we call it rock, paper, scissors."

"Good you know it then. Teaching you it was going to be my third gift."

"I don't understand."

"You will." The monk reached into his robes, "Now for my fourth gift, which actually is a gift in two parts, power and wisdom."

He pulled out and passed me an ancient scroll. I unrolled it to see beautiful illustrations but an undecipherable script. It was like his previous gift I did not understand what he meant by it. "I can't read this."

The monk said, "That is the story of Chenrezig. The Bodhisattva of compassion. He was about to enter an eternity of bliss when he heard countless souls crying out in pain. So he turned his back on Nirvana and chose to reincarnate a thousand times to help teach others the way of the Buddha."

"Why would anyone do that?" Andy asked.

"To help alleviate the suffering of others." The monk bowed and poured a little water ceremoniously in his bowl to clean it.

"So how does that help us?" I asked.

I waited, but the monk casually threw the water in his bowl over the edge of the cliff, stood up, dusted himself off, and bowed.

"Wait, isn't there more? I don't understand."

The monk did not answer but stepped backward off the cliff. We ran forward but could see no body falling, only a hawk soaring past on a thermal.

Chapter Twenty-Three

We spotted the temple at dusk. Covered in peeling black paint, it had a red roof sloped at an acute angle so the snow would slide right off. The black paint may have been an attempt to capture the warmth of the sun during the day, but I think it was more likely an indication of the darkness of the worship that occurred inside. Even as we climbed the last quarter mile, scurrying from rock to rock for fear of being spotted, I could feel a foreboding sense of wrongness emanating from the temple. It was not just my hesitation in confronting Amanda either. Hawks had been circling above us all day on the thermals, but now there was no movement in the sky. Animals shun the evil places of this world. I dared not look at the temple with my second sight. It was a cancer on the side of the mountain.

We snuck forward and paused at the last bend, crouched behind a rock, taking stock of the situation. The path ended in a single gate, which opened onto the courtyard of the temple. It was guarded by two men, holding AK-47s. On one side there was a sheer cliff plummeting downward.

"I think they are KLA. Kashmir Liberation Army." I told Andy as we crouched behind some rocks. "I read in the briefing that Amanda uses them for her muscle in exchange for funding their resistance. How are we going to get past them?"

"Can we do anything from here?" Andy asked.

I shook my head. There was no cover on the road leading up to the gates, and I did not want to start a fight at this distance. I also wanted to keep my magic for the temple. I couldn't afford to let myself be drained before I got inside—not with Amanda Singh to face. I had no idea how powerful she was, but she had been around for a while, and someone planning a major ritual to become an incarnation of a deity had to have some serious juju. What's more, this was her home turf. I asked Andy, "Can you hide us on the approach?"

Andy nodded. He looked tense but said, "No problem. What do we do when we get close?"

I pulled out my Beretta as a reply. Andy had brought my gun and katana through customs. Somehow his illusions were so good they could even fool metal detectors. I asked him how that worked, but he could not explain. It was like the alarms. He was able to fool any electronic equipment he chose.

Andy looked at my gun and raised his eyebrows. "Wow. Things just got serious."

What had he been thinking? Had he been having fun up till now? His capacity to not worry about things was really starting to grate. I reminded myself that I wouldn't grind my teeth but said, "So owing six million pounds isn't serious enough for you?"

"I didn't mean…"

"My apartment being blown up?"

"It was a turn of phrase."

"Take responsibility for your language please."

"I—"

"Just cover us," I said exasperated.

Andy nodded. A second later, the illusion was in place. We stood up and warily approached the gate. Even though we were under the illusion, it certainly went against every instinct I knew to walk up to two men armed with machine guns. Even cloaked we still had to be as silent as possible. Any bit of noise could betray us and dispel the illusion. I took the lead and held my breath. With each step, I was getting closer to killing someone. I had never taken a life before. I thought of the Buddhist monk we had met. He had given up violence. Could that be my way? I didn't want to kill anyone.

Yet I had to.

In my head, I heard my instructor saying just sight and squeeze. I took aim, but it didn't seem fair. I was a finger movement away from killing a man, and I wanted it to be fair? Was I crazy? They would blow me away with their AK-47s in an instant, if they knew we were standing there. They would lose no sleep either. I had become an agent knowing that I would have to kill people, but I had always envisaged it in a fair fight. This was just cold-blooded murder.

Andy nudged me. I glared at him. Nudge me again and I would kill him in a heartbeat. I turned back to the men, from twenty feet away I squeezed off a shot, aiming for the first sentry's head, for under the bulk of his jacket I couldn't tell whether he was wearing body armor. The other guard turned. The illusion dispelled. Up until then I had been pretending it was merely a training drill or a level of Halo. Yet, before this other guard had time to bring his gun to bear, I fired, looking directly into his eyes. I saw the bullet impact and knew that image would be with me for the rest of my life. The two sentries were down. I went over and shot them both again to make sure they were dead.

I ran forward toward the gate, ready in case anybody had heard the gunshots and were about to burst from the temple doors.

I took cover and kept my gun trained on the doors. I felt numb. I had killed for the first time. How could I justify the two deaths? I saw myself squeezing the trigger over and over again, and I realized I couldn't. The question became whether I was strong enough to carry the weight. I knew that I needed to do it, I was the only one in a position to stop Amanda Singh. It was the right thing to do, but I really expected more than this numbness. Maybe it was just my way of coping. There was a job to be done.

No one came through the doors. Our way to the temple looked clear. Yet, I put a hand on Andy's arm cautioning him to wait before we entered the courtyard. Although the light was fading, I put on my John Lennon sunglasses to see whether there was anything hidden in the courtyard. I did not want any surprises. Amazingly the glasses made me see as if it were the middle of the day and not twilight. They were better than any night vision goggles I had ever used.

Quentin never ceased to amaze me. He didn't tell me about this little surprise. The courtyard looked clear. The only thing I could see were two traditional stone lions guarding each side of the temple doors. It was safe to enter, but my intuition was telling me I was being watched. I looked high and around, yet there was no one there. I decided it must be the nerves from having just killed for the first time. There was nothing to do but keep on going.

We moved into the courtyard. The air felt crisp. I kept my gun trained on the door, ready if anyone came through. I heard a growl. Where had that come from? I took another step. The lions on either side of the door stood up. A low rumbling sounded in their throats.

"Aah Lynx? I think we may be in trouble."

"You don't say?" I answered Andy's fear-filled whisper.

The lions prowled down the steps and came slinking toward us. I emptied a whole round shooting at them, but the bullets pinged off their stone bodies. I grabbed Andy and ran toward the cliff. It was the only thing I could think to do. The nearest lion leapt, and I pushed Andy to the side. I turned and rolled onto my back as the lion came down on me. I simultaneously drew my power in and kicked out with both legs, using magical energy to power the move. Hours of yoga made me end in a shoulder stand, vertical, my legs reaching for the stars. Bruce Lee would have been proud of the result. The lion sailed over the edge of the cliff. I rolled to a crouch and watched it smash on the rocks far below. There was no way that lion was coming back.

Behind me I heard another growl. I turned and faced the other clawed beast. It stalked toward me slowly with intelligence. There was no way it would be falling for the same trick, I thought frantically. I was in trouble. How could I defeat a stone lion? Fire would not hurt it. Neither would wind. I could try to freeze it, but did not think that would work. I would need a sledgehammer to even hurt it in a physical fight. I made a mental note to pack some grenades next time. I was running out of ideas when an image of the Buddhist monk flashed in my mind. I remembered his gifts. I shook my head. It couldn't be.

The lion shuffled forward. I had to roll the dice. It was the craziest idea, but I was going to have to trust what that monk said, otherwise I was going to die. Andy would as well, and I really didn't like that idea. I took the scroll the monk had given me from the pocket of my jacket. Paper covers rock. I threw it in the lion's face, just as it raised a massive stone paw to strike me down. I cringed, but no blow fell. The lion was frozen. Power crackled out from the scroll. Blue lines of lightning covered the lion.

The lightning stopped. I reached out one hand to touch the lion's paw, and the lion crumbled away in a shower of dust.

"That's the biggest stake game of Roshambo I've ever seen." Andy offered me a hand up. He inclined his head toward the temple doors. "Shall we?"

I accepted Andy's hand. It felt good to be pulled up by a firm grip. The adrenaline hit me and Andy said, "Little bit shaky aren't we?"

I looked at the hand that he had just let go. Twenty espresso shots in a row wouldn't have hit me as hard. It was vibrating harder than an electric sander. I looked Andy in the eye. "I've never actually killed anyone before."

"Killing those guards was your first time taking a life?"

"Yes."

I will always remember him for what he did next. He didn't try to make it better for me or for himself, by giving me some pat advice. He simply took back the hand he had released and held it in his, while I exhaled deep breaths and tried to get my heart rate down.

Chapter Twenty-Four

The temple doors creaked like two cantankerous geriatrics as they opened. I should have put WD-40 in my pack, for I might as well have sounded the gong that stood by the door the noise was so loud. I put up a shield to ready myself for whatever lay waiting inside. It took a moment for my eyes to adjust. Before us stretched a vast wooden hall, dark but for two candles burning in front of a huge blue, black, and gold statue of Kali. Her four arms brandished curved swords— thicker and heavier than a normal scimitar, and the expression on her face was fierce. The statue dominated the central dais and apart from some black prayer mats lined in rows, the rest of the temple was empty.

"Are you sure we have the right place?" Andy asked, indicating the empty hall. "Maybe the dark ceremony is scheduled for next door."

"The guards were there for a reason." I answered tersely. I didn't have time for his attempts at humor. I could feel the energy building—something dark was brewing. It made the hairs stick up on the back of my neck. I heard something ever so faintly. I wondered whether I might be hearing things, perhaps my mind making up sounds from the wind rushing around the temple outside. It sounded like people chanting. I held up my hand, one finger raised, in the universal sign to keep quiet. Andy complied.

"Do you hear that?" I asked.

"I do. Where is it coming from?" Andy started to cross the great hall and I followed.

"It gets stronger near the statue." I tapped on the stone. "It's hollow."

Andy pointed out a trail in the dust behind it. "Look. I bet it moves to reveal a secret entrance."

We tried pushing it to no avail. "It could need a magical word."

Andy shook his head. "No, you saw those guards. There wasn't anything magical about them. It has to be mechanical."

"Don't be stupid. Amanda could easily have told them what to say. You don't need to have ability to get past a magic door."

He continued to examine the statue. "I don't think so."

"Shh, Andy I'm trying to think." Now what was the Sanskrit word for open or enter? I tried, "Uttana"

Nothing happened. "Pravisati."

The statue remained unmoved.

Andy leant against the statue. "Why don't you try abracadabra?"

"Don't be stupid. I don't have time for your games. What on earth could the password be?"

"I know it. I know it." Andy put up an arm like he was answering a question in class from the front row.

He wouldn't stop until I paid him attention. "You are skating on very thin ice."

"But I know the magic words."

I sighed, "Okay then. What are they."

Still leaning on the statue, he said, "O great Kali, I beseech thee, open sesame."

The jerk was making fun, but amazingly there was a whirring noise and the statue shifted backward, revealing a straight rock staircase leading downward. We could hear the chanting more clearly now.

I couldn't believe it. "You've got to be joking. Those were the magic words."

Andy looked at me impishly. "You could say thank you."

I shot him a look that signified anything but gratitude. I moved beside him and examined the statue. The arm he had been leaning against was shinier than the others, with no dust on it. I said, "It was mechanical."

"Wow Lynx. Your powers of observation are astounding. There I was thinking we'd finally found the entrance to Aladdin's secret cave."

I flashed him a smile. Why couldn't I remain angry at this man?

Moving downward, we came to the back of a cave, its vast mouth opened in the side of the cliff face. About a hundred worshippers were chanting and bowing before an altar, upon which lay the Koh-I-Noor diamond, displayed in the middle on a silken cushion. Even from this far away, I could see the way it sparkled. I could make out the words they were singing. It was Sanskrit for, "Come Destroyer Come. Let us bathe in blood. Come Destroyer Come."

Amanda Singh stood behind the altar in traditional garb. Hiding behind a column at the back, I put on my rose-tinted John Lennon glasses to see what was happening on an energetic level in the room. I could see Amanda directing the energies. A black wind grew arms and picked up one of the worshippers, tumbling him over the heads of the other bowing, chanting devotees. The wind carried him to the cave mouth and threw him out over the cliff. I could hear his scream fade as he plummeted to the rocks below. The energy in the diamond grew; we did not have much time—it was nearing its capacity.

I whispered, "Andy can you cast an illusion to make the worshippers not see me?"

"Sure. They are half in a trance already. It'll be super easy."

Another worshipper was picked up, and the diamond glowed brightly. Amanda changed her chant. The diamond rose from the altar, and a vortex grew around the jewel. We no longer didn't have much time. We were out of time.

I urged, "Do it now Andy."

Black energy flowed in swirls around the vortex. There was a rushing sound in my ears as I strode through the prostrate worshippers, whose chanting had reached a fever pitch. A portal formed around the diamond, and I felt a diabolical presence through the vortex. One that wanted to maim, hurt, kill, and would use anything to achieve its ends.

Amanda Singh looked tired but exultant as she stepped forward to pluck the diamond from the centre. Did she not realize what she was doing? If she took the diamond, she would no longer be in control. Compared to the Destroyer she was but an ant. I suspected all she saw was the power.

Out of my element, I had little to draw on in terms of power, but I still had a trick or two up my sleeves. I cracked two flares and dropped them to the ground. Amanda looked at me, bathed as I was in stunning red light. From the flares I drew in energy and hit her with all my might, imagining a huge fist of air punching her in the face. I used no word to direct the energy, but rather shouted a battle-cry, "KIAI." Using the pain as the energy tore through me to strike even harder.

Amanda's face crumpled. I'd broken her nose. She staggered back and seeing me, threw out her own energy in retaliation. I muttered, "Shield."

A gold light surrounded me, and while I braced myself for a battering, Amanda's attack, weak as she was from the ritual.

"On the floor Amanda," I ordered, "It's over. I'm arresting you in the name of Her Majesty the Queen, for the theft of the Koh-I-Noor diamond."

She looked at me with hatred and spat, "It is not stealing to take back your own property. The diamond was stolen from my ancestors first. It is mine by right."

She threw her energy at me again. It dissipated with a flick of my wrist. I warned, "This is your last chance. Lay on the floor with your hands behind you."

"Get her." She screamed at her worshipping followers.

"They can't hear you Amanda. Now don't turn this into a bad Bollywood ending. On the floor and I'll let you live."

She looked past me and threw her energy again, but this time she aimed it at Andy. He was thrust back against the back wall. I could not protect him in time. He smashed his head hard, and I could see his eyes glaze over. The chanting stopped around me. The worshippers rose. They could see me now. I sent out a magical shield straight away to wrap around the altar and diamond, like a huge beach ball. It wouldn't last forever, but it would stall Amanda and buy me time. The vortex grew inside, just as the nearest worshipper moved to hit me.

I dodged and another moved to grab me from behind. Bad move. I let him, that way both of his hands were busy while mine were free. Two quick turning elbows to his face and he crumpled. A snap kick to the worshipper's head in front of me, and I made enough room to open the tube on my back and draw out my katana.

Another worshipper threw himself at me in an attempt to tackle me to the ground. I reflexively stepped to the side and slashed, severing his arm. Instinct made me turn, and I skewered another coming at me through the stomach. He feebly pawed at me as his body went into shock. There was no time to think. I pulled the katana out with one hand and with my other grabbed my Beretta from its holster. I emptied the chamber sending men flying as I spun in a circle. I threw the empty gun at the next worshipper. It distracted him long enough for me to separate his leg from his torso with a vicious downward slash.

My breath came fast as I took in the space around me. For some reason the rest of the followers did not rush me. Instead four men pulled wicked curved knives from their belts. They smiled as they moved to engage me. These men were crazy. I bet they had been promised eternity in paradise for dying in Kali's name. They came in spinning their knives, and it was all I could do to keep from being hit. Yet I sensed the pattern of their attacks and sidestepping I slashed at an angle severing a head.

Thank goodness for the hours I had spent

sharpening the blade. It went straight through, and I attacked another before he had a chance to adjust, laying open his chest with a vicious cut. The other two quickly fell. I was covered in blood. I looked to see where the next attack would come from, but the rest of the worshippers fell to their knees. They bowed and started chanting, "She has come. She has come, She who is Death. She has come."

Wait, they thought I was Kali? I looked down at myself. Covered in blood, wielding a sword, maybe I could pass, especially considering I appeared out of nowhere in the middle of the room. I could roll with this. I turned back to Amanda.

She moved for the diamond, my shield finally failing. I hit her once more with a punch of energy, it tore through, and I was breathless with the pain as I watched her stagger. For the first time I noticed the sand circle drawn on the floor around the altar. It was like one of the colored sand mandalas that I had seen Tibetan monks draw except this one was from black and red sand. I suspected the red was from fresh blood and the black where it had dried.

Amanda crossed the line, smudging the circle with her back foot on the way. The vortex that was still spinning above the diamond seemed to roar, and two black tendrils shot out to grab Amanda. She screamed and tried to struggle, but the tendrils inexorably dragged her back toward the vortex. I sent a bolt of energy at the vortex, but Amanda was hauled through and the portal closed. I shuddered to think what fate awaited her on the other side.

I breathed deeply. The worshippers all bowed down around me. I was still half way across the room from the diamond. Time to pick it up. I was maneuvering my way through the ecstatic worshippers, when a huge shadow detached itself from the wall and took two strides to grab the diamond. My glasses still on, I could see the power that was there crackling in the fist of the one whom I recognized as the warlock. The one who ambushed us at Gordon's wine bar. From deep in the cowl of his hood I caught a glimpse of his golden mask. Black energy suddenly transfixed my arms like iron bars. I was cut off from my power. I struggled but could not move.

The figure laughed. "Well done Lynx, you stopped a deity coming through and let Amanda be dragged off to one of the greater hells. I hung back wondering how it would play out."

"Who are you?" I asked, as I saw Andy banded as well, being dragged by energy the man controlled toward the altar.

"Now that would be telling." Black lightning crackled out from his hands, and I felt searing pain rack my body. I mentally slapped myself. I would not check out. I accepted the pain and for a moment it receded. There must be something I could do. I forced myself to look around but then made the mistake of looking up, and fear engulfed me as I saw the warlock walking toward me. The pain became excruciating, and I could do nothing but scream until the world turned black.

Chapter Twenty-Five

The pain in my body pulled me from unconsciousness. I opened my eyes to see Andy asleep on the rock floor. We were in a small dark cell. After passing out, they must have dragged us here. I rose and tried the door, but of course it was locked. We must have been unconscious for some time, as I was dying for a glass of water. My bowler hat, boots, weapons, and glasses had been taken. I coughed involuntarily, and Andy turned over in his sleep. I coughed again, deliberately, this time louder. He blinked his eyes.

"Sorry, I didn't mean to disturb you," I said in a hoarse voice, suppressing a smile.

"Not to worry, I shouldn't be sleeping, anyway. Have to get up for breakfast. Some crispy bacon and eggs will go down nicely. Have you rung already for room service?" Andy said, as he rubbed his fingers gently around his temples.

I played along. "Yes it should be on its way. I hope you like your eggs poached."

"I actually prefer scrambled. Poached won't do at all."

"Sorry, I should have guessed you'd want your eggs to match your head. I will ring Jeeves and tell him to change the order with the chef."

Andy achieved a sitting position and managed to focus on me. "Seriously, how are you feeling?"

"Scared. Worried, but still in one piece. You?"

He rested his head in his hands. "I feel like I have the worse hangover ever. Yet I can't remember drinking."

"We didn't."

"I know. It was a joke."

"It wasn't a very funny joke."

Andy sighed. "I don't think much is at the moment. Very likely we will soon be killed."

Way to get my hopes up. I said, "I wonder why we're alive at all."

"Probably the warlock wants to gloat. It's what I would do."

"More likely to find out what we know and who we've told." I shuddered at the memory of the wizard's power. How could I fight that? I tried to touch my power, but there was nothing there. Somehow the cell dampened my abilities. I looked at Andy bravely trying to smile. "Will you hold me?"

Andy opened his arms, "Of course."

I collapsed into his chest, and our bodies seemed to mold to each other. He was surprisingly muscular. I snuggled in and realized his muscles weren't the only thing that was firm. I smiled and remembering the story about the strawberry, kissed Andy on the lips.

Andy returned the kiss with passion. I let go. His khaki shirt with all the pockets, which I know he chose to feel like an Englishman on safari, came off first. Rather than bother with the buttons, I undid the first couple and then pulled it over his head while still trying to kiss him. I looked down. His chest was smooth. I pushed my hand across it. Andy said, "I wax."

He did have that metrosexual look. I bet he spent

more on products than I did. I asked, "Everywhere?"

"No, but I do like to trim."

I couldn't remember the last time I had properly shaved. Oh well, if he judged, he judged. I pushed him back on the ugly, gray striped mattress and straddled him, letting my hair loose to fall and sweep over his chest while I unbuttoned my own shirt. His hands found their way under my sports bra, and then it was off and over my head. Shy, I pressed my body against his. He flipped me over, and I was lying on my back.

He kissed his way down to my navel. I was looking at a spot on the crown of his head where his hair had already started to thin and stroked that spot, with the lightest touch of my hand. He looked up to distract me. He grasped my unzipped jeans and knickers, and pulled them off together before I knew what was happening. He came back up to hold my face still between his palms. He looked me in the eyes and entered me. I arched my back, and with my head tilted back, I could see scratch marks on the walls someone had used to count their days in this cell. With each thrust, we erased one of those days of fear. The walls of the prison were momentarily no longer there, and I swear the mountain rumbled with my scream.

I dozed off for about five minutes. When I woke up, Andy was stroking my hair and staring at me. He was still sweaty. We both started to laugh as I shyly pulled on my shirt to cover my breasts.

I couldn't keep secrets from a lover. I took a deep breath and said, "Listen, I do have to tell you something."

"What? After that?"

I didn't know how he was going to react, but I did

want to be clear with him. "The Magus ordered me to kill you once the mission was over."

"Jesus, Lynx." He gathered his clothes to his chest. "Were you going to?"

"No." I had to be honest. "But I considered it."

He looked hurt. "You considered it?"

"I had to. It was an order."

It is hard to explain to a non-military person what that means.

He threw his arms in the air. "And you just blindly follow them?"

I tried to explain, "It's the way we are trained. It is treason not to."

He angled his head and asked, "Even if the order is illegal?"

"Oh grow up Andy. I haven't killed you, but I had to at least consider it."

He pulled his knees up to his chin and wrapped his arms around his legs. "That you would consider it, frightens me."

I hated the hurt puppy dog look, for I could not help but want to comfort him. How do men do that? I said reasonably, "Well it was on the table, but I wouldn't do it for the person you are."

"So if I were a different person, you would have murdered me?"

"Yes. No. Maybe." I didn't like what he was implying. "It's my job."

"That's what the Nazi prison guards said. Oh, I am sorry about the Jews, but I was only doing my job and following orders."

I didn't want him to think badly of me. I wiped a tear from my cheek. "I know."

Andy must have felt bad, for he put his arm over my shoulder and hugged me. He then started to laugh. "I don't know how you women do it. You just told me you were considering killing me and now here I am comforting you."

We stayed like that for a while and then Andy said, "There is something I have to tell you too."

"What?" I jerked away. Men were always like this. They first sleep with you and then it's all 'sorry, I like you, but I am gay, have two kids, three wives, am dying of cancer, or about to be sent on a mission to Mars.' Yeah right. Whatever. We aren't that stupid.

Andy though was looking down at the ground. "It wasn't my brother, it was me."

It was obvious, but I still asked, "You mean?"

Andy looked down at the rough stone of the cell. "I gambled my father's fortune away. I was meant to be in charge, but it went to my head and I ended up in debt."

"Why did you lie to me?'

He said, with the slightest shrug of shoulders, "Because I was ashamed."

I didn't understand him. He did get the bit that hacking a Van Gogh out of a frame was so much worse than what he did with his family money? I said, "I arrested you for breaking into the National Gallery."

"So?"

He was dense. It angered me that he still did not get that what he had done was wrong. "It really doesn't get lower than that."

"Yeah, but I thought if you thought that I did it for the right reasons…"

I finished his sentence, "That you could get in my pants."

"No." Andy looked confused. "Maybe."

He was digging his own grave. I looked at him with derision. "You're an arsehole."

"Hey." He tried his hurt look. "Just a minute a go you were telling me you had orders to kill me and you were keeping that a secret."

I really didn't follow his logic. "So?"

"Well, that's worse."

"How do you figure that?" My anger grew. "I didn't make something up and lie. I just didn't tell you something."

He started to flush red and said, "And that makes it better?"

I could not believe the gall of him to get angry with me. I stated the obvious, "Of course it does."

He raised his voice so that he was almost shouting, "How?"

I banged my leg with my fist. "It means I never lied to you."

"But you lied by omission," he growled through clenched teeth.

I asked him, "What's your favorite color?"

"Blue."

"Well until now you have been lying to me by not telling me that your favorite color was blue. Lying by omission is bullshit."

I didn't get to hear what Andy thought of my flawless logic, for we were interrupted by a key turning in the lock.

Chapter Twenty-Six

I wondered whether this would be our chance for escape. I readied myself to spring and overwhelm the guard, but a jolt of primal fear shook me when I saw the cowled warlock appear in the doorway. That he was so much more powerful than myself made icicles in my stomach, and I had to force myself to breathe through my fear.

The warlock spoke with some amusement, "I see you have been making the most of your time."

I was naked but for a loosely buttoned shirt. The rest of my clothes were strewn across the room. As I gathered them frantically, I realized I knew the Warlock's voice from somewhere. It hadn't registered in the Temple, but somehow now with the amusement in his tone, I knew it. I just couldn't place it.

He pointed at me. "You come."

Andy rose. He looked small and vulnerable, standing before the towering figure. "You can't take her."

"Very gallant." The wizard pointed at Andy, and a bolt of energy shot from his finger. Andy yelled obscenities as the purple lightning encased his body. Whatever wards stopped me from accessing my magic did not seem to apply to the warlock.

"Stop it," I shouted at the Warlock. "I will go with you."

He let the purple energy torture Andy for a few more moments, as if to make a point, before he snapped his fingers and Andy collapsed on the floor, thankfully still breathing and alive.

I stood up and faced the Warlock. "You didn't need to do that."

The warlock nodded his head in concession and replied, "I know."

A shiver ran through me, one not from the cold. "What sort of a monster are you?"

"The sort that will start again, if you don't act like a good girl, get dressed, and follow me."

The heat from my anger failed me and turned to embarrassment. I quickly pulled on my pants and buttoned my shirt.

I followed the warlock out of the cell. As we walked down a rocky corridor, I started to reach for my power, but the warlock must have sensed what I was doing and growled, "Stop that. There's a reason you're still alive, but I will kill you if I have to."

I knew his words were not an idle threat. One on one, I had no chance. I forced myself to relax. The adrenaline was making my heart thump, and I despised myself for clinging to his words. For if there was a reason I was still alive, that meant I had a chance.

"Good girl." The warlock swept onward, showing me his back. I hated his arrogance. He had dismissed me as any physical threat. Yet I couldn't risk trying to strike him. He was huge, and there were no primary targets I could strike with certainty, his spine and kidneys undetermined below the robe, and I knew there was no point grappling with him. I hated feeling powerless. I wasn't even wearing my boots. They'd taken them and the cold stone floor was making the toes curl on my bare feet. I slowed looking into a room that we passed. All it contained was a simple cot and had no other exit. There was no escape there. The warlock turned and grabbed me roughly on the arm. "Come on, no dawdling."

He held my shoulder, walked deliberately faster, and I almost had to break into a jog to keep up with his long legs.

The warlock led me to the cave where the ritual had been performed. I tried to break his grip, but he wouldn't let go. He took me to the cave mouth and stood silently, looking out at the view, while still holding my arm. A vicious wind blew and made a howling sound. I only had my shirt not my coat, and started to shiver.

"So why have you kept me alive?" I asked. Always try to take the initiative.

He turned to me and took a moment to answer, as if deliberating the right words. "To give you a chance at revenge."

"What do you mean?"

"I was there when your parents were killed. They were on duty protecting Princess Diana." The Warlock continued, "And were killed so the assassination could go ahead."

The words of the Oracle came back to me. I clutched my stomach as I asked, "Who killed them?"

"The Royals." He continued, "Well, not them personally, but they had it arranged."

The howling of the wind seemed to intensify, "How can you know this?"

The warlock flicked back his cowl. I almost didn't

want to look but could not turn away. The Mohawk was unmistakable.

It was Jensen.

It hit me harder than a kick in the gut. That he had been there for me when my parents had died, but then put me through such pain last night, was inexplicable. "Jensen, how could you torture me?"

"You needed to be taught a lesson. I've been planning this for such a long time, and you came along and spoiled everything. Last night I paced up and down, wondering what to do. It was only when a new plan came to me that the anger subsided." He smiled. "You forced me to change plans, but I see now that is a good thing. It gives us a better chance to take revenge for your parents and all the others the Royals have killed. I can use the power of the diamond to remove the whole bloodline. A curse that will kill the entire corrupt family and all the heads of state that will be at the upcoming wedding."

I shuddered to think that I had helped him create such a plan. "You can't do that. It will be anarchy."

"Yes. Anarchy in the UK. Johnny Rotten's dream." Jensen touched the green Mohawk standing up proudly on top of his head. How could we have all missed it? He was an anarchist through and through and proclaimed it proudly. "And I want you to be part of it, Lynx. Take revenge for your parents. I will tell you the full tale of what happened to them."

Jensen was offering me what I had always wanted, the tale of my parents in the days before Diana's death. All those years of unknowing undone and once undone I could have a chance at revenge. Yet... "You tried to kill me at Gordon's."

"You were asking all the wrong questions of all the wrong people, so I took the opportunity to stop you."

I felt like all the ground was being taken away beneath me. "You tortured Andy and I last night with magical pain."

"I punished you, Lynx. There is a difference. I could have killed you but I didn't." He held out his huge hand to me. "Come, take my hand, we will take revenge for your parents."

I took a step backward. "No. They wouldn't want that."

"Come on. I have seen the anger in you. I know they were taken away from you when you were far too young. Use that to join me. We will be unstoppable."

"No, Jensen." I held up my hands. "I'll never join you. They may have been killed, and if they were, I'll find their killers and bring them to justice, but I'll never kill innocents."

"There are no innocents, there are only the rich feeding off the toils of the poor."

"No." I know the only thing my parents would want was that their killers be bought to justice. They would never want to see innocents hurt in their name. Jensen disgusted me.

"If you'd done the things that I have done for Britain you would want to bring the Royals down as much as I do. It is so much more than your parents; they are but the tip of the iceberg. I hear them at night, all the people I have killed for the monarchy and the thing about it is, most of them don't blame me. Most of them don't want revenge they just want to know why. And it kills me that I can't tell them. I could get them to all shut up, if I had the answers, but every night they return. And every night I have to tell them I have no idea why I killed them.

He took a step closer to me. "People think anarchy is tearing everything down and just replacing it with chaos, but it isn't. I believe in people. People are essentially good. The only evil is the society that squashes them from freely expressing themselves as they truly are. Once we liberate them and take down the corrupt leaders, what a paradise we will build."

I looked at Jensen. He truly believed what he said. He was looking far away into a bright future that only he could see.

"I don't believe in what you believe in, Jensen. I can't. The present system may have its problems, but replacing it with chaos is not going to solve anything."

"Do you not have faith in the people?"

"I've faith that they want to build their lives in a stable world."

"Don't you care about your parents?"

"They wouldn't want this."

Jensen stopped as if hearing me for the first time. He closed his eyes briefly. Tears broke in the corners of his eyes. "So be it."

Before I could react he grabbed my arms in two mighty fists. "I am sorry, Lynx but I can't let you live knowing my plan."

He threw me off the cliff. I screamed and plummeted down into the chasm.

Chapter Twenty-Seven

I fell in darkness. I fell in silence. The world of light, color, and sound closed to me, and became but a memory. I fell until I fell no more. Cold earth supported me. A matched sizzled, and a candle was lit. In the light, I saw the Buddhist monk I had met on the cliff. He put his hands together and bowed. I raised myself to my knees and bowed back.

He waited to reestablish eye contact and then said, "Welcome."

"Thank you." I looked around me. "Where am I?"

"In the space between."

The monk sat cross-legged, hands lightly resting upon his knees. He had removed his mask, lost the jovial manner, and it was like I was seeing his pure essence for the first time. There was something formal to his replies. In some way I was being tested. I asked, "In the space between what?"

He nodded, as if my curiosity was good and now he could say more. He gestured up to the roof of the cave and around the cave walls. "This is the space that exists everywhere and nowhere. Between the stillness and the movement, between the sensation and the thought. Time no longer ticks, and if it did, well you would never ever hear it tock. I see you are seeking a name for this place. I have heard some call this the cave of dreams."

On the walls there was what looked like old paintings from forgotten ages. I got up and wandered over. I was surprised when I saw the pictures were moving. The closer I got, the less easy it was to make out anything. It was like a hundred projectors, all playing different movies, pointing at exactly the same spot. I touched the wall and with a shock my hand seemed to go through. The wall had no substance but for the pictures.

"I wouldn't suggest going through the wall. The cave is our link back to the world. We are safe as long as we stay within the confines of the cave."

I quickly pulled my hand back. "So the walls are made from people's dreams?"

"Yes. Though truthfully I do not know what is on the other side of these walls."

I sat so that I looked at him across the candle. It seemed appropriate. Once settled, I asked, "So am I dreaming?"

The monk looked disappointed and said, "No."

It felt like I was failing calculus all over again. "But we're in the world of dreams?"

"Yes."

So, I was in the dream but not dreaming. Maybe he meant I was lucid dreaming, that I was dreaming but aware and conscious. The monk threw a pebble and hit me in the face. What was that for? He must have seen my incomprehension, for he stated, "You are here as much as you are ever anywhere."

So pebbles hurt. I get it. A sudden chill went over me. "Am I dead? I remember being thrown off the cliff and falling, but I don't remember hitting the ground."

The monk smiled. I was asking the right questions

again.

"You are still falling, Lynx."

"What do you mean?" I patted the ground. "This seems pretty solid to me."

"Is it?"

For a moment, my senses were overwhelmed, with the rush of wind in my ears and the rocky floor of a deep gorge approaching fast.

I looked at him. "I am still falling, and this is my mind trying to cling onto life?"

"It isn't you who brought yourself here. It was me. Look in my eyes." I let my gaze rise to see deep into his soul. Before me no longer sat a monk in dirty robes, but a towering figure of golden energy. As a user of magic, I can sense another's power. This monk before me was so far out of my league. "Are you a god?"

The vision of his true form reverted, and he smiled, "No, I'm merely awake."

He gestured at the cave around us. "I have brought you here outside the reality of our normal space and time for a reason."

I shifted uncomfortably, "Which is?"

"You are to be given a choice."

"I don't get choices. I just follow orders."

"Not if you come and work for us."

"Us?" I looked up sharply.

"I can't tell you yet who we are, but I can show you the choices you face. Here is one path." The old monk leant over and with his thumb marked the space between my eyes.

A brilliant light enveloped me. I felt joy—such as I did not know existed. I could sense others around me. Two came to me in particular. They were my mother and father. I felt love pouring from them toward me. I was enveloped by it. Then just as it came it left, and I found myself once again looking at the candle in the dark. I was swamped with a feeling of loss. I sobbed and asked, "What's the other path?"

"I cannot show you, but it is a path you know, full of uncertainty and suffering. You return to your life."

"Why?"

"The world is falling to a terrible darkness, and few have the courage or ability to fight it. We want you to be a warrior for the Light, but you have to know the price. You have earned the right to let go of all the pain and join your parents. Perhaps one day to enter this world again. Yet we need you now."

"We?"

The old monk smiled. "Even though there are legions following the dark path there are the few who have banded together to fight them. Greater than your MI-23, we are non-political and inhabit many vocations in life. Some are priests, some are cleaners, mechanics, mothers. We are all who strive to make this world a better place for others. Those who give up their own selfish desires to help others toward the light."

"And you want me to fight for you?"

"We have few who have chosen the path of fire. I won't lie to you, Lynx, there is much pain and suffering that I see in your future if you choose to live. We're at a great crossroads, evil is on the march, and there are so few that stand to oppose it."

I allowed myself time to let his words sink in. I smiled. "So you are Good's chief head-hunter?

"Sorry?"

"Don't worry, it's a joke."

The monk smiled at me in the good-natured way of one who even though they may have missed the punch line, appreciated the attempt at humour. I was stalling. "Do I have to give up my current job?"

"Oh it is not like that. We won't pay you anything."

"So let me recap; there are no benefits or remuneration. I'll be giving up an eternity of joy and will have to fight the worst kinds of evil and suffer great pain."

"Yes. All life is suffering. The is the first great truth of the Buddha."

"It isn't a great sell you know."

I with all the fiber of my being wished to rest in the light that I had been shown. Yet how could I? I had to stop Jensen. I had to save Andy. Like Chenrezig, how could I move on, if by remaining I could help? I said, "I used your fourth gift to stop the temple lion, but I now understand the wisdom in the gift. Send me back to live."

He bowed his head. "So be it. The symbol of our order is a white lotus. By that you will know us. If someone comes bearing this symbol, please help them in anyway you can. Now be brave and strong. You have so much to offer this world, Lynx."

He blew out the candle, and all went dark.

Chapter Twenty-Eight

Free-falling toward the rocks at the bottom of the gorge, the thought flashed in my mind that I just made a huge mistake, but talons dug into my shoulders, and I heard a screech above me. My descent slowed. An impossibly large hawk had me in its grip. It did not have the strength to lift me into the sky, but like a furiously, flapping parachute, saw me safely to the ground.

The monk's voice sounded in my mind. "Remember you will never be alone. There are forces greater than you can ever imagine supporting your success."

The bird flew away. I sent out, "thank you," but there was no indication that the monk-hawk heard.

I allowed myself a moment to enjoy the warmth of the sun upon my face. The world sparkled. I spun in a circle of happiness, not caring when I stubbed my toe upon a rock. I was alive. Even pain felt good.

Though it did bring me back to reality. I was stuck at the bottom of this gorge, and somehow had to get back to the temple, stop Jensen, and rescue Andy. I sighed. Back to the grindstone. There was only one way up. I wished I had my boots. I was going to have to climb the cliff in my bare feet.

I studied the rock-face, trying to choose the best route. If I started climbing on the wrong side, I could end up with no way of going higher and a treacherous path back down. I traced a route that would lead me all the way back to the cave underneath the temple. I centered myself, felt for my first handholds, and heaved myself up, telling myself it was easy, just a matter of moving one limb at a time, while resisting the temptation to look down.

I'd never done such a climb without ropes.

About fifty feet up, I looked down and sincerely wished I could transform into a bird like the monk. Shape-shifting was one trick I had yet to learn.

Half way up, with my muscles aching, I heard a helicopter overhead. It landed at the temple. I pushed myself harder. They could be taking Andy anywhere. Yet I was too slow for about five minutes later, it took off again. It swept down into the gorge and away. I shrank against the cliff lest I be spotted.

Finally, despite the excruciating pain in my back and arms, I made it to the cave, flopped over the edge, and lay there breathing hard and sweaty, trying to get my muscles to stop shaking as I massaged my aching feet. The cave was empty and except for a sickening residue of bad energy, there was no evidence to show just last night there had been a major ritual performed.

Without any weapon, I had to be careful. I drew myself up into a seated position, folded my hands on my lap, and forced myself to meditate to summon my energy. After last night's exertions and the strenuous climb, I was shaking in my limbs, and my anxiety and fear for Andy was blocking the energy from flowing freely. It then struck me. I had slept with him. Oh my God, we hadn't even used protection. I mentally checked the date and sent a prayer to whatever deities exist that I hadn't ovulated. If Andy had gotten me pregnant I would kill him. He hadn't even raised the issue. Bloody men always leave it up to us. Butterflies churned my stomach. I had slept with Andy. I had thought I was going to die, so it didn't matter. Now I was going to live. Now I had to face him. What had I been thinking?

I feared Andy had been taken already, but I had to check. I made my way down the corridor to the cells as quietly as I could, even though it seemed no one was about. A set of keys hung on the wall. In a cupboard, I found my boots and pack. Andy's boots were there as well. I panicked. If they had moved him they would have let him have his boots, and if they hadn't moved him, had they killed him?

I got to the cell, found the right key and opened the door. Inside, to my relief, I saw Andy. He was staring at a rope on the ground in front of him.

"Lynx. Am I glad to see you." Andy scrambled up and gave me a hug. He didn't let go and seemed to be squeezing with all his might. "The warlock told me he'd killed you. That he had thrown you off a cliff."

"He did."

"He did?"

"Yes, but the monk we met on the way here saved me. What's with the rope?"

"Hold on—how did he save you?"

"Oh, he had a chat with me outside time, and gave me a choice between paradise and pain. I chose the suffering in this world. Then as a magical hawk he slowed my descent, so I didn't die. What happened to you?"

I could see Andy digest my explanation visibly and

a hundred questions flash through his eyes, followed by the realization that no explanation from me would ever be satisfactory. He gave up before he started. Good. The boy was learning.

Instead he told his story. "After the warlock told me you were dead, he let me know that they were all going from the temple and wouldn't be back for at least six months. He told me he was not inhumane, so he left me a rope for when the hunger got too much."

I looked at the rope on the ground in front of Andy and felt sick to my stomach. "He has turned into such a monster."

"You know him?"

I nodded, kicking the rope into a corner, "Unfortunately, yes. His name's Jensen. I know him well. He is a MI-23 agent. After my parents died, he would visit me. I always regarded him as some sort of uncle figure. That was until he threw me off the cliff. The horror of it is that I wanted to see some sort of madness in Jensen's eyes. That way I could excuse him. Yet, when I looked, all I saw was sadness when he threw me off the cliff. I remember those eyes, sadness, and incredible strength.

"He is not mad. He truly believes in what he is doing. So much so that he will kill whoever stands in his way. Even people he cares about. Such passion scares me. For I think back to the two guards yesterday, and I realize that I could be the same. I will kill if I think it is right. But the question is how do I know that what I am doing is right? That I'm not as misguided as Jensen?"

Andy looked at me for a long time before answering, "It's a fine line."

I felt a surge of anger at the inanity of his comment before actually appreciating his words. I was glad he wasn't trying to reassure me that I wasn't a monster. It was a fine line that I was walking, one that needed to be continually looked at and examined. I had gone into MI-23 hoping that I would be clearly on the right side, but the real world was murkier. I'd been trying to avoid the struggle to work out what was right for me in the moment. This was the twenty-first century. There were no set of rules by which I could navigate. The world was changing too fast. Maybe the only thing that was saving me from becoming a monster like Jensen was the fact that I was struggling to know what was right.

I grabbed Andy's hand. "Come on. Let's get out of here. We have to get back to England and stop Jensen from killing the Queen."

Andy didn't move. Instead he considered the back of my hand and stroked it with his thumb. "Wait, about last night…"

Coward, I could see he was testing the water, wanting to know what I thought first. I wasn't going to play his game. I took back my hand and just stared at him.

Seeing that there was no response forthcoming, he searched for something to say. "Ummm…It was really nice."

Cold fury rose inside of me. "Nice? It was nice?" The earth had moved. What a nerve he had. If that was all he thought, I had been so stupid. I could see what was coming so pre-empted it. "Look, I know you can't do your usual gotta-run-will-call-you-later routine, but don't worry I'm not looking for anything and even if I were, it certainly wouldn't be with the likes of you."

"I'm not looking to run," he answered. Although from the look on his face, I could see I had hit a nerve.

"What are you looking for?"

He shrugged his shoulders. "I don't know... To talk about it. I thought women liked communication."

"You think that describing making love with me as 'nice' is being communicative? What message are you wanting to get through?"

He put up a hand, palm facing me. "Wait. 'Making Love?' "

My cheeks burned. I was mortified. And it was obviously news to him. I screeched, "Sorry, what did you want to call it? Meaningless sex?"

He took a breath and spoke softly. "No it was more than that. Last night I thought it was going to be my last night on earth."

"So you just wanted to get off one last time, and I was the best option available?"

"No. I like you, Lynx."

Yeah, let's just be friends, arsehole. I like you. I have heard that one before. "Don't worry, you don't owe me anything. You've made yourself abundantly clear. It's not going to happen again. It's strictly professional between us from now on."

"But what if I want it to happen again."

Why did my groin betray me with a surge of heat when he said that? I growled, "It won't."

"Dammit. You're taking everything the wrong way. You're an amazing woman, and there is potential between us. I don't know exactly what I want, but I don't want to just shrug off last night."

So, he wanted to keep his options open. I could read the subtext. "All that happened last night is that we had some 'nice' sex."

"Look it was a poor choice of words."

"I made a poor choice altogether."

"You're so frustrating." Andy put his hand behind my neck and pulled me into a kiss. I tried to resist, but my body betrayed me, and I found my hands searching for purchase behind his head, rubbing my fingers through his hair. This was nice. Really, really, really, nice.

Chapter Twenty-Nine

Landing at Heathrow, I was nervous about having to face Customs. Worried they may have gotten to Toad and our passports might not work or worse yet, we would be arrested at the border. I whispered my fears to Andy in the seat next to me, but he laughed, saying that the Toad was too large and too powerful for anyone to put pressure on him.

How could he not be worried? I wish I could be carefree like Andy. I blamed my mind. It works overtime, weekends, public holidays, takes online work, and a second job, just to make sure it has thought through every possibility. I never get a moment's rest. I wonder what it would be like to live in the moment, savoring only what was before me.

The line at Customs was switch-backed and filled with people. I patiently joined the queue, maintaining the illusion I had cast. Glad they could not see my actual, sweating face. I kept on passing this one morose child being carried by his father. He stared at me each time we passed. The lady behind me kept on kicking her bag into the back of my legs. The longer we stood in line, the more I wanted to scream. I seriously don't know how smugglers do it. I swear someone makes the lines long and the service terrible so that anyone trying to bring in something is a nervous wreck by the time they actually get to the Custom official.

Lynx Somerton may have been nervous, but luckily Emily Elmsbury was excited to be home after a successful trip to Delhi, surveying the sight of a new soccer stadium that she was designing. She told the official that the humidity was unbearable, the food too hot to digest, and that the traffic made London in rush hour look like a leisurely jaunt down a country road. The bored official stamped her passport, and I was through.

In the washrooms, I assumed my own appearance. Superman has his phone booth; I have a toilet stall. Splashing water on my face at the sink, I still felt the need to ritually wash off the illusion. Now that I had arrived home, I allowed myself to feel some relief. Just make it to Bosley House and then the other agents could take over and go and arrest Jensen. Looking at my own reflection, I recalled the look in Jensen's eyes. He was certain he was doing the right thing. I washed my hands twice.

Andy was waiting for me outside. He had assumed his own form as well. I said, as we made our way to the taxi rank, "I don't know how you can be so comfortable with illusions. It feels so good to be me again. I hate being false."

"That's because you haven't learned how to enjoy them." His face lit up with a smile. "Perhaps I should take you to a hotel and show you how."

I punched him on the arm. "Stop that. We have to go to Bosley House and let the Magus know about Jensen."

He caught my arm and drew me in. "Yes, but after we save the world?"

I snaked my other arm around his waist, and

whispered in his ear, "You're incorrigible."

He put his forehead to mine, our lips almost touching and whispered back, "And you're corruptible."

I smiled coyly. "Maybe…we'll see."

I put my hand to his cheek and kissed him fully on the mouth. I didn't know what I was doing, but I didn't care. In the midst of all this madness, it just felt so damn good to not think about anything, and only feel his lips pressed against mine.

He broke contact first. "Come on. Let's go to a hotel before you report in."

I shook my head. "Can't do that. I told you I have to let the Magus know what danger Jensen poses."

"Okay. Report in and then we get a hotel room and hide from the world for days."

Sleep for a week more likely. Despite my tiredness, rest had eluded me on the plane. "Maybe. I have to check in and see what I need to do first. There will probably a mountain of paperwork."

"Is it always work first with you?"

"Of course." I hated that men never seem to understand or appreciate my dedication to the job. I pushed him away. "If you hadn't grown up so privileged, you might understand that some people like to be of service to others and put themselves last."

"If you grew up normally, you might value yourself more and give yourself a break from time to time."

Normally? Where did he get off? I can't believe I had just been kissing him. "I am in the military. What I want isn't the issue. It is Queen and country first."

"And you can live that way?"

We joined the line waiting for the taxis, and I knew my voice was loud, but I couldn't help it. "Stop trying to be my therapist."

"I wasn't trying to be. I am interested in what you think," Andy furiously whispered back.

"No you aren't," I said in the loudest voice I dared. "You are having a go at my choices. You are the same as every man. You undermine my life choice because it doesn't fit in with what you want me to do."

Andy winced as people turned and looked at us. He whispered back, "Granted, all I want to do is take you to a hotel and shag your brains out, but I still don't get this following orders thing."

I ignored his attempt to be charming. "That's because you are a selfish prat."

"I am not."

Great comeback kid. "When was the last time you did something just out of the goodness of your heart, not because it served you in some way."

He protested, "I am helping you."

"Yes and that is because you owe money to the werewolves. I am your only chance to see the end of this month," I said it like I was explaining something to a child.

"You think that is the only reason I am still around?"

"That and you want to get in my pants again," I challenged, "Tell me some other way you help others."

"I helped you save the world in Kashmir."

"It doesn't count."

"Why not?"

"Because I said so."

"Now you are the one that's being immature."

"Am not." I couldn't let him get the last word, "I..."

He put a finger up to my lips. "Shhhh. You can win next time."

I didn't have the energy to keep on fighting, and there was a side of me that kind of liked him taking control. I pushed down any comeback. We reached the front of the line, and he opened the door of the taxi.

A bit later, the taxi pulled into the sweeping drive of Bosley House. The tension peeled away from me. I hadn't realized how much I had been holding inside. All the way from the Himalayas, through India, I had been worried that Jensen might somehow appear and stop me. He was no longer the same man I had known growing up. I had seen behind his mask. I knew with conviction that he would do anything to make sure his plans came to fruition. The ends for him justifying any means.

"Follow me." I told Andy as he paid the cab driver.

"What?" Andy smiled at me. "I don't have to wait in the car this time?"

"Cute." I signaled for him to follow, letting him know by my tone that it was time to drop the act.

He did but looked worried. "Seriously, should I be coming in? After what the Magus ordered you to do."

I had already thought that through. "I won't let him kill you, Andy, and with the news we are bringing, I am sure that he will be more than reasonable."

"He still might want to make me pay and send me to prison."

"I know, but I will be on your side. It will be better if you turn yourself in." I looked him in the eye. "You don't want to spend the rest of your life running from this."

He flashed a nervous grin. "What's wrong with good old fashioned running? I get to remain free."

"And you will be hunted till the end of your days."

He put away his smile and though I could see the tension in his eyes, he said, "You're right."

I was so proud of him, I smiled. "Come on. We will face him together. With all that you have done, I am hoping for a pardon for you."

I offered Andy my hand. He took it, and we walked through the car park together.

Andy added, as we reached the door. "Understand though, all this noble turning oneself in doesn't mean I will knock back a reward if the Magus decides to give me one. We still have the werewolves to pay off."

"Hah! You think a government department in these times has that type of money lying around? Dream on." I reached over and squeezed his hand. "Don't worry, I'll think of something. Let's just get this over with first."

Entering the building, I made my way to the security gate, handing in my gun. Wharf Rat and Wish were on the other side. Great, what did they want?

I passed through the metal detector. "Let me through. I don't have time for your games. I need to see the Magus."

Wharf Rat pulled a gun and pointed it directly at me. I gathered my energy.

"Lynx, don't do anything stupid." Wish continued, "Please put your hands behind you."

"Not until you tell me what is going on."

Andy whispered beside me, "Let me know if we need to disappear"

"It won't help you, illusionist." Wish raised his gun and pointed it directly at Andy. "Now put your hands behind you."

"Every one calm down." I said, surely they would listen to reason. "I have to see the Magus. The Queen is in danger. Jensen is a traitor."

"Okay. If you put your hands behind you and let us cuff you, we will take you to see the Magus."

I nodded. If that was the price I had to pay to see the Magus, it was worth it. Surely the Magus would be able to see through to the truth of things. I released my magic and put my hands behind me. I ordered, "Do it Andy."

Andy unhappily complied. Wish cuffed us both.

"All right, now take me to the Magus."

Wish said, "Sure come this way."

He indicated the corridor to his left. I protested, "The Magus is upstairs. This is the way to the cells."

"Stop whining. Consider this payback for punching me."

"But you gave your word."

Wharf Rat made a guttural snort that I realized was his way of laughing. "You are so naïve."

I twisted to look for a way out. There was none. I asked, "How could you lie to me?"

"It was easy. I never have liked you. You don't belong in the agency. I don't know why you came back, but we aren't going to bother the Magus."

He came close. My hands were cuffed, but I still had use of my legs. I kicked him as hard as I could in his crown jewels. He doubled over in pain.

The security guards who had been standing nearby rushed over, and I was tossed to the floor with a knee in my back. Looking over I saw Andy was down too. He did not look happy. I should have let him stay in the car. I mouthed sorry to him and tried to fight, but it was to no avail. They led us away and put us in different cells. I pleaded with them to listen, but my cries fell on deaf ears.

Chapter Thirty

Wish and Wharf Rat led me to an interrogation room located deep in the bowels of Bosley House. A black bag, which stank like it had never been washed, had been placed over my head. Really? Was the bag necessary? It wasn't like I didn't know the way out. I had worked in Bosley House for the last three months. They were just being cruel. I tried not to think of the germs I was breathing in. My hands were still cuffed behind me with magical bonds, so I couldn't touch my power. I longed to break through and show them the mistake of treating me this way. I didn't like how Wish was holding my arm either. He was pulling it up, so I had to rise on my tiptoes to stop it hurting. They had taken away my boots, and the floor was slippery in my socks.

We reached the interrogation room. They sat me down on a metal chair and connected the cuffs with a chain that was bolted to the floor. I leant forward as they had taken my jacket and the metal back of the chair was bitingly cold through my blouse. I heard footsteps as they left the room and the door closed. I started to panic. Growing up on the moors, I hated not having fresh air. The bag on one side felt crusty, I wanted to recoil but had nowhere to go.

I could not say how long I sat there with that horrible hood stifling me. It might have only been five minutes, but it felt like hours. When they eventually came back and pulled off my hood, I was hot and teary. I took huge gulps of non-stale air, hating that they could see my weakness. I tried to compose myself as they took seats facing me, across the table. I was hoping that the Magus would be there, but it was just Wharf Rat and Wish. I looked over at the mirrored wall and could swear I could see someone through the one-way mirror, but I was probably imagining it. The only way out of this, for me, was through Dumb and Dumber.

"Are you ready to listen?" I asked, taking the initiative. Break their game. This was war. I kept my tone professional, as if I were wearing no cuffs and was their superior.

"Don't bother." Wharf Rat shook his head. "It's over Lynx. Jensen returned the Koh-I-Noor that you helped Raven steal."

The news filled me with dread. I hadn't thought that Jensen might come back and return the diamond. That would not look good for my claims he was a traitor. I had to explain, "We didn't steal it."

"I know," Wharf Rat answered. "You were conveniently on the gallery case. Well planned alibi that one."

"It's not an alibi. Jensen stole it for Amanda Singh. You have to listen—"

Wharf Rat slapped the table in front of me, causing me to jump. He growled, "I don't have to do anything."

"But…" Somehow I had lost the initiative.

"But nothing. Jensen told us how he tracked you down to the Himalayas and won back the diamond. He saw you go over a cliff and reported that you were dead. So it was a surprise when you showed up here.

What were you thinking? That you could just waltz back here and we wouldn't know what you had done? We hadn't heard from you since Magus had given you your orders. We thought you were dead, the smart thing for you to do would have been to stay that way."

Jensen returning the diamond was a masterful stroke. I was in real trouble, yet I still had to try. "I couldn't stay dead; it wasn't me who stole the diamond. It was Jensen. He is planning to kill everyone at the Royal Wedding with a curse."

Wish tapped a silver pen against the metal top of the table. "You need a better story. Jensen has already returned the diamond, and it is being fitted back to the crown as we speak."

"But the diamond is cursed." Wish rose and walked behind me. I shifted uncomfortably. I didn't like not being able to see where he was. I know that it was against the law to hit a prisoner, but I also knew the number of times that was abused.

"Yes. Yes." Wharf Rat continued, "We all know about the curse on the diamond. It's perfectly safe for the Queen to wear it. Only men seem to have bad luck when they possess it."

"Not that curse." Out of the far corner of my eye, I could see Wish leaning back against the wall. Good, he wasn't preparing to hit me. He was always a little more reasonable than Wharf Rat. I tried to talk to him as well. "There is a new curse that has been laid upon the diamond. At the temple of Kali, in the Himalayas, I witnessed a black ritual that infused the diamond with destructive powers."

"A new curse?" Wharf Rat took a sip of his coffee. They hadn't offered me any.

"Yes." I really could do with a drink. My throat felt scratchy after that horrible hood.

"You certainly can think on your feet." Wharf Rat played with the plastic lid of the cup not even looking at me.

I protested, "But it is true."

Wharf Rat's eyes swept up to meet mine. "Are we to believe after thirty years of faithful service to the Crown, Jensen has gone psychotic and wants to kill the entire Royal family? Or should we believe that one young woman got caught with her hand in the cookie jar? One young woman who owes six million pounds to the Werewolves of London?"

"Jensen is psychotic. Just look at him." Why couldn't they see? "And I only picked up that debt to save Andy."

"Psychotic?" Wharf Rat gave me a disgusted look, "I just had a meeting with Jensen, and he wept with relief when he found out that you were still alive. It had been eating him up that you had fallen."

"He threw me from the cliff when I wouldn't join him." I tested the strength of the cuffs trying to get up, but all I did was hurt my wrists.

"I saw his tears. They were genuine." Wharf Rat's face started to redden. He was genuinely angry with me. Great.

"How can you believe him?" I asked.

"I don't know. Maybe because he is a hero who has risked his life for this country, and you are a product of the I-generation, who only thinks about yourself." He leant across the desk, and I shrank back despite the cold of the seat. In my face he whispered, "I would kill for a shred of magical power, and it makes me sick to think that it has been gifted to a self serving-trollop like yourself."

"You won't even consider that what I am saying might be true?" I pleaded.

"Lynx, the only thing I want to hear from that serpent's tongue of yours is a confession. Tell us about Raven? Did you kill him? Was he in on the conspiracy when you betrayed him, or were you simply acting alone?" Wharf Rat placed a recorder on the desk and turned it on.

I leant forward and held his eyes as I spoke slowly into the recorder, "I didn't kill Raven. He was my partner."

Wish spoke from behind me, "We aren't stupid. We know you got a false passport from the Toad rather than report in to headquarters."

"I had to." I argued. I narrowed my eyes. "I had almost been killed and my apartment had been blown up. I didn't know who to trust, I had just found out that there was a traitor in MI-23."

"Yes, that was clever of you. Blowing up your apartment was a good way to erase all the evidence." Wish managed to sound bored.

"I didn't blow up my apartment." I was outraged. "It had all my memories in it. My parents left it to me."

"Look this is getting us nowhere. You are being deliberately uncooperative." Wharf Rat signaled to Wish. I watched him bring out a hexagonal box and place it on the table.

"Do you know what this is?"

I shook my head. "No."

"It's a hexant."

That did not make things clearer. I hated that I had

to ask, "What's a hexant?"

"It's a simple box that we are going to place in your cell tonight to keep you company." Wharf Rat bent over and took off the lid. "The thing about a hexant is that it is totally harmless while you remain awake, but once the lid is off, if you fall asleep, then it will feed on your magical abilities. You may drift off but when you wake up in the morning all your powers will be gone—forever."

"No." I looked at him in horror. "Why would you do such a thing?"

"It's not us doing it. It's you. All we want from is a confession. Let us know what you have done, and we will take that away. We don't want to strip your abilities away. I saw it done to one witch. She just sank into a depression and never spoke again. She stopped eating and just wasted away. So sad. Anyway, you probably can last tonight, but how many days in a row do you think you can remain awake?"

With that Wish jammed the hood over my head again. They led me back to my cell with the open hexant in their hands.

Chapter Thirty-One

Modern interrogation cells are painted white to aid in sleep deprivation. This is a particularly effective technique to break down the suspect's defenses, especially when combined with constant lighting and excessive noise. The lack of focal stimulus aids in disorientation. I knew all this, but it was still a shock to actually experience being locked in such a cell. The harsh fluorescent tubes were protected behind mesh, and there was a loud buzzing emanating from hidden speakers.

I sighed. No longer would white remain my favorite color. It was like Clockwork Orange when they spoiled Beethoven's Ninth for Alex. Being locked in here, made me desperate for color. When I got out, I would go on a spending spree of Mexican rugs. They had even dressed me in a white jumpsuit, the sort someone might wear painting a house. There was no clock either. I needed to keep myself awake till morning, but it was hard to stop my mind playing tricks, when I had no idea how slow or fast time was passing.

Since I was six, I had been taught many advanced meditation techniques, any of which could help divert my mind, but as I glanced at the open hexant, I knew I couldn't risk it. I had no idea how it worked and was worried that deep meditation could mirror sleep closely enough that the hexant would start stealing my power. I wanted to destroy that box, but I was still cuffed and could not reach my power. Instead, I just stared at it—wishing I were a Jedi and could crush it with my mind alone.

I slumped to the floor thinking that I should do some yoga, but my body rebelled. I just wanted to curl into a ball and feel sorry for myself. Not wanting to give in, I made myself go into a back bend. I hoped that might get the blood back to my head and stop me from feeling so tired.

The door to my cell opened. I rolled back down. I was ready to spring up and fight, but it was Andy, who they shoved inside. I closed my eyes in silent thanks at the sight of him. I had been imagining the worst, that the Magus may have Andy taken out the back and shot. I think it was lucky we had actually come to Bosley House, for many people had seen us arrested, and the Magus may have felt pressured to keep Andy alive. Well at least for the moment. Who knows what might happen when they transferred us to Skragrock. Most people sent there are forgotten. No one would know if Andy lived or died.

"Welcome to Chez Lynx," I said, rising from the floor and hiding what I felt inside. "*Mi casa. Su casa.* Would you like the grand tour?"

Andy dressed in a similar white jumpsuit, bowed ceremoniously. "Why thank you. You are too kind."

I put my hand out like a game show hostess. "Well here are the bunk beds. I have kind of claimed the lower one, but we can negotiate."

Andy said with a twinkle in his eye. "I say we wrestle for it."

He took a step toward me, but I pushed him away with my free hand and continued, "And over here we have the privy and basin. Amenities include flowing water, soap, and paper for all your wiping needs."

"And this…" Andy indicated the ground.

"That would be your pacing floor."

Andy strode one way past me and then turned. "Wow a whole five steps this way and then I turn and wow another five steps back again. That makes for some mighty good pacing."

"It also doubles as my yoga studio," I said ruefully, "And we get to do a lot of that for entertainment around here."

"And what's this strange lidless box." Andy indicated the box that I had kicked beneath the bed.

My face went cold. "It's a hexant. An eater of souls. Fall asleep and it will steal all your magical ability, permanently."

Andy nodded. "Aaah, so that is why they put us together."

I slumped back down against the wall. "That and they are probably watching to see whether we change our stories now that we are alone."

Andy looked up to the one-way glass observation window positioned on one of the walls. "Yes. They weren't big on believing us were they?"

"No they weren't." I put my face in my hands. "I am so sorry. I never meant for it to end like this."

Andy slid down next to me and put a hand on my shoulder. "Hey, don't give up."

"Do you have a plan for getting us out of here?"

He rubbed my back, which annoyed me. I didn't need soothing. I needed a way out. I didn't say anything though—some part of me needed the touch—whether I wanted it or not.

Andy's hand snaked up over my collarbone. "No but at least I can think of some things to do to keep us awake."

I pushed his hand off. "Not now Andy. Anybody could be watching. I am so frustrated with myself. I didn't think any of this through."

Andy left his hand out awkwardly between us. "You can't blame yourself for this."

I hate people telling me what I can or can't do. I grabbed his wrist and pushed his hand back to his own chest. "Why not? I should have realized what Jensen would do to cover himself."

Andy said, in what I took to be a gentle tone, "You can't be perfect all the time."

I really wanted to punch him. I really wanted to punch myself. "I can't be perfect any of the time."

"Why are you so hard upon yourself?"

I gripped my face with my hands. "I should be. If I had been harder, I wouldn't be in this mess. My parents never got arrested for being traitors. They would be so ashamed."

He grabbed me by my shoulders. "Look at me Lynx."

I didn't want to meet his eyes.

"Look at me," he commanded.

I raised my eyes, my chin still down.

Andy continued, "Don't give up hope. Winston Churchill once said that the merit of a man could be measured, if, when all the world looks set against him, he can keep on going."

"You made that up. Winston Churchill never said

that." I still could not help but smile. "And if you hadn't noticed I am a woman."

Andy wagged his finger. "Now you are being stubborn."

"Okay you win," I had to concede. I must be slipping. I was letting a man tell me what to do. He was right though. I had to keep on fighting. I would not let them break me. "Let's break this down into manageable problems. First thing we have to make sure neither one of us dozes tonight."

Andy nodded. "That is going to be hard. I haven't had any sleep since the plane from Delhi, and that was only a snatch."

"I am the same. I could sleep for days, so what do we do?"

"Exercise?"

"Stop being hopeful." I slapped his hand off my thigh. "I know what you're thinking, and its not going to happen with them watching."

Andy shook his fist as if at God.

Just then the grille on the cell opened up. A guard said, "Here's your food."

I got up and took the two trays. Looking down at the food, I guessed the white goop was potatoes, the brown stuff some sort of stew, good old frozen peas and carrots mix for veggies, and some yellow stuff they were passing for custard. It wasn't an inspiring dish at all, but even though I didn't want to touch the food, I would eat. I must keep my strength up.

"Thank you." I called through the grille. I knew the guard. His name was Vinny. He had two kids and was a big Chelsea fan. He seemed embarrassed and did not meet my eyes. He turned and walked away. It was so strange being on this side of the bars. It would be less shameful if no one knew me.

As I took the trays to Andy, I felt something on the bottom. I signaled him over to the bottom bunk where we had cover from the glass window. I whispered, "There is something underneath the tray."

Taped to the bottom were a number of pills, a lock pick and a note, which read, *"Keep faith. Not everyone believes Jensen's story. I can't move now because the Magus has his eye on everything, but in the morning you are being transported to Skragrock. Be ready to move then. Enjoy the caffeine pills. I was monitoring the interrogation, so whatever you do—don't Sleep."*

It wasn't signed.

Andy said, "Well that makes staying awake easier."

I looked at the note and the pills. "Can we trust it? It could be a ruse."

"True." Andy considered the pills in my hand. "But if they really wanted us to ingest something then they could have put it in our food or water or just come in and forced us to take them, and why give us the lock pick as well?"

"You're right." I replied, "Bottom's up."

We each took a pill, made a toast, and swallowed. I immediately felt a rush, but that's what always happens with me. My body was a walking advertisement for the placebo effect. It would take at least half an hour before we could know for sure if the pills were legit.

Andy turned to me. "While we wait, how about a game of I-spy?"

Faced with a totally blank white room I don't think I have ever laughed as hard.

Chapter Thirty-Two

Wish and Wharf Rat refused to listen. The morning's interrogation had gone in endless circles. They continued to deny my request to talk with the Magus, and I maintained my stubborn silence when they badgered me to confess. I was exhausted when they led us down the corridor to the transfer van. I stumbled more than walked. We were manacled at both wrists and ankles. Only the sharp pressure of the lock pick hidden up my sleeve gave me hope. Wharf Rat was digging his fingers into my arm as he pulled me along, and I could not summon the energy to protest.

Two officers waited at the loading bay, ready to take us to Skragrock. After checking our shackles, they mostly threw us in the back of the prison van. No mind your heads here. The van was stark metal and cold.

"You could have made this easier on yourself, Lynx. All you needed to do was confess." Wish had one hand on the van door ready to slam it closed.

"I can't confess to something I didn't do." I sat up and shrugged, pretending nonchalance whilst seething inside.

Wharf Rat and Wish had been impervious to even entertaining the idea that Jensen was the traitor. From the glances they had made toward the two-way glass during the interrogation, I knew Jensen had been watching. Sending me to Skragrock was a message. He wouldn't allow me to discredit him. He would brook no doubt being placed on him. Not this close to the finalization of his plans.

Wharf Rat said, "I almost believe you."

It was the most that they had conceded. "Enough to take away the Hexant?"

They were still carrying it, and it had been present the whole time in the interrogation room. The box filled me with fear. Even if I were going to Skragrock, where I couldn't use magic, it was still different from having my talent ripped away.

Wharf Rat played with his earlobe with one hand, "Aah Lynx, I made that up. It's just a cheap junk box I found in Chinatown. I have found it extremely useful in gaining confessions."

We could have slept all night. I wanted to kill him. "You bastard."

Pursing his lips, Wharf Rat replied, "I know."

I locked my loathing of them in a safe place inside me. I would deal with that later. This was my last chance to convince them of the danger. They surely had to see the bigger picture. I pleaded, "Look whatever you think about me, put a tail on Jensen. You have got to stop him."

Wish shook his head. "Can't do that."

I should have known that would be his answer. I asked, "Why not?"

Wish moved forward. "Well since Raven was killed, someone had to step up and lead our section and seeing as he returned the diamond and all…"

"The Magus made Jensen the section chief?" I could not believe it. Of all the stupid things the Magus could do. Really?

"You got it in one." Wish's eyes traveled up and down my body, as if in farewell and then he dismissed me. He turned away and walked off.

I felt oily, but still yelled, "You are doing the wrong thing."

Wish turned back and nodded. "We often do. It's the nature of the beast. However, I think the fact that Jensen returned the diamond is enough for me to close the door on your pathetic little life."

Wharf Rat just had to chip in, "Sorry it didn't work out for you, Lynx. We'll see you in twenty years."

The officers slammed the van doors. I heard them fastening the padlock on the back. I didn't like that the light wasn't working and the only air was from a small grille in the roof. I could just make out Andy seated on the metal bench at the side. I pulled the lock pick from where I had hidden it in my sleeve. It didn't take me long to free myself from my cuffs, and then I started to work on his.

He asked, "Do you think the chauffer will be providing snacks?"

I smiled despite myself. "Check the mini-fridge for champagne, and I'll buzz him."

We were both free of our cuffs as the van began its journey. Andy looked around rubbing his wrists. "Now what? How are we meant to get out of here?"

"I am not sure, but let's wait till we get a bit of the way out of London. If we hop out of the van in traffic, we will have the police after us in no time."

"Good point. And the way CCTV is everywhere now, it wouldn't be long until we were picked up again. I don't think I could cast an illusion that would cover us from every angle."

"Let's try and get some sleep and break when they make a stop. They can't drive all the way to Scotland without a couple of stops."

"It ain't the Taj Mahal, but I'll try," Andy quipped.

I let the opportunity to point out that the Taj Mahal was a mausoleum slide, and watched him stretch out on the bench. Despite how tired I was, I popped the remaining caffeine tablets. I did not want to miss out on the best chance to escape. Every bump in the road jolted me up and down on the hard floor, but I managed to find a meditative peace and reached out to lights left on in bathrooms, elevator music playing in empty lifts, the blinking hieroglyphics on wireless routers, and the residual heat in electric ovens, to help me rebuild my energy on the drive.

About three hours later the van stopped. I nudged Andy awake. We heard two doors slam.

"This is our chance." I said. "We must be at a rest stop somewhere."

I gathered my power. It was so sweet after the cuffs had cut me off. I stood by the rear door and was positively crackling. I released my will and said, "Push."

I must have drawn more power than I thought for the rear doors flew off the van. They came crashing down to land twenty feet away on a BMW three series. The car alarm screeched in protest.

"You could have just opened the doors." Andy admonished me as he climbed out of the van. "We could have then closed them and they would be none the wiser until they actually reached that Skragrock place."

"Shut up and cast an illusion over us." I saw the

two officers come running back out of the service station, where they had stopped for supplies.

Andy waved his hand and the officers stopped. They drew their guns, but I could see we had disappeared in their eyes. The officers looked like they wanted to take a few shots, so I pulled Andy behind a car. However, they didn't fire. They ran past us in the direction that they must have guessed we were heading. Andy commented as we stood up, "You're lucky I am so good at this."

We watched the two terribly peeved officers come back and look incredulously at the blown out back of their empty van. They went and grabbed the back door off of the BMW.

I nudged Andy as they called in the escape. While these two were mundanes, it might not be too long before someone from the agency turned up, and I wanted to be long gone by then. Too many people had ways to track us that I didn't like.

We jogged down the road, and I turned for the center of town. From the look of things, I guessed we were on the outskirts of Peterborough. The fastest way to get back to London would be the train. Hopefully heading straight back would be the last thing they would expect us to do. Now all we needed were some clothes. Unless we were posing as a painting company, the white jumpsuits were way too conspicuous.

Chapter Thirty-Three

Pulling into King's Cross Station, I tousled Andy's hair to wake him. He looked cute in the gray suit we had found for him in a Salvation Army donation bin. I was dressed in an early 70's, orange, paisley, sleeveless jumpsuit, and had matched it with a halfway decent, brown, leather jacket. I loved this station. I could almost hear the steam engines from times past, huffing in pleasure as they came to rest, transporting me to an age where steam was king. A time when the class you traveled was inversely proportional to the amount of luggage you carried. Where one was expected to drink tea, eat scones with jam and clotted cream, and make up stories about the other travelers in the carriage.

Stepping off the train, I looked up. The steel roof seemed to fall away from the walls, like some sort of reverse steel and glass waterfall. It made me want to dive up to the sky and be lifted away from all the bustle.

Finding Andy's hand behind me, I sidestepped some Harry Potter fans trying to drive their luggage carts into a pillar.

"Hello, Lynx." A familiar voice broke me out of my reverie.

Stepping from behind the pillar was Quentin. I spun three-sixty degrees. He was alone. At least, there were no other agents that I could see.

"Don't worry. It's only me," Quentin said, confirming my assessment.

I calculated in my head. "It was you who sent the note."

Quentin inclined his head slightly. "It was."

I really should tell him that it had not been fashionable since the eighties to wear jeans and a denim jacket. I relaxed. "How did you know we would be on this train?"

"I didn't," Quentin admitted. "However, if I was right about you and you were indeed innocent, it was a simple matter to figure out how you would most easily get back to London from Peterborough to clear your name. Google Maps helped."

I couldn't hold back any longer. I swept Quentin up in huge hug. "Thank you. Thank you. Thank you."

"My dear, it was the least I could do."

"We really do appreciate it," Andy added, standing somewhat awkwardly off to the side.

"I do have some bad news." Quentin looked down at his feet and shifted from side to side.

"What?" I asked.

"Since your escape they have raised your status to Most Wanted. There is a capital order out on you both."

"What's a capital order?" Andy asked.

I felt cold. "A capital order means that if an agent so chooses, they can justifiably shoot us in the back, if they think it is too risky to arrest us."

Andy put up his hands, and my heart died a little as he half-turned away. I knew it even before he opened his mouth. "This is getting too dangerous for me."

"You can't back out now," I told him. I did not want him to go. How could he?

He grabbed me and explained, enunciating each word, "I did not sign on to get shot in the back."

I shook my arms free. "What about the werewolves?"

"I'll take my chances with them, over MI-23 gunning for me any day." Andy looked at me. "If you are smart, you will come with me. Let's at least get to the continent where we will have a chance."

I shook my head. "I can't."

It wasn't just my oath to protect Britain that was stopping me, or even my desire to live up to my parents' names. I knew beyond doubt that I had to stop Jensen. I could never live with myself if I walked away.

"Come on, we have a good thing going. Give Quentin the information and let's stay alive."

"I said, 'I can't.' "

"Are you crazy?"

"Of course not."

"Then stop trying to be a martyr like your parents and do what is right for yourself."

I resisted the urge to slap him. "How dare you bring my parents into this?"

"Isn't this what it is about?" Andy wagged his finger in my face. "*You* have some sort of a death wish."

I tried not to screech. "A death wish? This is about duty, about seeing something through. Sure I am willing to die to make this world a better place, but I do not have a death wish."

Andy let his hand drop. "I hate to leave you."

"I can't come with you."

"Well, I guess this is goodbye."

We stood looking at each other awkwardly. I

glanced sideways at Quentin, and Andy took the opportunity to turn and walk away.

"Andy…" I started. I didn't want to be without him.

He turned back. His shoulders were ever so slightly hunched. "Yes."

I steeled myself. What was I thinking? I was fine on my own. I didn't need this man's help. "Good luck."

"Thank you." He almost seemed like he wanted to say something as well, but after a moment's thought, Andy simply said, "…you too."

I watched as he disappeared into the crowd.

"Coward." Quentin looked at me with a raised eyebrow.

How did Quentin know how I felt? It wasn't cowardice anyway. I protested, "I couldn't let him stay. What if he was killed?"

"That would have been his choice. If you had let him know how you actually felt."

I tossed my hair back. I hadn't had time to braid it since being arrested. "He would have still gone."

"You don't know that." We stood awkwardly before Quentin picked up the backpack beside him. "It's been a hard week for you, hasn't it?"

"That's an understatement." Even the first week of basic training wasn't as bad as this.

"Let's go and get a cup of tea. I'm afraid I have some other bad news."

How much worse could it get? I glanced once more in the direction that Andy had gone. I couldn't see him. It felt like someone was swinging a meat cleaver inside my heart. It was my own fault. I should have protected myself. I said, "I don't know how much more I can take."

Quentin, God bless him, must have read my face, for he said, "Come on. I am sure we can find an adequate café that serves some decent tea. Then, I'll tell you the rest."

We ensconced ourselves at a table of a cafe, looking out at the people rushing to get to their platforms in time for their trains. I never understood why they bothered, when nine times out of ten all that they were rushing for was an excruciatingly long wait as British Rail was once more behind schedule.

I ordered Earl Grey. Quentin got a latte. Once our drinks arrived, he said, "The bad news is that Jensen has been placed in charge of the security for the Royal wedding. The Queen asked for him personally because he returned the Koh-I-Noor."

"So…" I knew what he was saying but wanted to hear it from him.

Quentin tapped the table nervously, as he glanced about to see whether there was anyone listening, before whispering, "Every agent and police officer will be at his disposal to make sure that you do not disrupt his plans. You are going to have a very hard time getting anywhere near that wedding."

I put my face in my hands, my elbows on the table, and let out a groan. "It keeps on getting harder."

"Hey buck up," Quentin said as he put a napkin on his lap. "Did you know that they believe Boadicea is buried under platform nine? She faced the Roman army for Britain. You, surely, can face Jensen."

I took a breath in. Quentin was right. There was no use feeling sorry for myself. I just needed to do what must be done.

Quentin passed his backpack over the table to me. "All is not lost. I did manage to put together a little care package for you."

I could see why he had never been made a field agent. It was the worst hand off I have ever witnessed. He was as subtle as a mallet. I took the backpack and glanced inside. There was a gun, money, a crystal, my bowler hat, glasses, boots, and a file marked Top Secret. I took out the gun and tucked it in the waistband at the back of my jumpsuit making sure the leather jacket covered it. I trusted Quentin, but was wary that Jensen might somehow know where I was and if anyone showed, I wanted easy access to my gun. I asked, "What's the file?"

Quentin was digging his little finger into his ear as he answered, "Oh just the security arrangements for the wedding."

I smiled. The man was a gem. "You know I can't thank you enough."

Quentin stopped waggling his finger in his ear. "Stop Jensen, clear your name, and that will be all the repayment I need."

The fool had gone, replaced by a man of deadly seriousness. I forgot how well he played the absent-minded professor. There was something else. "I hate to ask, but there is one other thing you could do for me."

Quentin nodded. "Name it."

"The file on my parents' death."

Quentin took his hands off the table. "What about it?"

"Could you get it for me? I asked in the repository, but it was marked Magus's Eyes Only."

Quentin took off his glasses, breathed on them, and

wiped them on the bottom of his T-shirt. Putting them back on, they didn't look cleaner just smudged. "You don't want to go digging at old wounds, Lynx."

Those wounds had closed over a long time ago. "It isn't that."

"What is it then?"

"It was something Jensen said." I paused, unsure how much it was safe to tell Quentin, then thought I may as well spill all. "He said the Royals killed my parents to get at Diana."

"I think," Quentin said slowly, "that he has watched too many conspiracy documentaries."

"How can you be sure?"

Quentin did not answer me, and I wondered whether I should read something into his silence. Finally, he asked me a question, "Are you having second thoughts about stopping Jensen?"

I took the time to check in with myself before I answered. I owed Quentin that. Once I was sure, I said, "No it's the right thing to do. I just want to know the truth about my parents as well."

"I don't know the truth." Quentin drummed the table as he thought about what he wanted to tell me, before he continued, "But I do know that Magus asked me before your parents went to France to equip them, so that they would be ready to face a possible traitor within MI-23."

"So…"

"So it could very well be the fact that they got too near Jensen, and he ended up killing them himself."

I thought back to my conversation with Jensen. What Quentin was saying didn't quite fit. There was something about Jensen's words that had struck me as true. Well at least that he believed it. He may have been a traitor back then too, but I don't think it was he that killed my parents. I asked, "And the files?"

"They were marked Magus's Eyes Only, so I cannot access them. However, I'll see what I can do. I just can't make any promises, Lynx."

I needed to see them. I needed to know. I set my face to a blank mask and said, "That's all I ask."

I owed my parents that much.

Chapter Thirty-Four

Threadbare olive carpet, an old box TV, and dusty horizontal blinds offset a bedside lamp with a shade that smelled from the days when smoking was allowed in hotel rooms. The bathroom, not much bigger than a cupboard, contained a basin with an obligatory drip. An electric kettle, plastic mug and sachets of powdered creamer, coffee, sugar, and tea rested on the countertop.

I did not fit in this room and felt vaguely repelled by everything I touched. God knows who did the cleaning. I laid some newspaper down upon the bed and removed the gun from my waistband. I stripped and oiled it. After putting it back together, I lay back on the bed. I had nothing to do but wait. Wait and hope that some inspiration would hit. I had no idea how to get Jensen. No idea how to bring him down.

Restless, I took a shower but got out quickly. The water oscillated from steaming hot to ice cold without a warm balance. Drying myself in front of a fogged out mirror, with a threadbare towel. I wondered why Andy had felt impelled to go. I know it was petulant, but part of me wanted him to be so in love with me that he wouldn't care about being under a capital order.

Surely I was worth it.

I wiped the mirror and appraised myself. All I could see were my faults. Not large enough in the chest. No high cheekbones, I had a square face. I needed to shave my legs and trim in-between. My shoulders were too muscular, and my knuckles were calloused from punching the bag. My eyes were a little too startling and all knowing for men to feel comfortable. My hair was depressingly straight, and no matter what conditioner I used, it never had any bounce. I know I shouldn't hold myself up to the ideals of those stupid glossy magazines I devoured in my lunch break, but it was hard not to. I wrapped myself in the towel. It barely made it around my waist. I swear I have seen facecloths that are bigger. I went back to the bed and picked up the phone. I needed my aunt.

The old darling had made one concession to the modern age. A telephone in her kitchen, the odd man out among the jars of the spice rack. I'd insisted on it when I moved out. I knew she was a powerful witch, but I couldn't help but worry about her. She was awfully old. She looked like an old Queen Victoria back in Queen Victoria's age. She had agreed to the phone, if only for my sake. Of course it was one of those old style dial phones. There had never been any electricity at the house growing up. It was reading by oil lamps for me, and for the lack of television, I am eternally grateful. I was lucky to have lived my life, and not lie around watching one.

I used the phone in my room. I didn't trust the crystal and wanted to minimize its use. If Quentin could listen in, who else might be out there? Hearing the phone ring at the other end, I could imagine the brisk tone of the phone jolting my aunt away from the stove where she was preparing a delicious supper. I knew she would grumble her way across the kitchen to look at the object that was so obtrusively clanging with ire. It would ring once more to break her out of her distaste, and she would pick it up if only to shut it up. I heard her answer, "Hello, Lynx."

"Hi, Auntie Bonnie. How did you know it was me?"

"You're the only one I have ever given the number to, so of course it would be you."

That was the type of love you could only get from family. I said, "It's so good to hear your voice Auntie…"

"What's wrong?"

"How do you know there is something wrong?"

"You only installed this thing to ring me when you needed help."

"I installed it for you," I said indignantly.

"Come now dear. I may be old, but…"

She had a point. I did need her. "Oh Auntie it is awful. I've been declared a traitor, and all the other agents are hunting me. One of them is the real traitor, and he is planning to kill the whole Royal family, and I'm the only one who can stop it from happening."

"And?"

"What do you mean, 'and?' I just told you I'm being hunted and have to stop an assassination.'

"Lynx, love, I know you, and that is just run of the mill work stuff. You'll sort it all out in the end. I've complete confidence in you. Something else has happened that you don't want to talk about."

She had complete confidence in me. I wish I had complete confidence in myself. I thought about it though, she was right, something else was bothering me.

She continued, "Is it something to do with a man?"

I took a deep breath in and let it out. It was hard to talk about. I never understood that. Why was it hard to say the words? I forced myself, "I met this guy on the job. He was a thief, but I could see the good in him. We slept together. Then when we came back to England and found out we had a capital order on our heads, he ran away."

"Has he been trained like you?"

"No. He's just a thief."

"So you expect him to risk his life to stay with you?"

I considered her question. "Yes. I'd protect him."

"Have you considered how that would make him feel?"

I ventured, "Powerless?"

"And afraid. It's easy to judge him and make it all about you, but I would like to think that I have raised you better than that. The poor man is afraid that he will die when faced with opposition that he has no idea how to combat. I'd say that he is not being a coward but being rather clever in doing what he needs to do to stay alive."

"But I need him."

"To finish the job?"

"No."

"I think you're being a little bit selfish, Lynx."

I *was* being selfish. Andy had done the right thing for him. I wanted to be with someone like that, someone I wouldn't have to worry about but it still hurt that he had gone. I didn't like the way this conservation was going. My aunt ought to be on my side and tell me how bad he had been, "But Aunt Bonnie…"

"Hush dear. What you really want is to be loved."

I knew it might turn out like this, my aunt had lived for many years and always managed to get to the heart of matters. I agreed, "Yes."

"Do you really expect to get the love you want from a man you only just met?"

What she just said was frightening close to the title of the self-help book I had bought. I grumpily said, "No."

"So you want my sympathy for expecting someone to give what they aren't able or in a position to give?"

"Yes."

"Well you have it, dear. I'll always be here for you."

Sometimes sharing is enough. My aunt was right. I knew it, she knew it, and she was there to give me a metaphorical hug. I did feel a little silly, but that was the great thing about my aunt. I didn't have to be perfect with her. She made it okay to be a little messy. If only I could extend that into the rest of my life.

"Well, dear, I shouldn't keep you from saving the country. All my love. Come and visit when it is over."

"Thank you. I love you."

With that I hung up. Time ticked by as I lay back and stared at the ceiling, thinking about Andy. This would not do. I sat up and grabbed the newspaper. The front page was titled, '*48 Hr Countdown To Royal Wedding.*'

Forty-eight hour countdown to disaster, more like it. I flipped past the news and looked at the obituaries. Maybe there would be something for Raven. Under Funeral Notices, I found a service for Stephen Gattick, at Highgate Cemetery. Few people knew Raven's real name. Real names have power, which is why we all choose a pseudonym in the agency. I guessed it didn't matter if people knew Raven's real name now.

I was glad of the choice of Highgate cemetery. Raven loved that place. The most haunted graveyard in England, it was home to at least one master vampire. I had to go to the funeral and pay my respects. But how could I, when MI-23 would be there?

I couldn't cast an illusion—there were too many powerful people who might see through it. I would need something more powerful. A good old-fashioned disguise.

****

There was a pharmacy across the road. When people think of disguises they think of latex masks, wigs, and make up. The truth is most people can spot a fake mask or too much make up or a wig. Think how easy it is to spot when a man wears a wig to cover up his baldness and who doesn't notice thick smearings of foundation? No—I would buy some hair dye, it was time to go black. After choosing a semi-permanent dye I needed to get something appropriate to wear at the funeral. All the MI-23 people were used to seeing me in black leather pants, T-shirt, and a jacket. It was time to get a little black dress, a veil that hung from one of those black circular straw hats, and some heels. The boys would never recognize me, especially if I finished the outfit with Grace Kelly sunglasses and a scarf.

I entered a dress shop. It was one of those where the retail staff were way too effusive, from the moment you walk through the door. I ignored their enthusiasm and found the perfect dress, some warm stockings, a pair of scary looking heels, a circular hat with a veil, and a short, waist-length, black jacket. I walked out of the shop and then had to return. I had forgotten a purse to finish it off. I needed somewhere to hide my gun.

Chapter Thirty-Five

I cursed my choice of heels as soon as I got to Highgate. The mud offered no resistance to the heel and every step made my calves ache. Seriously, how do people dance in these things? I missed my boots.

It took me a while to find the spot, but when I did I saw Raven's funeral was still being conducted. From a surreptitious spot behind a headstone, I could see the Magus saying a few words to the agents who had shown up. There was no family, which I found a bit sad, but it was to be expected. Raven had been almost two centuries old, and everyone he had grown up with was dead.

I wanted to pay my respects but needed to wait until they were done. I turned and wandered around the Gothic beauty that was Highgate, admiring the dying overgrowth that obscured weathered, marble angels and gravestones. The place felt uncared for, but that was deliberate. The trustees encouraged the haunting quality of Highgate. It brought more tourists. It was also something that I think magical types felt oddly comforting. The veil here was somewhat thinner than most graveyards, and I guess the idea that one could still touch the real world after death was somewhat consoling. Most people were frightened there was going to be no life after death. We were frightened by the fact that there was.

After an hour of wandering around the paths, I returned to the spot where I could observe Raven's plot. The people had dispersed, but I was cautious for there could be a trap. I had a single daffodil in my hand. I don't know why I chose a daffodil. I could not think of Raven having a favorite flower, and if he did, it would probably be something manly like a black rose, but somehow the daffodil had seemed appropriate at the flower shop. I could not see anyone, so I went up to the grave. His coffin had already been lowered and covered with soil. I let the daffodil drop down.

I surprised myself by starting to cry, "Goodbye Raven. I know we didn't get on all the time, but I promise to find your killer."

As the tears flowed, I was glad of the veil.

A cawing disturbed my grief. A murder of ravens looked down at me from an elm growing near his grave. They were focused on me in a spooky way. There were at least twenty of them. I didn't know what to do. Part of me wanted to run.

One flew down and landed by the grave. It dropped something from its beak, which glinted on the ground. It was a diamond ring. I picked it up, and the whole flock took off with cacophonous cawing. I put the ring upon my finger. Surely it couldn't be. My mind went back to the Oracle saying there were those watching this world of pain waiting to help. Still a whole murder of them? Raven always did have a sense of humor. I wondered what he thought I could do with the ring as I smiled at the sky.

I had one more grave to visit. The last time I had been was with my aunt. I didn't like to go on my own. I should have gone each year upon the anniversary of their death but had missed the last couple of years. The guilt weighed on me. Yet, I was still angry they had died. Amanda and Peter Somerton. They were buried near the grave of Douglas Adams, and I was thankful there were no tourists around. I realized something had changed inside of me since meeting the monk. I had never really thought about the afterlife. I took it for granted that my parents were gone. That I had to hold on tightly to their memories for otherwise even they would fade. Now I don't know how to explain that experience of the light, but some how I felt like I didn't have to hold on so tight. That they were in a better place, they would always be remembered, and that one day we would meet again.

I arrived at the grave and knelt down. I didn't know how to pray, so I simply spoke like they were there. "Mum. Dad. I think you are somewhere good. I hope you are at least. I'm doing my best to be the agent you hoped I would become. I may have even found your killer, but things are so much murkier than I thought they could be. I hope I'm doing you proud."

"Touching." A deep voice sounded behind me. "Now stand and put your hands up. I knew you couldn't resist coming here."

I rose slowly with my hands held high. I had my Beretta in my handbag but wouldn't have time to draw it. I turned to see Jensen standing behind me.

A fury deep inside me. "You killed my parents and now have the audacity to confront me at their grave."

"Where did you get that idea? I had nothing to do with their deaths."

"That's not what Quentin said."

"You would believe that nerd? You know he used

to be a warlock, delving into black magic."

"And what are *you* now?"

"True, but sometimes the pot can call the kettle black because it knows its own kind. Quentin will say whatever to manipulate you into doing what he wants."

"What he wants is for me to stop you." I looked at Jensen with cold fury. "And it wasn't only Quentin, the Oracle told me too."

"Really? Are you sure? What exactly did he say?"

"That I was on the track to find out who killed my parents."

"And I told you. You know not to take the Oracle's words literally." Jensen seemed agitated. "Look it wasn't me. Yes, I killed Raven. Yes, I'm going to off the Royal family. But no, I didn't kill your bloody parents."

Dammit. Jensen wasn't lying. What he said had the ring of truth about it. I wanted it to be him. It would make things simple. I wasn't going to accept his word that it was the Royals. Maybe there was even another traitor in MI-23. "Do you have any proof that it was the Royal family?"

"Of course not. I would have let it out ages ago if I had. So are you going to join me? It's your last chance."

"I told you before…"

"Well, now it is time for me to arrest you."

The only warning I had was a roaring sound, as he sucked in energy from all that surrounded us. I threw up a shield, just in time. Purple energy arced toward me. He was so strong. I was driven down. My shield started to cave, yet as it did, a heat started to build in my necklace. The tree of life started to glow and a yellow energy flew out at Jensen, to blast him back so that he smashed into the crypt behind.

To each side of me stood two beings of light, and they poured energy into my necklace. I was aglow with magic. I'd never felt such power. Jensen lashed out with a dark whip of energy, but it simply cracked ineffectually upon the glowing shield surrounding me. The tree of life heated, and a series of balls of energy shot out at Jensen. He raised a shield in time, but each ball pushed him back. I'd not even thought about what I was doing. It was the beings beside me teaching me how to use their power.

Jensen rose from where he had fallen. "You may have won this one, Lynx, but you'll not get anywhere near the wedding. Once anarchy reigns, I'll take the time to track you down. This I swear."

I did not reply but let the excess energy flow to my hands building energy—ready for another strike. Jensen snarled and ran.

The two beings beside me held out their hands. I tried to hold them, but they were insubstantial—they were fading and there was nothing to hold onto. As they vanished in the air, I heard them whisper "Daughter."

I tried to answer, but they were already gone.

Chapter Thirty-Six

Back at the hotel, I threw on some jeans and a black cotton blouse. I've never been a real tomboy, dirt always freaked me out, but I love comfortable clothes, and my boots felt delicious after those heels. I don't understand how women wear heels everyday. Is the look worth the sacrifice of comfort? Not that I can talk. I endure waxing, even when I don't have anyone to appreciate the results.

It was time to leave this dump. I couldn't risk staying. Jensen might be following or tracking me somehow, and while I had foiled him at the graveyard, it was only the interference of my parents' spirits that enabled me to survive. I threw everything into the backpack Quentin had given me, minus those hideous heels, which went straight in the bin.

Half of me wanted to make a stand and lure Jensen into a trap. It would be easier than trying to figure out a way into the wedding. However, Jensen had years on me. There was no way I could defeat him using magic. One day I might be as powerful. I really didn't know my true potential, but even if that day came, it was a long way off. I'd no idea how to stop him, but my best chance was to wait for the wedding and hope he would be too distracted to see me coming.

After making sure no one was following, I ducked down an alley and lifted up a grate. Under London there were almost as many ways of getting around as above. A whole city exists below. I dropped into the dark passage. Trying not to think of the rats, I took out a flashlight, walked to the end of the passage, and down three flights of concrete stairs. An old metal door confronted me.

I turned the handle, but the door wouldn't budge. I mentally kicked myself for still having no WD-40 in my kit. I put my shoulder into it, and the door finally popped open with a bang.

I walked through to the platform of a deserted, unused tube station. There are over seventy abandoned tube stations underneath London, and while the official story is that most of these have been demolished, in certain cases demolished means the main entrances have been filled with cement, but the whole station remains underground and unused. When I say unused, I mean unused for their original purpose. Many of the homeless flee the cold weather above and find their way into under-London, not to mention the supernatural community down here. I trod carefully, not wanting to step accidentally on any discarded needles.

"Who's there?" From the shadows rose a girl with blue hair and as many piercings as the Country Women's Association's National Embroidery Day.

"Hello Charlotte. Mind if I use the office?"

Charlotte stayed with my aunt and I, after her mother, a local Devon matriarch, asked for help. Charlotte had been practicing the lower forms of witchcraft and in doing so strayed toward the dark side. My aunt accepted her into our home and taught her enough about witchcraft that Charlotte would not do any harm, nor be harmed. But Charlotte was Charlotte and wasn't one for convention. Even a witch's home was too straight for her, and she soon left for London. Firmly fitting into various subcultures, she rejected any pretense of a normal life.

Later, when I actually moved to London myself, she laughed at me when I told her there was always a room for her at my apartment. She told me she would prefer if instead we were to remain friends. We stayed in touch, meeting every few months. She was a dab hand in assisting with ritual magic and a natural born potion mixer. This abandoned tube station was her home base, and I was relieved to find her. Charlotte shrugged and spat, "'S'pose so. Didn't recognize you with your new mop. Black definitely isn't your color. Watcha up to?"

"Oh, just trying to work out a way to break into the Royal Wedding," I said with nonchalance.

Her face widened with a grin. "Welcome to the dark side."

I knew she would like that, but I had to rain on her parade. "I have to admit I'm there to save the Royal family."

"You always were such a square." She sniffed. "Well I guess it's a free country."

"I've heard rumors."

"Well we try our best, despite the establishment trying to push us down." She smiled at me. It was the same old game with us, a delightful pattern. Her taking gentle digs. She indicated the old stationmaster's room down the platform. "You can use that office."

"Could you do me a favor?"

Charlotte stuck her little finger in the corner of her mouth and said, "Depends."

She looked so coy, I could not help but smile. "Could you keep a look out?"

"What for?"

I didn't want to give her the full story, but I had to let her know the danger. "There's a warlock who doesn't like what I'm doing."

"Is he dangerous?"

"Exceedingly." I could see she was taking my statement lightly, and I needed her to be serious but knew that wasn't going to happen. Still I tried, "If you get any whiff come running. Do not try and take him."

"All right. All right. Don't brown your panties. Just one thing."

"What do you need?"

"A hug."

Charlotte broke again into one of her vast smiles. I opened my arms and pulled her in. She grabbed me around the waist and lifted me. She swayed to one side and then the next. Building momentum, we toppled over. I couldn't help but laugh. Any interaction with Charlotte was like wrestling a bear. The stress of the last week fell away.

"Thank you." I grabbed her by the shoulders and looked into her eyes.

"It's nuthin." Charlotte pushed herself up and walked away, obviously a little embarrassed by the affection. My smile turned into horror as I became aware of the rubbish I was lying in. I jumped up and watched as Charlotte secured the door I'd come through with a heavy metal drop bar. She must have previously welded it in place as a security measure. As she did so, I saw her mutter a few words activating a ward. The metal bar would stop any of her friends dropping in and the ward would let us know if Jensen came. She then jumped down onto the abandoned rail and took a seat in the middle of the tracks. I shuddered as she picked up a rat and talked to it.

I knew what she was doing. They were her eyes and ears, if anything came by the way of the old rail line, they would let her know.

A quick kick and the rotting door to the stationmaster's office gave way. Charlotte stole electricity from the grid, and I was pleasantly surprised that the lights in the office still worked, although they gave off a smell of burning dust as they heated up. Inside the office there was a swivel chair with no back. Its rusty spine stuck straight up. On the pockmarked desk lay a 1960's playboy. The woman on the front actually looked real compared to the airbrushed fantasies of today.

I used the magazine to brush dust off the desk, but it was a bad move as I sneezed. Pulling up the broken chair, I slapped down the file for the Royal Wedding security. Time to study. There must be some way into the wedding. I had to find it. I had to stop Jensen. I turned the first page.

One hour in and I wished I'd had the foresight to bring a coffee. Two hours in and I made the mistake of trying the Women's facilities—the less said the better. I don't know how Charlotte puts up with the muck. Three hours in, I gave up. Jensen knew his stuff, and he knew I was the main threat. He had plugged every hole that an agent might use to get inside. It was unfair. He pretty much had written the manual on infiltration for MI-23. I'd one chance left. I took out my communication crystal and called Percy at MI-6.

"Lynx." Percy sounded distant. I wondered whether it was because I was underground. He continued, *"I've been hearing rumors."*

"You know those rumors aren't true." I didn't want to say too much on the phone, but I did need Percy on my side.

"I treat every rumor just as it is—a rumor—neither true nor false until proven otherwise."

Okay, so he was sitting on the fence. *"I need your help."*

"And..."

Better to just lay it out straight. I asked for what I wished for, *"I need you to help me get into the Royal Wedding."*

There was silence on the other end, and then Percy said, *"You don't ask for small favors, do you?"*

"I know. Please. You are my only hope. I wouldn't ask but Jensen is planning to kill the whole Royal Family."

"And why am I to believe that you're not actually planning the same?" Percy asked.

I had no idea how to convince him. I simply said, *"You know me Percy. How could I possibly do anything like that?"*

"Jensen would probably say the same thing."

"Think Percy. How long has Jensen been an agent? He has become jaded. He is the leak in MI-23 and believes that anarchy is the way forward for Britain. What possible motivation could I have?"

"There is a capital order out on you."

"I know. Please Percy."

There was silence on the end of the line as he considered. Finally he said, *"I could never refuse a pretty girl."*

"You'll do it?" Relief flooded into me and was immediately replaced by worry. Now I had a way in, but the larger problem of how to stop Jensen loomed.

"Yes. Let me see." I could hear him tapping away at a computer. He offered, *"We are arranging the delivery of the flowers for the wedding. I can substitute you for one of the drivers, then we could hide you, perhaps in the Abbey shop until the ceremony?"*

"Yes. I cannot move until Jensen actually threatens the Royals." I needed for the Magus to see Jensen had turned traitor.

"Okay, be at Osborne House, 10 Devonshire Square, at ten in the morning."

He cut the connection. I pulled a picture of the Koh-I-Noor from the file and from my pocket dug out the ring the raven had dropped at the grave, a plan beginning to form in my mind.

Chapter Thirty- Seven

Jensen had made certain security at the royal wedding was as tight as a glam rock-star's pants. Even the flower deliveries were to be made by military personnel. What he hadn't counted on was anyone taking my side. Thank God for Percy. And thank God for Charlotte too. She was taking such delight that I was on the wrong side of the law. She offered to guide me through the maze of tunnels under London. After a terrifying night with the rats at Charlotte's station, I was a bit reluctant, dreaming of fresh air and no scurrying beasts, but it wasn't worth the risk. So after making our way through under-London, we emerged, via a drain, a block away from Osborne House.

I bought an espresso in a can at a convenience store and used their bathroom in an attempt to make myself as presentable as possible. Plaiting my hair into one straight ponytail at the back, I could hardly recognize myself with my dark, dyed hair. Still I placed my bowler hat on my head, put on my John Lennon sunglasses, and chugged the too-sweet coffee, steeling myself for the day ahead.

A young man from MI-6, whom I recognized as one of Percy's assistants, met me outside Osborne House. As I tried to remember his name, he said, "Lynx, good to see you again. Percy has briefed me. You'll make one of the deliveries of flowers this morning."

"Good to see you too," I said lamely. My obvious memory lapse was even more glaring, with his use of my name first thing. Chadwick? Charlie? Something like that, some name that sounded like it was out of the 1920s. I envied that he had been briefed. Still, I bet he would have known my name anyway. He was that sort, earnest in a scary way.

He seemed not to notice and continued, "I wish I were going myself. I love a good wedding. My cousin got married last fall and it was the best fun ever for the family. It was like Christmas, just without the fights."

I laughed, covering the fact that I hadn't really been listening but rather ticking off names in my head. "I've never actually been to a wedding."

"No one in your family tied the knot yet?" he asked good-naturedly.

"There is no one in my family."

He gave me a concerned look, one that I had gotten all my life from those luckiest of people who have relatives that love them. I could see on his face the disbelief, as he asked, "Surely you have some relatives somewhere?"

I answered, trying to not get angry at his implication that I was not an orphan as I claimed, but had merely misplaced my family. "One elderly aunt, but she is way beyond the marrying age."

That and she thought every man she had ever met was an idiot.

"Well a wedding is a grand thing you know."

He gave me that look, and all of a sudden I realized where he was steering the conversation. It was difficult to find someone compatible when you were a spy. How do you explain to a partner why you disappeared for two weeks or why you have to leave at three a.m. in the morning without them becoming suspicious? He was being quite cute about it, but it was a valiant attempt by him to let me know that he was a serious lad, who believed in the thing that he believed all women believed in, the sanctity of marriage. I felt like patting him on the cheek and letting him know I hadn't seen a romantic comedy in years and thought that long walks on the beach were better done alone. Yet I didn't have the heart. He pulled out his card and handed it to me. In that moment I remembered his name without looking at the card, it was Carlton. He said, "If you ever want to get together sometime, let me know."

He obviously was too low on the pay grade to have heard about the capital order. I smiled. "I'll let you know."

I could see by the beaming smile that he thought that meant a yes. I should have just been truthful and told him he had no chance, and I had smiled because I was flattered. It was nice to be wanted. I sent a dark angry psychic glare Andy's way wherever on the continent he now resided.

We arrived at the van. It was already loaded with flowers. To my surprise Carlton got in the passenger side. "Are you coming?"

"Yes. Percy said that you will be staying, as part of the security at the ceremony, so I'm to drive the van away as soon as the delivery has been made."

That made sense. Good work Percy. Besides, there would be few one person details today. Almost everyone would have a partner. It was part of essential security protocol, for it's so much harder for anyone to betray the security of the wedding when you have a partner. Watching the watchers was only sensible.

Driving, we passed through three different security checks to even get anywhere near Westminster Abbey. Already there were people lining the streets, ready to wave their little plastic Union Jack flags for the thirty seconds the Royal couple would take going past in their coach. I watched as an Alsatian sniffed a mailbox checking for bombs. Police, Army, Special Branch, everyone and everything was turned out today.

I breathed a sigh of relief when the badge Percy had left for me worked, despite, my fears to the contrary. At each checkpoint, it was scanned, and I was waved through. Thank you, Percy. It was awesome to have a friend who actually comes through. My thoughts rested darkly for a moment on Andy. I shouldn't be disappointed in him, but I was.

We arrived without incident at Westminster Abbey. After setting down the delivery, I thanked Carlton and promised to ring him soon. What an idiot I was. I need to learn to say no. Yet what harm could come of one coffee? I slipped into the Westminster Abbey shop. The plan was to hide in the cleaning cupboard, until the service started. Adapting what Andy had taught me, I thought mop-like thoughts and cast what I hoped was a successful illusion. If anyone came checking, they would open the door and see a mop and bucket. I settled down for a long wait but was startled by a knock on the closet door.

I thought, perhaps, it could be Percy, with a change of plan. I dispelled the illusion and opened the closet door. Percy was there but standing behind him were a platoon of men, holding guns pointed straight at me.

"Don't move, Lynx," Percy instructed.

There were no options. I couldn't stop the hail of bullets they could unleash. A shield against such force would only stand a short while. I looked at Percy, "What have you done?"

Percy shook his head. "Don't look at me like that. I didn't betray you. You already did that a long time ago to yourself. Jensen was worried that you would contact me. He showed me the surveillance footage of you with your illusionist lover visiting the Toad to get out of the country."

"I had to stop Amanda Singh."

"Yes. He told us how you murdered her." Percy held up cuffs and threw them at me. "It's game over love."

I reluctantly put them on. I could see there was no arguing. "You're making the biggest mistake."

"Back in the closet, Lynx. The media has started to arrive, and we don't want to cause any alarm by marching you out of here."

I didn't move and with the cuffs on, I guess Percy felt safe enough to come close. He grabbed my jacket and said, "Have it your way."

I looked him in the eyes and kneed him as hard as I could in the groin. "You're an idiot."

He crumpled to the ground, swearing under his breath. All was still for a strange moment, then he made a signal to the men. They closed in on me, beating me with the butts of their guns. The world started to spin. I collapsed.

Percy called, "Enough."

He stood up and walked over and kicked me in the stomach. I couldn't breathe. He picked me up and threw me back in the cupboard. "For the sake of our previous friendship. I won't let them beat you to death. Even though I ought to. I can't believe you had a part in Raven's death. After all he did for you. "

So that was it. I couldn't believe he thought I had anything to do Raven's death. "I never…"

"Save it, Lynx. No more lies, darling, I just can't take them. It's over." With that he slammed the closet door and with a sinking feeling, I heard them drag something heavy in front blocking my way out. There would be no kicking the door down for me. I spat out a mouth full of blood and tried not to weep as fiery agony from the beating spread over my body.

Chapter Thirty-Eight

In the dark recesses of the cupboard, I wanted to throw up. I shook my cuffs ineffectually. I tried leaning against the door to open it, but whatever they had put in front of it was too heavy for me to move. I patted down the shelves, but all I could find were cleaning products, and I was no MacGyver. I yelled until my voice went hoarse, but my cries were lost in the heavy stone of the Abbey.

I was alone.

My ears rang from the blows. I'd failed. Even the thought of the Magus, apologizing profusely, with me holding the biggest "I told you so" in history, since Hitler's teacher told his mother that there was something not quite right with her child, held no satisfaction. I wish they'd knocked me unconscious. Anything would be better than lying in this dark with the pain of my thoughts. It wouldn't be long before Jensen attacked. There would be no one to stop him. With the power of the diamond behind him, he would wipe out all opposition. I screamed in frustration. It came from the depths of my being.

I heard a scraping sound outside. Whatever was in front of the door was being moved. Someone swore with the exertion. Great they were coming for me. Had that much time already passed? I stood up, not wanting them to see me defeated and in that moment I realized I wasn't. I was standing. I started to laugh. No matter what they threw at me, I was upright. They may have won, but they hadn't taken away my will to fight. I may not be the agent my mother or father had been, but I didn't need to be. I wasn't perfect and may have failed, but I was proud. I had done everything in my power to do what was right. I could hold my head high. I let go of expectations. I would never give up. No matter the pain. No matter what anyone else thought. No matter that I was badly beaten and locked in a cupboard.

I put my handcuffed hands in front of my face and formed them into fists. Whoever was coming for me through the cupboard door had better be ready for a fight. One leg hurt, but I balanced on the other. I was going to go out *Karate Kid* style.

The door opened. I saw a dark outline and I reacted. A beautiful, front, snap kick into the figure's face.

The person fell back, and I leapt out into the light, ready to take on the world.

"Jethus Lynx, dat hurths"

I looked. It was Andy, half bent over, pinching his nose. He stood up straight, blinked his eyes twice, and removed his hand. He sniffed, but no blood came out. I felt mortified. I didn't know what to say. Andy filled in the gap. "Look I'm sorry I ran out on you before, but there is no need to kick me."

"I didn't know it was you."

We stood looking at each other for an awkward moment.

"I was kind of at least hoping for a 'Hi Andy. Thanks for saving me.' "

"Of course. I'm just stunned that you're here." I

took two uneasy steps, slipped my arms over his neck, and wrapped him in a big hug. "How?"

"I knew you would try and stop him at the wedding. I wandered in here trying to plan what to do when I heard someone screaming in the closet, and kind of thought it could only be you."

I slipped my cuffed hands back over his neck, took a step back. "No. I mean how are you here?"

"You're talking to the greatest illusionist alive and you ask how? Let's just say you aren't the only one who can do an Archbishop of Canterbury illusion."

"That's not what I meant." He was being deliberately obtuse. I looked at him. "I thought you'd fled the country."

"First things first." Andy held out a lock pick. "Wait until you're all clear, kid."

I held up my hands, and he unlocked my cuffs. He was right. It wasn't time to worry as to why he was here. It was time to stop Jensen. Though one part of my brain started singing in a child's delighted voice, *He's here because he loves you. He's here because he loves you.*

"You look a right mess," Andy commented breaking me out of my reverie.

I felt my face heat up. I feared looking in the mirror. I could feel the blood crusting on my face. The beating had left me sore, and I could barely stand. How the hell was I going to go and stop Jensen? I steeled myself. If I had to hobble to the wedding I would.

Andy delved into one of his pockets and jingled a flask. "Care for a drop?"

I looked on in wonder. It was a flask like the one the monk had given us on the mountain. How had he come by the monk's rescue remedy here? I took the flask from him and knocked back a gulp. A wondrous fragrance filled my head, a golden light ran through my body, and my hurts faded away. I could feel a rib that was broken start to mend.

"Better?" Andy questioned.

"Better," I agreed. "Where the hell did you get that from?"

"I was at the ferry terminal in Dover ready to depart when I kind of changed my mind. I didn't want to run away anymore, and the thought of you tackling all this on your own just didn't feel right. I turned around and directly behind me was a Tibetan Monk holding a white Lotus. He bowed, gave me the flask, and walked away. The thing of it was no one should have been able to see me with my best illusion up. I was invisible to everyone."

I wiped my face with my hand.

"Just let me…" Andy took a handkerchief from his pocket, wet it with some bottled water he grabbed off the counter of the gift-shop, and started to dab at my face cleaning it. I felt like I was three.

I caught his wrist. "Stop that. I feel better. It doesn't matter how I look."

"Au contraire. If a guard sees you with all that blood on your face, you won't get anywhere near the wedding."

He had a point, so I let go and couldn't help but smile as he gently began to wipe the blood away.

Chapter Thirty-Nine

Andy wanted to come with me. He thought he could be useful as a backup, but I persuaded him to stay in the gift shop. The Magus would be on the look out for any illusion, and if Andy cast one I didn't want to come in, as it were, shining a beacon. Besides, if things went bad, I didn't want to have to worry about protecting him. Also, and I didn't want to admit this to Andy, I didn't really have a plan. I was going to wing it, and I wouldn't have time to let him know what I was going to do.

My first problem was how to approach the wedding without getting shot. There were two security men on the door of the approach from the cloisters. I walked toward them, my head down, hoping they were still on the lookout for someone with blonde hair. Yet as I approached, from inside the abbey I heard the Archbishop of Canterbury say, "If any person here can show cause why these two people should not be joined in holy matrimony, speak now or forever hold your peace."

Jensen's voice boomed out, "I have an objection."

The gasp from the audience would be reverberating around the world, as millions viewed the wedding live on TV. The two guards, at the door I was lining up to come through, turned to see what was happening. I took my chance, came up, and put a hand on each of their backs, whispering, "sleep."

They collapsed, and I made it in the Abbey proper. I may have been in trouble even then, but for the fact that all the security was focused on Jensen. These were the best men in the realm, but they still could not help but be distracted by a huge, mohawked punk standing on a pew in the middle of the crowd raising objections.

From the doorway, I put on my rose-colored glasses and saw a dark power pulsing in the Koh-I-Noor, which the Queen was once again wearing in her crown. The energy was flowing into Jensen, and he had a huge dark shield around him. Men were moving to take him down, but they were still too far away—he would have no trouble causing major mischief.

Jensen strode past frightened guests and leapt from the pew into the aisle. He announced to the whole assembly, "I've an objection to all Royalty and all politicians."

I had to stop this now, but the Magus got there first. I saw him rise from his seat and even from where I stood, I could feel the power in him. The Magus said, "Stand down, Jensen."

Jensen turned to him and replied, "Too late for that little man."

With the power of the Koh-I-Noor behind him he struck out. With my second sight, I could see the dark energy rushing at the Magus. The Magus held for the briefest moment before he collapsed on the ground. While he was perhaps the greatest living wizard, the power infused in the diamond was the power of Kali, and no human could stand against the power of a goddess.

All the audience would have seen was an old man

collapsing. The security agents were about to engage Jensen, but I knew we were moments away from Jensen unleashing his magical power in front of the world's cameras.

I knew I couldn't beat Jensen in a one on one power struggle. Tied to the diamond he was way too powerful. Even without the diamond, he was way too powerful. So I did the one thing I could. I pulled out the diamond ring that the ravens had dropped on the ground, Raven's last gift to me. As I've said before, sympathetic magic is not one of my strong suits, but as I had been in the temple when Kali was raised, I already felt a connection to the energy that Jensen was using. In my mind I established a link between the small diamond in my hand and Koh-I-Noor on the Queen's crown.

Jensen was controlling the flow from the diamond, but he had neglected to bring with him a focusing object. With the diamond in my hand, I hoped to wrest that control away, if only for the briefest of moments. For when Jensen realized what I was doing, I wouldn't have the power to stop him from wresting it back again. I threw all the energy I could into the diamond I held and muttered, "Disperse."

The link from the diamond in my hand to the Koh-I-Noor held. Millions of years ago the diamonds had been lumps of carbon. Then pressure from deep within the earth pounded them into a crystalline form. In many ways they were just stored energy. I released that energy, cracking the very crystalline structure, so the gem in my hand shattered, and through the link I had established in my mind, so did the Koh-I-Noor in a thunderous roar. A shock wave of energy poured out, blowing out every light and candle. In my one brief moment of control, I released all the energy Jensen was planning to use. The abbey went pitch black.

Still wearing my glasses, I was the only one moving in those first seconds of darkness, apart from some heroes throwing their bodies in front of the Queen. I could see exactly where Jensen stood. He was turning toward the Royal Family, and while he no longer had the power of the Koh-I-Noor diamond behind him, he still had enough brute magical strength to destroy them all, and the only one who could have stopped him, the Magus, was down. I still did not have the power to take him, but I had a card up my sleeve. I saw him draw in energy as I leapt and landed on his back. He growled and reached up behind, to pull me off, but at that moment I spun my bowler hat.

We appeared in the Repository. The Keeper was shelving some volumes quite near where we arrived. She looked at us both and said, "Oh dear."

This was the only part of my hastily, cobbled together plan that I was worried about. I didn't know what Jensen could do to her, but I hated that I might be putting her in danger. I said to the Keeper, "Please go hide. I don't want you getting hurt."

"My dear, I am a being of spirit. I'm in no physical danger." She tilted her glasses. "You, on the other hand, might have bitten off more than you can chew."

I could feel the animosity rolling off Jensen. With one hand, he threw me off his back onto the ground. I managed to roll to minimize the damage, but my arm felt numb from where it had hit. I sprang up and faced him.

He growled, "What did you do?"

I could try and get him angry in the hope that he would make a mistake, but the only line I could think of was, "I couldn't stop you, so I did the only thing I could. Take you where you can do no damage."

"And you think that bringing me here is going to stop me doing damage to you? I am going to kill you for spoiling my plans, then take that stupid bowler hat from your head and go back and kill the Queen."

I knew that if I merely spun the hat now, I would pull him back with me. So I didn't answer, I punched him in the face. I wanted to see how good he really was.

He laughed as blood started to well from his nose. "Well that was unexpected. I must say, Lynx, you hit like a girl. Now I'm going to tear you in half for getting in my way."

He came at me. I hit him again in the face, but he shrugged off the blow and slapped me hard with one of his huge meaty hands. I was stunned. As I blinked tears from my eyes, he caught me in a big bear hug. He started to squeeze, and I felt like I couldn't breathe. My training kicked in. When someone much bigger has a hold, I knew to attack the weakest point, usually that means the little finger.

I grabbed his and pulled it back, rather than letting it break, he released his grip, and I rolled putting the Chesterfield chair between him and me. I was in trouble. There was no way to defeat him in a fair fight. He was too strong. I was fighting way out of my weight class, and despite all my training, he had years of experience on me. I smiled. I wasn't planning to fight fairly.

I came around the Chesterfield, used the arm as a launch pad, and tried a flying kick at Jensen's head. He easily moved out of the way of the kick, caught me, and slammed me to the ground, landing on top of me. My body shook with the impact. I was winded and couldn't breathe.

"Stupid move, Lynx. You telegraphed that move from the moment you came out from behind the Chesterfield. What were you thinking?" He didn't give me a chance to answer, as he put two meaty hands around my neck and started to choke me.

I had him right where I wanted him. With one free hand I snapped a handcuff onto his wrist. With my other, I spun my bowler hat. We were back in Westminster Abbey. It was still dark, and it seemed everyone was shouting.

I was almost blacking out from the pressure of Jensen's hands, but I reached my power and threw him off me with a surge of magic. His instinct was to reach for his power in return, but in that moment, I croaked out the word, "Freeze."

He froze and I saw realization spread on his face of what I had done. The cuff, even on one hand, stopped him from reaching his magic. I took one step toward him. The lights came on. I was hit, from the side, by two Royal Security officers, taking me down. As they snapped cuffs on me, I watched with satisfaction as four of them tackled Jensen to the ground. I sighed with satisfaction—the Crown hadn't gone down on my watch.

Chapter Forty

The paving below my face and the white walls of the Cloisters to either side were all I could see. Six security men were carrying me the back way out of Westminster Abbey, keeping things far from the prying media at the front. I laughed, thinking of the ones who were carrying Jensen in a similar way. They had drawn the short straw. The laugh turned slightly hysterical. I had no idea what the security men were thinking. It was over, that was all that mattered. The relief was flooding into me. It was over. I didn't mind or really care what happened to me next. I'd faced my demons and come out the other side stronger than ever. My parents would've been proud.

"Excuse me," I heard a voice cry. I tried to turn my neck, to see whether I could see who was calling, but there was no way to look behind me.

I was unceremoniously dumped on the ground, the hard cement cool against my bruised cheek. There was a tear in my eye, from the pain. Behind me I could hear angry voices. Then someone knelt down and uncuffed me. I shook my wrists, pressed myself up, and turned. There, peering down at me was Quentin, wearing a Bazinga T-shirt underneath a pinstriped suit that he must have purchased for the wedding. His badge was still in his hand and some miffed security men stood behind him. They were obviously disappointed and a little embarrassed that they'd tackled the wrong person, and were compensating for that, by giving Quentin and I suspicious looks. The power of Quentin's badge held them back. I blew them a kiss.

"Care for a hand?" Quentin reached down to pull me up.

He got me to standing and stared for a moment at my face. "God, have they done a number on you."

After the fight with Jensen, I must have looked a real fright. I felt for tender spots on my face. "I'll live. No permanent damage."

Quentin beamed at me. "Well done. I knew you could pull through."

I gave him a hug. "Cheers. Thanks for never doubting me."

"How could I? You were absolutely brilliant."

"What's happening inside?"

"They fixed the breakers so the electricity came back on and now they are continuing with the wedding. Good old royalty, the show must go on and all that. The official story is that one crazy stood up shouting objections and then a fuse blew. In the confusion the Queen's crown dropped and needed repair. So she isn't wearing it anymore. I suppose they will find some sort of huge cubic zirconium to replace the Koh-I-Noor and none will be the wiser. The press are having an absolute field day."

"What about Jensen?"

"They are taking him out the back to a police van. Wish and Wharf Rat themselves are under orders to transport him directly to Skragrock."

"Can I see him before he leaves?"

"I don't see why not, but we'll have to hurry."

We scurried out back as fast as we could. They were loading Jensen in the van.

I went over. Jensen saw me and said, "Come to gloat?"

I looked at the man who used to bring me birthday presents and could not help but feel a well of sadness within my heart. "No. There is no triumph here, only tragedy."

Jensen softened and whispered to me, "I did what I thought was right."

"I know," I sighed. "That is the tragedy."

I watched as they put him in the van. The desire for any sort of revenge had slipped far, far away.

"Well done, Lynx." A familiar voice sounded behind me.

I turned to see the Magus standing there. Two beefy security guards flanked him. The bulge of their shoulder holsters was obvious under their suits. I asked, "Wedding over?"

"Yes, onto the reception at the palace in a bit." He tipped his head. "Near thing that."

"You feeling better?"

"Yes. Many thanks to you for stopping him, from me and from the Queen. She wants you to know that while she can't acknowledge publicly that there was any incident, she would very much like you to know that she is pleased."

"What?" Quentin interjected, "No tea at the palace?"

The Magus took off his glasses and cleaned them with his handkerchief. "No. I'm afraid she very much blames Lynx for the disastrous state of her crown."

I smiled. "Well next time I stop an assassin I'll pay

more attention to protecting the Royal property as well."

"You could throw in world famous department stores, while you are at it."

The Magus placed his glasses back on his face and it took me a moment to realize he had just made a joke.

"So…" I started.

The Magus read my mind, "Yes, your name is clear now. The capital order is obviously rescinded, and while officially I cannot acknowledge your achievements, you are in my debt."

There was one thing I did need to do. I asked, "Would it be all right then if I had the next week off work?"

The Magus looked taken aback, but Quentin whispered something in his ear, and he said, "Aah of course, the werewolf thing."

I nodded.

"I take it you have a plan."

"Yes, I just need a little time off work."

"Granted then, good to see you sorting that one out on your own. It isn't a good state of affairs for one of our agents to be owing money to loan sharks."

I hardly heard what he was saying. For sauntering along the corridor came the Archbishop of Canterbury.

I made an instant decision in my mind, a decision for myself and for my career. I pretended to stumble and bumped into one of the security guards that stood beside the Magus. I lifted the gun from his holster. Before anyone could realize what I was doing. I let loose two shots. They looked behind in horror as the Archbishop of Canterbury fell to the ground.

The Magus wrapped me instantly in a flow of

magic. I could not move and could hardly breathe. He shouted, "Have you gone mad?"

I tried to squirm, but his grip was too strong. I shouted back, "It's the illusionist."

The Magus dropped me in an instant. We hurried over, and there was Andy spitting blood from his mouth, the Archbishop of Canterbury no longer. There were two bullet wounds in his chest. He looked up at me with sad brown eyes and said, "Why?"

"It's better than a cage Andy. It's better than a cage."

I knelt beside him and held his hand as he tried to say something else, but the life went from his eyes, and I closed them shut.

The Magus stopped and looked at me. "Thank you Lynx. I wasn't sure whether you would do it or not."

I stood up and saluted. "Just following orders, sir."

"It's a dirty business we are in Lynx. One man's life weighed against the good of the country."

I looked at him and saw the pain with which he spoke. Here was a man who could start a war with a phone call and in fact probably had. I did not judge him. I had entered a world where there were no longer blacks and whites. "I understand, sir."

"We just can't have that sort of thing happening, the break in at the National Gallery. What you have done today will get around the magical community and no one will even dare think about another theft."

"I understand."

"Good. I didn't want you to think that my order was unnecessary or cruel in any way. I just order what needs to be done."

"Of course."

I thought for a moment he was going to touch me on the arm, but British propriety weighed forward, and he firmly clasped his hands behind his back. Then the next thing he said turned my blood to ice. "I am glad you can follow orders, so unlike your parents. They quibbled when they should have been strong and it was for that reason you understand…"

I felt ice in my stomach. To what was the Magus alluding?

"Did you…" I couldn't even ask the question.

He put on a grim frown as he looked at me. "Every decision I make is for the good of the country."

Guns were great levelers when it came to the magical community. A bullet was still a bullet, whether it was ripping into a magician or a mundane. I started to raise my gun. The Magus wasn't even looking at me. He was looking at Andy's dead body. All the nights spent crying, all the Christmas's where it has just been me and my aunt, all the pain at the loss screamed at me to pull the trigger.

I dropped the gun and ran.

Chapter Forty-One

I wore a black bikini top under my barely buttoned red silk blouse. I know it was slightly unfair, but I was going to use every advantage I could. Even with the John Lennon rose colored glasses, I had to be careful not to make a mistake. One wrong call and I could be all in, with a 1 in 52 card coming up for my opponent on the river. I had to choose wisely. Still I had made it to the final table and there were only two people left to beat. Then I would have enough money to be cleared of debt to the werewolves.

The Oracle had tipped me off. Using the insurance money from my flat, I was on the richest poker cruise in the Caribbean, the buy-in, one million dollars U.S.

I surprised everyone by making it to the final table. Why do men think they are better card players just because they risk it all? That's gambling. What I was doing wasn't gambling. It was grinding my opponents down until in exasperation they tried to bluff me, and then the rose colored glasses came into their own. I currently had the largest stack, so it wouldn't be too soon before these two had to make their move.

I leant forward deliberately. I made a bet of twice the pot to open the round. I was getting cocky. I shouldn't really bet Ace Ten, under the gun, but they were suited, both hearts and there were only three of us left at the table.

The player to my left, a large man, who looked like an over eager turtle with glasses, checked his cards, and limped in with a call. I put him on Queen Jack off suit. He was hoping for a lucky flop and had probably been paying more attention to my chest, than the cards. I leant back stretching my shoulders and watched his eyes follow me.

The other player at the table wore a gray hoody and had it pulled up, covering his face, large sunglasses hiding his eyes. He predictably raised the pot. Through my glasses I saw him shaking his head. He had nothing. I re-raised.

The over eager turtle folded. Gray hoody had one move, he called all in. With my small raise at the start he would be expecting me to fold. He had only half my stack. I could afford to call. Watching his face, I did. I turned my cards over, and he hit the table. He tossed his hand on the table. Jack Nine.

The flop came and gave neither of us anything. The turn gave me a ten. His only hope was a Jack on the river. It didn't come. The crowd buzzed with noise. I was the favorite for the win, although I suspected that had more to do with my cleavage than anything else.

I had come here with the insurance money from the apartment. There are strict laws in most countries against any use of magic on the gambling table. That we were one hundred miles from any shore, cruising the Caribbean made me feel better. I don't like to have late library books let alone break any law. Some would say I was cheating. I liked to think that I was just using what natural God given talents I had to win money off gamblers and fools.

Gray hoody took off his glasses and pushed back

his hood to reveal dyed spiky blond hair. He nodded his head at me and said, "You are impossible to bluff, I was all covered up and you still picked me. How do you do it?"

"Oh I just have a knack for picking up tells," I said off-handedly.

He left the table. Obviously miffed. He would be going over in his mind everything he did, to see whether he had done anything that could be construed as a tell. It was probably cruel what I said to him. Still he left with over a million in prize money, so I wasn't going to feel too sorry for him.

I dismissed him from my mind. One to go. Over eager turtle had about a quarter of the chips I had. I smiled at him. Heads up.

It was no surprise that we were the last two left at the table. He rubbed a Jade Tiki that he wore around his neck. The Tiki is a Maori luck god, and I wasn't sure where this one had come from, but the shaman who made it had imbued the icon with power, or at least a deep connection to the spirit world where that power resided. I don't even know whether over eager turtle even knew what he wearing. Sure on some level he kept on rubbing it, but as with most mundanes, their subconscious knew more about the mystical world than they did. If I told him that it actually was shifting the cards in his favor, he would not have believed me.

Now was the time to pull out the big guns. I did not want to take on over eager turtle's luck god, so with respect to Andy, I was going to take care of the final hand with an illusion. It was over before anyone knew it. The pair of aces in over eager turtle's hand, somehow transformed to deuce seven when he lay them down on the table, and the call of all in looked like a massive mistake. I won the hand easily. Over eager turtle looked sick but didn't want to say anything. I left him scratching his head. He must be wondering whether he was going mad.

A sense of relief hit me. I had just won $15 million US, in the biggest poker tournament ever in the Caribbean. I could now pay off the werewolves. I wasn't going to die. I smiled as they dumped a huge pile of cash on the table and posed for a promo pic.

Chapter Forty-Two

Standing at the nose of the huge ocean liner, it was hard to resist the urge to play Titanic. I did feel like I was queen of the world. I instead got out my crystal and phoned the werewolves. It took a while to connect. There was a funny ring on the other end.

"Hello?" A tentative voice sounded in my mind.

"Is that Weasel?"

"It is. Who is this?" Weasel's voice firmed.

I could hear a lot of background noise, clinking glasses, and loud talking. *"It's Lynx."*

"Aah that explains it."

I went away from the nose of the ship, seeking respite from the wind and asked, *"Explains what?"*

"Well Dave and I are having a couple of pints at our local. The man next to me taps me on the shoulder and asks whether my name's Weasel. Ready for a fight, I said yes, but all he does is hand me this phone and said it's for me. It's his, but when he answered it, a voice on the other end of the line told him to pass the phone to the big guy in the suit, standing next to him, named Weasel."

I didn't know the spell could do that. *"Don't you have a phone of your own?"*

"No, can't stand them. Only person I ever want to talk to is Dave, and he is usually within a couple of feet." Weasel sounded like he took a long slurp of a

pint and then continued, *"So what can I do for you young lady? You still have two days left before we start hunting you down. I hope you aren't ringing for an extension."*

"Sorry to disappoint, I'm calling to let you know that I have your money."

"You do?" Weasel's voice shot up.

"Don't sound so surprised."

"Ha-ha. It's not that. Dave owes me a fiver. I backed you as a resourceful one. Where are you? Can we come and pick it up?"

"That might be a bit difficult. I'm sailing in the Caribbean as we speak. Looking at an amazing sunset over the water. Cruising into Nassau tomorrow."

"Well nice for some innit? Hope you have one of those drinks that comes in a pineapple, with those little umbrellas. Nassau is a little too far for us, but our employer does have an account in the Bahamas. You could deposit it when you get in. Have you got a pen?"

"No, but I do have an eidetic memory."

Weasel let me know the bank details and then said, *"Well done Dorothy. Been a pleasure."*

"Sorry to deny you your witch flesh."

"Ha-ha I was only saying that for show. Got a reputation to uphold. Truth is I prefer a nice rare steak any day..."

"Bye Weasel. I hope I never see you again."

"Click those heels."

Weasel cut the connection.

My way back to the suite went slowly. Plenty of people wanted to shake my hand and congratulate me on the way, and I had to delicately decline an invitation for dinner from the captain. Finally I made it. I pushed my card into the lock and went inside.

The Archbishop of Canterbury was lying back on the king size bed. He asked, "Everything went well darling?"

"Cut it out, Andy." I smiled. Jensen was wrong about me. I would never just follow orders. I had taken the chance and cast an illusion the moment I saw Andy at Westminster Abbey, making it seem like I was shooting him. Luckily, Andy caught on and played dead. It was the only way I could keep him safe and out of prison. Even if he had escaped, he would always be looking over his shoulder. It was the only way I could see for him to remain free. I was just happy that no one had been able to see through the illusion.

I had changed and was glad I didn't pull the trigger when I had the Magus in my sights. I know he had my parents killed, I just know it. Yet revenge was not my goal. I wanted justice, and there was no way I could be the person I wanted to be if I played the game the same way as the Magus. I wanted to protect people, not the 'country' and if I pulled the trigger on the Magus I would never have the opportunity to do anything with my life except run.

Andy reverted to his normal face and asked eagerly, "Did it though?"

I asked, "Did what?"

He turned his face into a smile, "Come on. Stop teasing."

I decided to put him out of his misery. "You are looking at the new poker champion. I phoned the werewolves, and we are free."

He popped a champagne bottle that he had ready beside the bed and poured two glasses. "Well this deserves a toast."

I kicked off my heels. "Do you know where the origin of the word toast comes from?"

"No. Do tell." Andy made some space as I lay down next to him on the bed.

I explained as he started unbuttoning the rest of my blouse. "Well back in Roman times it was customary to put a bit of toast in the goblet to make the wine taste better."

"Taste better…"

"Don't knock it, think of the charcoal filter we use nowadays to purify water. This is the same only they used burnt bits of bread, and there were plenty of impurities back then within the wine."

"Are you suggesting we do that to this gloriously expensive champagne?"

"Not at all—I think you should kiss me."

"Are you sure you don't want to go kinky and do it with the archbishop?"

I know there isn't a future with Andy. I am not blind. He will end up wandering off, and I won't try to stop him, for I love him for all that he is. I still owe him. Plucking the strawberry, I ran my finger over his chest. "Actually, do you want to take confession?"

"The Anglicans don't do that, but all right."

I laughed and felt at peace with the world. I still did not know whether the monarchy killed my parents in collusion with the Magus, but I planned to find out. Maybe I would discover that Britain was ruled by a corrupt machine. If I did, then I would figure out what to do. For now, I was content with the knowledge that the solution Jensen had attempted was wrong, and I stopped him. I'm not talking biblical wrongs, the 'thou shalt' stuff, but rather the wrong I felt inside when I saw those men burnt at the Tower. There was no acceptable outcome for me to justify such an atrocity. I didn't believe in sacrificing the few for the sake of the many. It didn't mean I wouldn't kill if necessary. I just wouldn't do what didn't feel right. A little death of spirit occurs when we follow only what we have been told to swallow, rather than listening to the wisdom of our own hearts. When I listened to mine, it said that Britain might not be the mighty nation it once was, but for the values of decency, respect, and a nice cup of tea, I would gladly give my life.

The people of Britain could go to sleep happy knowing that their world was safe. That is something that neither Jensen nor the Magus would never understand. I would fight for people like Mr. Adams, so that he could rebuild his store and go to work to keep away from Mrs. Adams. I would fight for all the decent people out there trying to make the world a better place by the quiet bravery of their lives. My job was simple. I was there to keep the people of Britain safe, so they could enjoy the magic of fish and chips and a pint at the pub on Friday nights.

A word about the author...

With ancestors who were pirates, James inherited a restless soul. Born in Australia, he currently lives in a Zen temple in Toronto with his wife and purple bear.

Thank you for purchasing
this publication of The Wild Rose Press, Inc.

If you enjoyed the story, we would appreciate your
letting others know by leaving a review.

For other wonderful stories,
please visit our on-line bookstore at
www.thewildrosepress.com.

For questions or more information
contact us at
info@thewildrosepress.com.

The Wild Rose Press, Inc.
www.thewildrosepress.com

Stay current with The Wild Rose Press, Inc.

Like us on Facebook

https://www.facebook.com/TheWildRosePress

And Follow us on Twitter
https://twitter.com/WildRosePress

www.ingramcontent.com/pod-product-compliance
Lightning Source LLC
Chambersburg PA
CBHW051522260626
47170CB00003B/745